TARGET FOR REVENGE

LAURA SCOTT

Copyright © 2020 by Laura Iding

All rights reserved.

No part of this book may be reproduced in any form or by any electronic or mechanical means, including information storage and retrieval systems, without written permission from the author, except for the use of brief quotations in a book review.

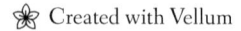

Created with Vellum

CHAPTER ONE

January 18 – 7:04 p.m. – Washington, DC

"You're up to your pretty eyeballs in danger."

A deep voice from the shadows sent Sun Yin into instant attack mode. She executed a roundhouse kick, aiming high and hitting her mark. A muffled oomph gave her a surge of satisfaction. She danced to the side and kicked again, only this time her foot was deflected away, sending her off balance. With the grace of a ballet dancer, she spun and found her center before striking again, determined to neutralize the threat.

"Sun! Stop! It's me, Mack."

His words came a second too late; her next kick hit him square in the chest. He grunted but didn't strike back, although if the man in the shadows really was Macklin Remington, he could have easily held his own against her.

"Stop already! I didn't come here to hurt you."

She went still, every sense on alert. It was impossible to see his face clearly in the darkness. Was this guy really Mack? It would explain why he hadn't fought back. Yet why was he lurking in the shadows outside her house? "Where did we last meet?"

"The Mensa roundtable in Geneva, Switzerland."

Sun let out a deep breath and relaxed her guard. No one knew the details of her Mensa group meetings, except those who were there. "Why hide in the shadows, Mack? I could have killed you."

"Yeah, right." He stepped forward, revealing his tall, broad-shouldered frame and blond hair. He dismissed her assertion with a wave of his hand. "We've sparred too many times for you to beat me. I know all your tricks."

They'd often fought as teens, verbally and physically, so there was an element of truth to his statement. She stared at him, trying to understand why Mack was here in Washington, DC. The last time she'd seen him was more than five years ago, at her last Mensa roundtable. They'd practically grown up together in the Mensa boarding school they'd both attended, until they'd gone their separate ways.

"Aren't you going to invite me in?" Mack asked.

"No." She and Mack had spent more time fighting than getting along, and she was in the middle of a case. He'd broken her heart by dating her best friend, Abigail, and she still hadn't forgiven him. She wasn't in the mood for a trip down memory lane. "Why are you here? What makes you think I'm in danger?" She didn't point out that her job with Security Specialists, Incorporated put her in danger every single day.

"Sun, please. Let's go inside." Mack glanced around the area. It was dark and cold, a hint of January snow in the air. "We need to talk."

She didn't move. "About what?"

He blew out his breath, a puff of smoke forming in the

crisp air. "You're being targeted. Someone is going to great lengths to find you."

A shiver of apprehension shimmied down her spine. "How do you know?"

"Because they found and attacked me." Mack's voice turned grim. "Thankfully, I managed to get away relatively unscathed. I came here to warn you."

"You played right into their hand," Sun said in a rare spurt of anger. "You led them straight to me."

"No, I did not. Give me a little credit, will you? I took precautions to avoid being followed."

She didn't believe him. Oh, she believed he'd tried his best not to be followed, but Mack wasn't an undercover operative the way she was. Her current role within Security Specialists, Inc. had taught her a lot about staying under the radar.

"Thanks for the warning." She was anxious for him to leave. "I'll keep that in mind."

When she moved toward the door, he caught her arm. She could feel the heat of his hand through the sleeve of her thin coat. It took all her willpower not to toss him over her shoulder like a bag of bricks.

"Sun, please. I'm worried about you." Mack hesitated, then added, "I think they're really searching for your mother."

Her heart stopped, and her breath froze in her chest. Her mother had escaped North Korea long ago, before Sun was born. But the current regime maintained lengthy memories and did not tolerate defectors.

If there was the slightest possibility her mother was in danger, Sun needed to be prepared. "Come inside, then."

"Gee, thanks." Mack's sarcasm wasn't lost on her, but she ignored it.

Moving quickly now, she unlocked the door and went inside, Mack following close behind her. As always, she did a quick sweep of her house, looking for anything that may have been disturbed.

Paranoid? Maybe, but if Mack was telling the truth, there was good reason to be. After clearing the house, she returned to the kitchen, flipped on a light, and faced Mack.

Oddly enough, he looked older, wiser, more serious, and more muscular than she'd remembered. In her mind, he was always the pesky kid who constantly teased her. He'd treated her like a little sister, while she'd secretly wanted more.

The way her pulse kicked up proved she wasn't as immune to him even after all these years as she'd have liked. Brother, remember? She needed to keep him firmly in the annoying-friend bucket. Anything else was unacceptable. He preferred cute perky blondes like Abigail. Steeling her resolve, she tipped her chin. "Start at the beginning."

Mack pulled out a chair and sat, rubbing the center of his chest where one of her kicks had landed. "You've been practicing."

She stared up at the ceiling for a moment, praying for patience. "If you're not going to tell me what you know, then leave. I'll figure it out on my own."

"Still stubborn, aren't you?" Mack offered a crooked smile. "I've missed your sass." When she scowled, he went on. "I was in Central Park, New York, when two Asian men attacked me. One held me in place, punching and hitting me, as the other demanded to know where you were. They used your full name, Sun Yin-lee. I didn't answer them and was able to get away. Still, I heard enough of their own personal conversation to be concerned."

"Like what?" Intrigued, Sun dropped into a seat across from him.

"They mentioned a North Korean defector going by the name of Hana Yin-lee." Mack's expression turned serious. "I remember you mentioning your mother's name was Hana."

"Yes." Her voice sounded faint, and she worked hard not to show her deep, visceral reaction to the news. "What language were they speaking?"

"A North Korean dialect." Mack leaned forward, resting his elbows on the table. "This is serious stuff, Sun. Sounded to me as if they're seeking revenge, for what I'm not sure."

The knot of fear in her stomach tightened. "Revenge against my mother? Or me?"

"I don't know," Mack admitted. "Possibly both. This must have something to do with those devoted to Kim Jong-un."

Her stomach tightened to the point she felt sick. Kim Jong-un was known to be a brutal dictator when it came to finding and executing those he considered traitors. He had no qualms about doing so, even killing members of his own family.

Living here, halfway across the globe in the United States of America, wouldn't protect them if Kim Jong-un wanted her or her mother dead.

Weren't there rumors, though, of him being sick? Not that Sun expected those who served the regime wouldn't still carry out his orders.

"I need to warn her of the danger," Sun murmured, thinking fast. She hadn't seen her mother in years, specifically to keep her safe. The timing couldn't be worse as the FBI had hired Security Specialists, Inc. to find intel on a potential nuclear threat coming from North Korea. She had, in fact, just come from a meeting with a North Korean defector known as Hyun-woo.

A coincidence? She didn't believe in them.

"I agree," Mack said. "When do we leave?"

"We?" She gaped at him in surprise, momentarily forgetting he was there. "This is my problem, not yours."

"Wrong answer." Mack's expression tightened, and for the first time, she realized how far he'd come from the prankster he'd once been. He was only two years older than her twenty-nine years but looked very much like a man determined to do what he felt was best. "I was attacked, Sun, which means we're in this together."

Every instinct in her body rebelled against the idea of teaming up with Mack, but there was no denying that he was in danger too. Those men had attacked him in Central Park.

Because of her.

And Kim Jong-un's insatiable thirst for revenge.

JANUARY 18 – 7:15 p.m. – Chicago, IL

Professor Jarek Zeman stood staring out the window of his condo, watching the rippling water of Lake Michigan. He'd been searching for Hana recently, and with the help of a private investigator, he had finally gotten his first big break.

To learn after all this time that Hana was last seen in Geneva, Switzerland, was crazy, considering that was where this had all started just over thirty years ago. He'd met her here, in Chicago, but she'd come from Geneva to study here in the US.

Not once had he stopped thinking of Hana. Stopped yearning for what they'd once had. But she'd pushed him away, insisting he must leave her alone for his safety and hers.

Honoring her request was the hardest thing he'd ever done. And to this day, he called himself all kinds of a coward to have given up so easily.

Well, not anymore. The cancer scare had convinced him there was no time to waste. He was going to find Hana and make her understand how important she was to him. Of course, there was always the chance she'd moved on to someone else. Was married with children. A family.

The family he'd been denied. Oh, he knew Hana would have wanted him to find someone else, but that had proved impossible.

Without hesitating, he turned from the window and sat behind his computer. He booked the first available flight out of O'Hare to Geneva, Switzerland.

It was time to put the past to rest and look forward to the future.

JANUARY 18 – 7:17 p.m. – Washington, DC

Mack wasn't sure what irritated him more, Sun's timeless and graceful beauty or her ridiculous stubborn streak.

He'd always been secretly fascinated with her. Oh, he'd tried to treat her like a younger sister, but it hadn't worked out very well. The whole time he'd dated her best friend, he'd thought of her. Sun was as tough as ever, determined to prove that her petite, slender stature didn't hinder her ability to fight. The way she'd kicked him in the stomach and the chest with surprising force made him smile.

All hint of humor faded when he thought of Sun being in danger. He'd done his best to cover his tracks in getting here. Had taken twice as long as normal in order to make sure he hadn't been followed.

But the truth of the matter was if he could find Sun, so could others. Especially Kim Jong-un's men.

If that's who attacked him. If not for his own expertise in martial arts, that little encounter may have ended much differently. He'd pretended to be helpless to get as much information as he could, before fighting back and breaking loose.

He hated the thought of Sun being placed in a similar situation. He cleared his throat. "We need to move. Now. Tonight."

Sun stared at him through her dark slanted eyes. "It's not that easy. I have other commitments."

"Nothing more important than your life."

She grimaced and nodded. "Okay, but we can't go far, not until I connect with my boss and maybe our FBI contact."

"Feds?" He lifted a brow. "Impressive."

"Private company, actually, but we do a lot of work for the Feds." Sun rose to her feet. "Better to call him from the road. I'll be ready to leave in ten."

He didn't doubt her statement, Sun was always precise. Rubbing the back of his neck, he tried to ignore the deep sense of foreboding.

Sitting here in her kitchen felt a lot like being one of those goofy rubber ducks in a shooting gallery, just waiting to be picked off.

He sighed. At some point, he'd have to tell Sun the entire truth about why he was here. The attack in Central Park was only part of it. Not yet, but soon. His phone buzzed silently. He scowled at the number displayed on the screen and let the call go to voice mail.

He didn't have time to talk to his boss.

Right now, nothing was more important than getting Sun out of here.

Mack rose and began pacing the length of the kitchen. He watched as the seconds ticked by slowly. He felt certain Sun would want to head straight for Geneva, the last known location of Hana Yin-lee, but he couldn't let her do that. There was too much going on here, in DC.

Somehow, he needed to convince her to stay put. How he'd manage that, he had no clue.

It would be easier to stop an active volcano from erupting.

He scrubbed his hands over his face, the lack of sleep catching up with him. When Sun returned carrying a small duffel, he was relieved. "Ready?"

"Yes, but we need to head out the back, just in case."

He silently approved of the strategy and eased ahead of her. "Allow me."

"I'm not helpless," Sun protested.

"I never said you were." Why did she have to argue over every little thing? He admired her stubborn streak, but at times like this, it was maddening. "But if something happens to you, who's going to warn your mother?"

That silenced her, at least for the moment. He peered through the window first, making sure no one was around. He'd checked out the entire property while waiting for Sun to come home.

Which reminded him. "Where's your car?" he asked in a hushed tone.

"Why do you think I have one?"

He ground his teeth together in frustration. "Because you were always partial to Jeeps, and there's one registered under Security Specialists, Incorporated, which is the private company you work for."

She stared at him in the darkness for a long moment. "And how did you know that?"

"You're wasting time," he said curtly. "I don't have a vehicle. I flew in from LaGuardia and took the Metro here. Just tell me where you keep the Jeep."

"I pay for a parking spot a few blocks from here." She gestured with her hand to open the door. "Let's go. May as well find out sooner than later if you're right about not being followed from New York."

He bit back a sarcastic reply, pulled a gun from the shoulder holster that was under his winter jacket, and stepped outside. He'd had to use his credentials and lock it up to fly here, but Sun didn't ask about how he'd managed that. Instead, she appeared relieved to see the weapon.

Even though he felt certain she was equally armed and dangerous.

Mack led the way through her small fenced-in yard, heading to the gate that opened into an alley. Sun was close on his heels, covering his back. He opened the gate and slid through, keeping a sharp gaze out for any hint of a threat.

Moving silently together, they lightly ran along the edge of the alley to the next cross-street. From there, Sun gestured to the left, and he allowed her to take the lead. He had no idea where the parking place was.

He'd studied maps of DC and could easily bring them into his mind, but that wasn't the same as knowing everything around them. From what he could tell, Sun had been living here for at least two years now.

So close, and yet so far.

The wind coming in from the north was sharp, stealing his breath. The streets of DC weren't all that different from those of New York, and lights from various homes slashed through the darkness.

They went more than a few blocks, taking a variety of turns, then retracing their steps. Once again, he was impressed with Sun's ability. Earlier, she'd approached her house in a similar manner, coming in silent and quick.

She paused at a corner coffee shop. "That's the parking garage."

He nodded, raking his gaze over the four-story parking structure sitting across the street. "Which level are you on?"

"I pay extra to be on the ground floor, easy access in and out." She stared out at the structure. "It occurs to me that if you found the Jeep, others might have too."

"Maybe." He couldn't deny the truth in her statement. Then again, his job granted him access to a wealth of resources most people didn't have. He held out his hand. "Give me the keys, I'll go in and check it out."

"No. You stay here, I'll go."

He was getting mighty tired of her obstinacy. Why had he ever thought it cute? It wasn't. At least Abigail had been sweet and nice. Which was likely why their relationship hadn't lasted more than six months. Cute and perky only took a relationship so far.

"Wait. Use your key fob from here." Maybe he was being paranoid, but that's what happened when you learned the woman you grew up with was in danger.

Sun dug in her pocket and pulled out her keys. She pointed the fob in the general direction of the structure and hit the button.

The resulting explosion shook the earth beneath their feet, sending them backward onto the unforgiving and frozen ground. A ball of fire lit up the sky.

For a moment he was stunned speechless, then he

scrambled upright. He grabbed Sun's arm and drew her onto her feet.

"Let's go," he said hoarsely. "Hurry!"

Without hesitation, they turned and ran in the opposite direction from the burning vehicle.

Mack found himself being grateful her Jeep had been rigged to blow rather than her house.

Or they'd both already be dead.

CHAPTER TWO

January 18 – 7:54 p.m. – Washington, DC

"This way." Sun grabbed Mack's hand and tugged him around the corner and down two blocks before turning into a narrow alley. She knew the neighborhood far better than he did, and she always had a backup plan. Not that she'd expected her car to blow up with the click of her key fob.

The regime knew where she was.

The realization was horrifying, but she couldn't afford to worry about it now. She and Mack needed to get far away from the explosion before the cops and fire trucks arrived.

She could already hear the faint wail of a siren in the distance, which galvanized her into moving even faster.

To his credit, Mack allowed her to take the lead without complaint, easily keeping pace with her. She headed toward a rather rough neighborhood that wasn't too far. The duffel bounced against her hip, and she didn't argue when Mack took the bag from her. It occurred to her that he was still in prime physical condition, maybe even more so since the last time she'd seen him. At the end of the alley, she made another turn and led them down a street with several low-budget homes lining each side of the road.

After three blocks, she slowed her pace, mentally counting the houses. Passing the fourth house from the corner, she raked a quick glance over it, checking for any signs it was compromised. She couldn't see anything out of the ordinary, but that didn't mean much.

If Kim Jong-un and the regime had sent assassins after her, they wouldn't sit in the living room with the lights on, waiting for her to arrive.

Mack slowed his pace, matching hers, waiting with uncharacteristic patience for her to make the next move. She went past the house and turned at the next corner, intending to approach her secondary hideout from the rear, just in case.

The lack of pedestrians was concerning. In this area of town, the cold weather didn't keep people from buying or selling drugs, gathering at street corners with said drugs or liquor, finding a myriad of ways to get into trouble. It was almost as if there was a pall hanging over the neighborhood, a warning of bad things to come.

Normally, she wasn't the type to believe in bad omens. But fear for her mother's safety had dredged up decades-old superstitions.

The wail of sirens grew louder, and she could see the orange glow in the sky behind them from the car fire. Time was running out. She eased through the property of the ramshackle two-story home located behind her safe house, coming to a stop in the shadow of an ancient cherry tree. Mack slipped in behind her, remaining silent as she once again checked the place she used as her backup safe house.

It appeared undisturbed.

Sun stepped forward, but Mack clamped his hand on

her arm, preventing her from moving. She shot him a narrow warning glare over her shoulder.

But his gaze was focused on the dilapidated house beside them. She frowned, following his gaze to understand what had caught his attention. Then she saw it. The barest flicker of a light from the upper level window. It was off so quickly she could have imagined it.

She hadn't. And neither had Mack.

Someone watching? Or was the person upstairs simply one of the residents living there?

She blew out a silent breath, relieved he'd noticed the light before they'd made a mad dash for the safe house, even as her stomach knotted with frustration.

No one knew about this place. It wasn't under her name or that of Security Specialists, Inc. If someone was watching her backup safe house, how had it been found?

No clue, but their options were limited if she couldn't access the items and extra funds she'd hidden inside.

Torn with indecision, she tried to come up with another plan. It was tempting to break into the house where they'd seen the light, if only to find out who was up there. Confronting your enemy was often the best way to know exactly who you were dealing with.

Mack touched her arm, drawing her gaze. He leaned down, his mouth near her ear. "We need a diversion."

His suggestion sparked an idea. Dropping to one knee, she patted the ground, searching for a rock. The ground was frozen, but thankfully there wasn't a lot of January snow to deal with, just a few patchy areas that hadn't melted during the heat of the day when temperatures managed to sneak a degree or two above freezing.

Closing her fingers around a large rock, she eyed the

window, estimating the distance. Mack plucked the rock from her hand.

"You decide whether or not to make a run for the place while I distract whoever is up there," he whispered. "I'll go around front, hopefully draw him that way."

Since she knew where she'd hidden her things, including the safe house key, she nodded. "Okay."

Mack slipped back in the direction from where they'd come. Staying put was difficult, but she had to trust he'd do what was necessary.

Sending up a quick prayer that he'd be safe, she waited until she heard the loud crash of the rock sailing through one of the lower-level windows. Instantly, the light in the upper window flashed on as the person up there went to investigate.

Without hesitation, she ran, keeping to the shadows as much as possible. Kneeling beside the porch, she found the key and quickly inserted it in the lock. Seconds later, she was inside the safe house.

There wasn't a moment to waste. Without using any lights, she made her way through the kitchen and into the living area, to a specific floorboard along the wall. Wedging her fingernail beneath the lid, she flipped up the floorboard. She pulled out the cash and disposable phone, along with the keys to a backup vehicle.

Less than two minutes later, she was back outside, making a mad dash to the shadow beneath the cherry tree.

Her breath hitched in her throat as she crouched in the shadow.

Where was Mack?

JANUARY 18 – 8:22 p.m. – Washington, DC

After tossing the rock through the window, Mack dropped behind a small pine tree as a dark figure emerged from the doorway of the house. He couldn't tell the gender of the person standing there, but he could make out the outline of a something small and dark in the guy's hand. Likely a gun.

How long would Sun need?

He lifted his arm and threw a second rock directly at the figure standing in the doorway. It hit its mark, right in the center of the chest. In return, the guy fired the weapon, aiming in Mack's general direction.

Well, okay, if that's the way he wanted to play. Mack waited another ten seconds, then lifted his weapon. He didn't like killing people, especially since he didn't know for sure this guy was their enemy, but he would do whatever was necessary to protect Sun.

Before he could pull the trigger, another gunshot echoed loudly. He ducked at the same instant Sun sprinted toward him. A smile tugged at the corner of his mouth as he realized she was the one who'd fired at the guy in the doorway.

They needed to get out of here, pronto.

Another gunshot rang out, even as the wail of sirens echoed through the night. When would the gunshots garner attention? They couldn't stay behind the small pine tree for long.

Sun peered through the tree branches and lifted her weapon, aiming carefully. He tensed, ready to run. Upon hearing the crack of gunfire, followed by a howl of pain, Mack stood and ran down the street with Sun hot on his heels.

With a burst of speed, she passed him, which was good as he would rather protect her back from the guy in the doorway. A bullet would have to go through him first to get to her. The way the guy had yelled out meant she hadn't tried to kill him, only to slow him down. He liked her aversion to killing unless absolutely necessary, it was his philosophy as well. He gladly followed Sun. This time, she headed down another street, then cut through more backyards as if she knew exactly where she was going.

Oddly enough, he was exhilarated being with her, despite the lack of contact over the past five years.

They'd nearly blown up in a car bomb and had now been shot at, yet he felt reasonably confident they'd find a way to escape the bad guys nipping like Chihuahuas at their heels. As crazy as it sounded, he wanted to grin like a loon.

Sun slowed to a walk as she approached a corner tavern. Before he could ask what they were doing there, she crossed the parking lot to an old, rusty dark-colored Chevy.

"Get in," she said, pulling the driver's door open. He didn't hesitate to get into the passenger seat, tossing the duffel into the back.

"Yours?" he asked incredulously as she inserted the key into the ignition. Despite how rusty the vehicle looked on the outside, the engine started right up. And moments later, they were out on the street, heading away from the source of the fire.

"Yes." She frowned at him. "There's no way anyone should know about my backup safe house."

He wasn't sure how to respond to that since it appeared someone had been watching the place. "What about Security Specialists, Incorporated?"

"I never told anyone I work with about it. It's always been a backup for me, personally, just in case of situations like this. It's a tactic I learned from my mother." Her scowl deepened as she navigated the side streets, taking so many turns it made his head spin.

"I suppose it could be a coincidence," he said, knowing full well that wasn't likely.

"Maybe." She took yet another turn. "To be honest, I'm surprised there was only one guy watching the place."

"Only one that you saw." He twisted in his seat to look out the back window. "There could be others."

"I know." Sun's easy acceptance of the possibility sent a warning chill down his spine.

Whoever had come after her had more resources than he'd anticipated.

How long before they were captured, or worse, silenced for good?

JANUARY 18 – 9:01 p.m. – Chicago, IL

Jarek Zeman paused in front of the airport gate, glancing at his watch. His flight to Geneva, Switzerland, was due to leave within the hour.

But now there was a delay posted on the screen. With no specific time designated for takeoff.

Despite the hour, the Chicago O'Hare International Airport was always teeming with people. They might not have quite as many citizens as New York or LA, but Chicago could hold its own with the other major cities.

Frustrated with the delay, he turned away from the counter. A man of Asian descent caught his attention, making him frown. The guy looked familiar, as if he'd seen him before. Maybe going through the TSA security checkpoint.

Jarek knew it wasn't unusual to see familiar faces in an airport, after all, they were all flying somewhere, and it was entirely possible for him and the Asian to be on the same flight. But a warning tingle had him turning into the closest restroom, his heart thudding painfully against his sternum.

Was it possible he was being followed to Geneva? And if so, why? Because of Hana?

Staring at his reflection in the mirror, he silently rebuked himself for being paranoid. It had been thirty years since Hana had left him. Three decades! Why on earth would anyone follow him now?

Unless he'd somehow triggered the dangers of the past by secretly searching for Hana. It seemed impossible, but according to Hana, she would never be safe, which was why she'd left him in Chicago all those years ago.

Fully expecting him to move on with his life, without her.

And he had, until his recent cancer scare had made him realize what he might be missing.

What if going to Switzerland caused harm to come to Hana? Bitter fear lodged in his throat.

As an English professor, he wasn't an expert at all this cloak-and-dagger stuff. Yet there was no denying he had the distinct sense he should try to leave this area of the airport without letting the Asian know he was onto him.

But how?

He splashed cold water on his face, then came up with an idea. Albeit an outrageous one. If he was right about the Asian tailing him, he needed to do something drastic.

Emerging from the restroom, he pulled out his phone, staring down at the screen as if reading a text or an email. From the corner of his eye, he noted the Asian had taken a seat at the end of a row, holding an open newspaper up so that it partially covered his face.

Not enough, though, to prevent Jarek from recognizing him.

The newspaper was the *New York Times*, which piqued his interest. Why not the *Wall Street Journal*? Or the *Chicago Tribune*? Was the man originally from New York? Or just preferred the *Times*?

Maybe he was making too big of a deal out of the Asian's choice of reading material. What did it matter? Jarek turned and idly walked in the opposite direction, glancing at various kiosk stands pretending to look for food.

When he was far enough down the terminal that he couldn't see the Asian any longer, he ducked into a bar and waited for the guy to emerge.

It didn't take long. Ten minutes later, with the *Times* tucked under his arm, the Asian strolled by as if he didn't have a care in the world.

Jarek wasn't buying his act.

He could only think of one way to get out of the airport without his tail following his every move.

Turning toward the bar area, he abruptly clutched his chest and moaned. "Help me," he said in a strained voice. "My chest hurts. Please, help me!"

Instant pandemonium broke out around him as patrons sprang into action.

"Call an ambulance," someone shouted.

"Where's the defibrillator?" another asked.

He continued moaning as people crowded around him. He noticed the Asian scowl in his direction before taking several steps away.

Still, Jarek knew he wasn't safe yet. When someone arrived with one of those portable defibrillators, he hoped and prayed they wouldn't shock him into having the heart attack he was pretending to have. After being checked out from head to toe during the cancer workup, he knew his heart was actually in good shape.

Thankfully, they didn't. Within ten minutes, the ambulance crew arrived. Two EMTs young enough to be his kids, if he had any, quickly packed him onto a gurney and wheeled him down the airport terminal. Through a slit in his eyes, he could see the Asian watching him go by with obvious displeasure.

Jarek didn't relax until they'd stuffed him into the back of the ambulance, slammed the doors shut behind him, and drove away. He felt certain he was being taken to Loyola Medical Center as it was the best place to go for cardiac care, and not far from O'Hare.

As the EMTs checked his vital signs and asked questions about his health history, his mind whirled.

If his searching for Hana had placed her in danger, he needed to find a way to warn her.

Before it was too late.

JANUARY 18 – 9:25 p.m. – Washington, DC

Sun gripped the steering wheel of the old Chevy with both hands to keep them from shaking bad enough for Mack to notice.

Her goal had not been to kill the person at the ramshackle place, only to scare him or her off.

But her bullet had hit flesh and bone rather than the wall or doorframe.

There was a sour taste in her mouth. What if she'd shot an innocent person? Someone who wasn't mixed up in all of this?

Her mind veered sharply from that thought. It was too much of a coincidence that an armed person had come outside after being on the second floor overlooking her safe house. An armed man who'd taken a shot at Mack was hardly innocent.

Innocent until proven guilty, reminded a tiny voice in the back of her head.

"Do you have a destination in mind?" Mack asked, interrupting her troubled thoughts.

"Out of DC," she responded curtly. She thought about the motel she and her boss, Jordan Rashid, had used a few months back. Clarksville was about halfway between DC and Baltimore. It wasn't that late, but she wanted a few minutes of peace and quiet to regroup.

They needed a plan. A way to reach her mother before anyone from the North Korean regime found her.

And she needed to call Jordan to let him know she may not be able to work the possible nuclear bomb case, although she hated disappointing him. This particular case was right up her alley.

Being torn in two directions, between her work and her personal life, reminded her of the series of events that had unfolded just a few months ago when Jordan had been trying to infiltrate a terrorist cell only to have his daughter kidnapped and held for ransom. Only to learn his daughter had been captured by the same terrorists.

Was she walking into a similar scenario? Something created by the regime to keep her from uncovering the truth about a possible nuclear threat?

"Sun?" Mack's deep voice had her glancing toward him. "Are you okay?"

She shook her head. "We're going to head to Clarksville, but we're taking the long way, just in case we've picked up a tail."

"What's in Clarksville?" His tone was curious, as if there was something important they were heading toward.

Instead of something dangerous they were running from.

"A hotel I know that will take cash no questions asked." She shrugged and headed onto the interstate, going west instead of east. "We need to think this through."

He was silent for a long moment. "You mentioned a job you were supposed to do for the Feds. Could the bombing of your car be related to that?"

"Anything is possible, but I don't think so. I wouldn't have gone to get the car if not for you showing up on my doorstep." She hadn't intended to sound accusatory, but the words had an edge to them.

"I didn't do this, Sun." His voice was low but intense. "I would cut off my arm rather than put you in harm's way."

Despite her loner mentality and suspicious nature, she leaned toward believing him. Sure, he'd broken her foolish heart, but that was her problem not his. Considering the history between them, she couldn't believe Mack would physically harm her. "You really don't have any idea who attacked you in Central Park?"

"None, other than how they spoke a North Korean dialect, the way I told you." He sounded disgusted with himself, but she knew that escaping two skilled attackers had been more than enough for him to handle.

Mack was just as smart as she was, and he also picked up languages without difficulty. It was one of the traits they shared during those early years in the Mensa school.

That and the lack of having any family. Her mother had sent her to the school, then disappeared, returning only on a rare occasion.

Why was she thinking about that now? There were

bigger issues to be concerned with. "We have to assume they're from the regime, and that means anyone who had the misfortune of interacting with me is in danger." Including Jordan and Diana and Sloan and Natalia, the other members of Security Specialists, Inc.

Even Bryn, Jordan and Diana's young daughter. She felt sick to her stomach. Why had she thought she could live a normal life? After leaving LA, she'd felt certain living and working in Washington, DC, wouldn't be a problem.

Yet here she was, on the run from a monster who would stop at nothing to get what they wanted.

Which she knew with sick certainty was to kill her, and her mother.

Along with anyone who tried to get in their way.

CHAPTER THREE

January 18 – 10:12 p.m. – Chicago, IL

Jarek waited until the medical team—having determined by numerous test results that he wasn't having an acute heart attack—left him alone. He slipped from the bed, grabbed his clothes, and disappeared into the bathroom to change. He had to rip off the EKG patches, which made him wince as several chest hairs came with them. In the distance, he could barely hear the faint beeping of an alarm, likely triggered from removing the patches.

He didn't feel safe here. Frankly, he didn't feel safe anywhere.

Thankfully, the emergency department was busy, and he'd heard a couple of staff members talking about the steady stream of patients. Too busy to notice the alarm until it was too late, he hoped. His leaving was doing them a favor, one less person to deal with. And he knew there was nothing wrong with him, at least physically.

Mentally? His inability to let Hana go may qualify him as mentally imbalanced.

Moving casually, hoping no one would notice, he

headed toward the nearest exit. Without a car, his choices were taxi or rideshare. Taxi was safer as he could use cash, so he went through the doors leading outside, an icy breeze hitting him in the face.

They didn't call Chicago the Windy City for nothing.

He moved toward a shivering guard standing near a valet stand. Valet parking was all the rage with hospitals these days, and this poor guy did not look as if he was very happy about it.

"Any chance you can call me a taxi?"

"Yeah." The guard pulled up a radio and spoke into it, before turning toward him. "Taxi will be here shortly."

"Thank you." He gave the guard a five-dollar bill for making the call. While waiting for the taxi, he tried to think about where to go.

Returning to his condo didn't seem like a smart move. If the Asian had followed him to the airport, he had to have known not just where he lived but that he'd made an airline reservation for the flight to Geneva.

How was that even possible? Oh, he understood his knowledge of all things technical was sorely lacking, but still, it seemed crazy to him that they'd followed him to O'Hare so effortlessly.

The thought of the Asian knowing every move he made caused a sick feeling to settle in his stomach. Would the Asian have gone all the way to Geneva, Switzerland, with him? He had to assume so.

The taxi pulled up beside him. Jarek bent over to get a good look at the driver's face. He was of Hispanic descent, but he still hesitated, wondering if it was possible the Asian was still somehow tracking him.

"Where to?" The driver's tone held impatience.

"The DoubleTree Hotel." It wasn't his usual type of

place, over the years he'd gotten soft, preferring to stay in four- and five-star establishments, but desperate times called for equally extreme measures.

As the taxi driver navigated through traffic, he considered his next steps. How could he get to Geneva to find Hana without anyone following him?

He needed a new identity. Something that would throw off the Asian and whoever else might be out there watching him. Could he borrow one from a friend?

As he pulled out his phone to call one of his faculty friends, he hesitated, then opened the window and tossed the cell phone out. The taxi driver eyed him warily in the rearview mirror as if he might at any minute turn into a lunatic.

A valid concern, the way he felt at the moment.

"Change in plan." He leaned forward. "I need you to take me to Oak Park and Washington Street."

The driver frowned. "That's a long drive."

He pulled out a one-hundred-dollar bill. "I'll make it worth your time."

The driver's eyes widened, and he nodded. "Okay, yeah sure. Oak Park and Washington Street. No problem."

"Thank you." Jarek sat back against the seat feeling good about his decision. Geoff Webber wouldn't be happy to see him at this hour, but his long-time friend and co-faculty member would certainly help him out.

He closed his eyes, knowing this was merely a temporary reprieve. He had to find a way to warn Hana of the danger.

Danger he'd likely brought thundering down upon her.

JANUARY 18 – 10:23 p.m. – Clarksville, MD

Mack kept a keen eye on the headlights behind them as Sun drove. A tail wasn't out of the question, but he was confident they hadn't been followed. He was impressed with her resourcefulness, having both a second safe house and a backup vehicle at her disposal. He didn't know of anyone else who had that type of fallback plan. Sun had obviously come a long way since the last time he'd seen her.

She'd be a perfect agent for the federal government, especially considering her eidetic memory, much like his, but she had chosen instead to work the private sector.

To make more money? Maybe, but money hadn't been that important to Sun, at least when they'd been growing up.

Things could have changed. And he needed to come clean about his current role in this case. He hadn't lied about being attacked by two North Koreans in Central Park or about how they'd mentioned her mother as a traitor, but he hadn't been completely honest with Sun about why he'd come to DC so quickly either.

His role in the NSA was classified, although that wasn't why he hadn't told her. Deep down, he was afraid she'd refuse to work with him once she knew the truth.

And that wasn't an option. Not anymore. No way was he leaving her to deal with this mess alone.

Seeing her again made him realize how much he'd missed her.

"Tell me about your case for Security Specialists, Incorporated," he said.

"The motel is coming up at the next exit." She didn't so much as glance at him. "I'll get the room, you'll need to wait in the car."

"Must be a secret, huh?"

"Yes." Her simple response made him smile.

"Okay, I get that. Just want to be sure your current case isn't tied to the car bomb or the guy stationed outside your safe house."

She didn't respond for a long moment. "Did you notice if he was Asian?"

"No, I never got a good look at him." He eyed her warily. "Did you? Was he North Korean?"

"Maybe." She shrugged. "I didn't get a good look either, but it's a reasonable assumption based on what happened to you in Central Park."

"True." He twisted in his seat as she pulled into the motel parking lot. "I don't think we've been followed."

"I hope not." Sun looked perturbed. "I went to a lot of trouble to have access to a backup vehicle that has no connection to my name. I'm still irked they found me at the safe house."

"The name on the safe house is different from the name on this car?"

She sent him a withering look. "Of course. I'm not stupid."

He lifted a hand in surrender. "I never said you were, Sun. No need to be so prickly."

In response, she pushed open her door and climbed out of the Chevy. She slammed the door with more force than was necessary, then headed inside. He rubbed the back of his neck, wondering why he'd been unable to forget her over these past few years. Sun was as different from Abigail as night was from day.

Which is why he'd gotten bored and ended things with Abigail.

Whatever. Being in a relationship wasn't important, keeping Sun alive was.

And hopefully finding out if the threat of a nuclear bomb being in DC was real or a hoax.

JANUARY 18 – 10:41 p.m. - Pyongyang, North Korea

He bowed deeply before the presence of the Supreme Leader of North Korea, his palms damp with sweat.

"What news did you bring me?"

The words were spoken in North Korean, but he knew the Supreme Leader could speak some English. Not that he was about to test that knowledge.

His body was trembling enough.

As before, there was something off about the Supreme Leader. But looking him directly in the eye was inviting instant death.

A fate that may await him still.

"Speak!"

His mouth was dry, but he managed to croak out a response. "We have discovered she is using the name of Hana Yin-lee. We believe she is in Geneva, Switzerland, but have not found her location as of this moment."

The silence was agonizing, and he was braced for the Supreme Leader's wrath. He kept his head down in the expected gesture of obedient servitude. He would stay here for hours if necessary.

"You must find the traitor and bring me evidence of her death."

The order was not surprising, it was exactly what he'd expected. The tightness in his chest eased a bit. "Yes, Commander."

He still didn't move, not until one of the Supreme Leader's men touched his shoulder, indicating he could stand. He wiped his damp palms on his pants, hoping his internal terror wasn't visible for all to see.

Failing to execute his assigned task would result in a swift and merciless death.

Followed by the deaths of his entire family.

A high price for failing the Supreme Leader.

JANUARY 18 – 11:04 p.m. – Oak Park, IL

"Let me out here," Jarek said when he spied Columbus Park.

"But this isn't Washington Street yet, I think it's a couple of blocks up ahead," the driver protested.

"This is fine, thank you." He paid the man his fee, along with the extra hundred, before sliding out of the back seat. The driver sped off, and it occurred to him that he should not be so frivolous with his cash.

How long would he need to live on what he was carrying in his pocket? Hopefully, Geoff would be willing to loan him more.

Along with allowing him to borrow his identity.

Asking such a thing would not be easy. No matter how your friends might offer to help you out of a jam, allowing their identity to be used for travel purposes was a serious request.

One Geoff may very well refuse.

If Geoff wouldn't help, then he hoped his colleague would allow him to stay for what was left of the night.

He strode down the street toward Geoff's residence, sweeping his gaze over the area to make sure the Asian didn't pop out from behind a tree. His paranoia was getting to him, but considering the possible implication to Hana, he had little choice but to move with great caution.

Which was why he was approaching Geoff's place from the rear, rather than from the front of the property.

Geoff's backyard was fenced in, and at fifty-seven years old, it had been a long time since he'd performed the physical task of scaling a fence. But he wasn't going to let that deter him. He exercised on a regular basis, did some strength training, and used the elliptical three days a week, how hard could it be?

Much harder than he'd ever imagined. Jarek knew that if anyone saw him struggling to get up and over the fence with the grace of a wounded buffalo, the police would be here in a heartbeat.

When he finally dropped down to the ground on the other side of the fence, he stayed in a crouched position, gasping for breath.

It was entirely possible Hana would have no use for the old and out of shape professor he'd turned out to be. Maybe once this was all over he'd go to the gym and hire a personal trainer. Surely fifty-seven wasn't that old.

There were no lights on in Geoff's home, making him wonder if he was out of town for the holiday rather than simply being asleep.

He swallowed hard, unable to comprehend what he'd do if Geoff was gone and unavailable to assist him.

Moving as silently as possible, he crossed the well-manicured lawn and knocked at the back door. The sound was incredibly loud to his ears, and he found himself praying the Asian wasn't within hearing distance.

No response.

He rapped again, louder. Geoff lived alone, too, although he'd been divorced, while Jarek had never married.

His heart had always belonged to Hana.

After what seemed like eons, he heard the thud of footsteps. A wave of relief hit hard. Geoff was home.

The door swung open, revealing a sleepy man who looked extremely grumpy. "Jarek? What on earth are you doing here at this hour?"

"I'm in danger and need help. Please, Geoff, don't turn me away."

The annoyance faded, and his colleague took a step back, allowing him to enter. "You're always welcome to stay in my guest room, Jarek. What sort of danger?" Geoff frowned. "And how did you get over the fence?"

"It wasn't easy. I'm not as young as I used to be." For the first time in hours, Jarek felt safe.

For now.

He glossed over what had transpired at the airport, and thankfully Geoff was too tired to press for more. As Geoff led him upstairs to the guest bedroom, it occurred to Jarek that anyone digging into his personal life would easily find that he and Geoff were work colleagues as well as friends.

He swallowed hard and silently prayed that he hadn't brought his danger to Geoff's doorstep.

The sooner he could convince his friend to allow him to borrow his identity long enough to fly to Geneva the better.

JANUARY 18 – 11:18 p.m. – Clarksville, MD

After convincing the desk clerk to take cash for the room, Sun returned to the Chevy where Mack was patiently waiting. He seemed to have more patience now than when they were younger, another sign of how much he'd grown and changed.

As she had. Physical attraction aside, she no longer cared about who Mack spent his personal time with.

She slid behind the wheel and tossed him a key.

"I'm going to park the vehicle in the back, near the dumpster, where it can't be seen from the road."

"Good idea."

She wasn't sure why she felt like Mack was humoring her. The way he'd reacted instinctively after the car bomb exploded and again at her compromised safe house indicated he had some sort of professional training.

More than just sparring at the gym to keep in shape.

What had Mack been doing these past few years? Last she'd heard, he'd been some sort of computer geek.

Hacking skills that were useless to her at the moment as a computer hadn't been something she'd stashed at the safe house. Something she'd have to reconsider once this current threat has been neutralized.

She thought about her meeting with Hyun-woo, the North Korean defector who claimed to have information on an impending nuclear attack. Not a bomb being set off directly from North Korea, but a small nuke that had been smuggled in to be used here in DC by supporters of the regime, under Kim Jong-un's orders.

Personally, she found that hard to believe. How could anyone possibly smuggle something like that into the US? Even a small nuclear device wasn't easy to hide. It seemed far-fetched, but she knew Jordan and Sloan were being paid to find out what was truth and what was merely an embellished story, boasted about by those who believed the regime was all powerful.

If such a plan was in place, she feared the upcoming presidential inauguration was the perfect time to strike.

Just over thirty-six hours from now. Not a lot of time, considering she'd already narrowly escaped two attempts on her life.

And that didn't count the possibility of her mother being in danger.

"Buck for your thoughts," Mack said in a low voice as they headed into their room. They had room number ten, the last one in the row, and the only room that provided two ways to escape.

His comment made her smile. They'd always bet a buck on everything they did, competition between them hot and fierce. "I really need to call my boss."

"Understood." Mack stood behind her with the duffel as she unlocked the door. "Are you concerned about a trace on your phone?"

"No, I have a disposable phone with me, just need to plug it in and get it validated so I can use it."

His eyebrow levered upward. "That stash of yours was pretty complete."

"Did you expect anything else?" She closed the curtains to cover the window, then turned on the bedside lamp.

It took longer than she thought to get the disposable phone working, and when she did, she learned she had missed a voice mail message from her boss. Even more frustrating was that Jordan didn't answer.

She left a terse message. "Call me at this number ASAP."

Mack sat on the edge of one of the beds, regarding her thoughtfully. "Speaking of calls to make, do you have any way to contact your mother?"

"Not directly." It pained her to admit she hadn't spoken to her mother in the past five years and hadn't actually spent time with her for even longer. The last Mensa meeting in Geneva, Switzerland, she'd only used a disposable phone to contact her mother, not daring to use anything traceable. Although they did have an anonymous answering service number they'd both memorized to use in case of an emergency.

"Your disposable cell is probably safe," Mack pointed out.

She looked up with sudden suspicion. Was there more to Mack's presence here in DC than he was admitting to? "Is there a reason you want me to call my mother?"

Mack didn't look away, holding her gaze steadily. "No, Sun. My only concern is to keep you and your mother safe."

She desperately wanted to believe him. Knowing Mack as long as she had, the thought of him turning on her was too painful to contemplate.

Once, she preferred working alone, but after partnering with Jordan and Sloan in preventing a terrorist act on the anniversary of 9/11, she'd come to appreciate having someone watching your back.

Someone like Macklin Remington.

But she hadn't seen Mack in just over five years.

Every muscle in her body went still as she tried not to panic.

What if he'd decided to go rogue? Play for the dark side? How did she know he didn't plant the car bomb himself? If she remembered correctly, it had been his suggestion to try to use the key fob from where they were standing.

Lord have mercy, had she placed her trust in the wrong man?

CHAPTER FOUR

January 18 – 11:58 p.m. – Geneva, Switzerland

Hana Yin-lee approached her apartment building with hesitation, the tiny hairs on the back of her neck tingling in alarm.

She'd sensed she was being watched since earlier that morning. Geneva was no longer a refuge. She never should have returned here after her last trip to North Korea, which had been a weak attempt to deflect suspicion before making her next move. Unfortunately, it hadn't worked. She must be slipping. She should have left the moment she'd caught a glimpse of a man with distinct North Korean features leaving the coffee shop she passed earlier today.

Now it might be too late.

She'd defected from North Korea more than thirty years ago, but she knew her recent work continued to put her in danger. Still, she'd taken every reasonable precaution and was good at her job.

Unfortunately, she knew better than most that there was no such thing as absolute safety. Her ties to North Korea were such that those who despised her would never rest until she was dead and buried deep beneath the soil. It was the main reason she'd used her resources there to mine important information that was so desperately needed. The only glimmer of hope she clung to was that no one in the regime knew about her daughter, Sun.

And she would gladly take that secret to her grave.

From the corner of her eye, a glimpse of movement. Nerves stretched to the limit, she reacted instinctively, spinning and pulling her knife, then slashing at the man who'd leaped forward in an attempt to grab her. Her blade struck flesh, but he didn't utter a sound. Instead, he fell into a fighting stance, ready to strike again.

Her martial arts training was by far her greatest strength, one she'd gifted her daughter. Most men used brute force in an attempt to cause harm, but so far, she'd managed to successfully beat them.

Please, Lord, provide me strength and knowledge to escape!

The North Korean attacked again, a knife in his hand and a glint of anger flashing in his eyes. She waited until the last possible second to strike, using her foot to disarm him, then spinning and kicking again, catching him beneath the chin. The knife flew from his hand, his head snapping back beneath the force of her kick.

Without stopping, she struck again and again, using every bit of training she possessed, hitting hard and fast without giving him time to collect himself. When he fell and hit his head against the unrelenting ground, his body went limp and blood pooled beneath his skull.

Hana instantly turned and ran from the apartment building, knowing the location had been compromised. How Kim Jong-un's men had found her, she had no idea.

But they had.

She didn't understand, why had there only been one man rather than the traditional two-man team? Unless the other was upstairs waiting for her in the unit.

She wasn't about to stick around long enough to find out.

When she was far enough away from her apartment, she caught a bus and headed for the Geneva station where she kept a locker full of cash, a disposable phone, and a fake passport. No gun, but she couldn't take one with her anyway.

She couldn't put off going to the United States any longer. Not the way things had escalated. She could only hope and pray it wasn't already too late.

JANUARY 19 – 12:14 a.m. – Clarksville, MD

Mack eyed Sun warily. Even after not seeing her for the past five years, he recognized her moods and knew something was wrong.

Was it possible she didn't trust him? Despite how he'd worked alongside her these past few hours?

She had good instincts. Better than most. It could be that she'd sensed he was holding back. Well past time to come clean. He drew in a deep breath. "There's something I need to tell you."

Sun jumped up from her seat and dropped into a fighting stance. "I knew I shouldn't have trusted you," she accused, her eyes flashing with fury.

"Whoa, Sun, that's not it at all." He winced at how badly he'd handled this. Sitting on the bed, he lifted his hands, palms forward, in a gesture of surrender. "I'm not here to hurt you but to keep you safe. And to help with your case of the potential nuke."

Her mouth dropped in surprise, but then her expression tightened. "Who do you work for?"

"NSA." He held her gaze. "You want to see my creds?"

"Yes." She didn't relax her guard, and he very carefully opened his winter jacket and pulled out his billfold and badge.

He held them up for her to see, then set them on the bed beside him. Once again, he raised his hands in the air. "I swear on the Bible that I'm not here to hurt you, Sun."

"How much of what you told me was a lie?" she challenged.

"None of it." He thought for a moment, then added, "I was attacked in New York's Central Park, and I did fly in from LaGuardia. I took the Metro to your place, but when you weren't there, I circled the area, looking for clues as to where you might be. When you walked up from the Metro stop, I felt certain you must have been meeting with the North Korean defector, Hyun-woo."

She stared at him without blinking. It was just as unnerving now as it had been when they were kids. "That's how you knew about my role with Security Specialists, Incorporated."

"Yes. Your boss, Jordan Rashid, reports to Clarence Yates, the Deputy Director of the FBI, correct?"

She nodded but still didn't relax. A tough nut to crack.

"After the attack in Central Park, I went to my boss, Ken Tramall, to request a leave of absence so I could come find you. Turns out, Tramall knows Yates and felt certain that a second pair of hands, one that could also understand North Korean dialects, would be a good thing to have working the nuke case. Sounds like Tramall worked with Yates in the past, loaning out an agent to participate on

Yates's multiagency task force with great success. I snapped up the chance."

"And you didn't tell me all this right away because—?"

He grimaced. "I was worried you'd kick me out of your place and off the case."

"I still can." She still didn't relax her fighting stance, and he could tell he'd ticked her off big time. "I trusted you, Mack."

"I still trust you more than anyone I know, Sun." He spoke from the heart, even though he sensed she wasn't in the mood to hear it. "When I learned you were in danger, I wasn't going to let anything stop me from coming here to back you up. In fact, I was prepared to resign my position on the spot if Tramall didn't approve my working with you." Learning about the possibility of a nuke being in DC had been an added bonus. Not that he wanted a nuke to go off here, but the ability to work with Sun had been too good of a chance to pass up.

With infinite slowness, Sun relaxed her guard. He lowered his hands yet made sure to keep them within view. He trusted Sun but had sparred with her often enough to know that beating her in hand-to-hand combat wasn't a piece of cake.

In fact, they were about dead even in the competitions they'd done over the years.

And if anything, she appeared to be in better shape now than she had back then.

"What do you know about the nuke?" Sun asked. "Do you have more intel than I do?"

"Doubtful, as I wasn't at the meeting with Hyun-woo. What did he have to say? Anything concrete about where we might find this thing?"

"No." Sun tipped her head from side to side as if

working kinks from her neck. "He was scared to death, kept looking over his shoulder as if he was expecting men from the regime to show up and grab him."

"What was the point of meeting with him, then?" Mack felt certain there had to be more.

Sun crossed over and picked up his badge from where he'd set it on the bed. "NSA, huh? For how long?"

"Six years," he admitted. "Remember when I told you at the last roundtable that I was doing computer work? That's how I started with them, but after eighteen months, my affinity for languages got me promoted into an agent role."

"Agent, huh?" She tossed the badge and billfold back onto the bed. Still moving slowly, he picked them up and returned them to his pocket. "I'm going to verify your story when Jordan calls me back."

"I know." He wouldn't expect anything less.

There was a brief pause. "He claimed no one within the North Korean regime would want to bomb the US, especially not in Washington, DC."

It took a minute for him to switch gears. "Hyun-woo said that?"

"Yes." She lifted a slender shoulder in a shrug. "Claims that the regime doesn't want a war with us, which is exactly what would happen if a North Korean nuclear bomb went off on US soil."

"There's an element of truth to that," he acknowledged. "Kim Jong-un isn't stupid. The US military would squash him like a bug."

"My thoughts exactly." Sun began to pace. "But why would there be any chatter about a nuke at all, then? A scare tactic?"

"Maybe." It was difficult to understand what went on in

a criminal mind. "But what's the fun of that? Thirty-six hours of fear, but then the suspense is over."

She halted mid stride. "The NSA thinks the presidential inauguration is the target?"

"Yes, that seems to be where a terrorist would get the biggest bang for his buck." He grimaced. "No pun intended."

Sun nodded slowly. "If there's any possibility of there being a nuke here in DC, we have to find it. While dodging the North Koreans, if that's who has come after me."

"I know." And they didn't have much time.

The clock was ticking. No way would anyone in the White House call off something like a presidential inauguration without a really good reason backed up by hard-core facts.

Neither of which they had at the moment.

JANUARY 19 – 12:36 a.m. – *Clarksville, MD*

Sun's phone vibrated. Recognizing Jordan's number, she answered. "It's about time you called me back."

"I know, I'm sorry we've been playing phone tag. Diana isn't feeling well, so I waited until she fell asleep." Jordan's voice was barely a whisper. She knew Diana was pregnant, and so was Natalia, Sloan's wife. The guys at Security Specialists, Inc. were settling down to be quite the family men.

Where that left her, she wasn't sure. Certainly, they needed to support their families, so it wasn't like they were going to shut down the business.

At least, she hoped not.

Not her problem at the moment. She decided to get straight to the point. "I got your message. Were you calling about the NSA involvement in this?" She kicked herself again for missing his call, must have been when her Jeep exploded. She'd been a little busy then.

"Yes, I didn't want to give you all the details on a voice mail, just in case. I spoke to Ken Tramall at length about the possible attack."

She grimaced, knowing he was right about not leaving details on a voice mail. "What did Tramall say?"

"Just that he had an agent who could speak flawless North Korean and was very interested in helping us on this case. Why? Is there a problem with the guy? We can send him on the first flight out of here if needed."

"No, it's fine." She let out a soundless sigh. She knew no one in the federal government really believed a nuclear bomb had been smuggled into the city without someone hearing about it. Jordan obviously considered this mission somewhat of a wild-goose chase.

And wasn't that what Hyun-woo thought as well?

"Is there something wrong with the agent?" Jordan asked.

"No. As it happens, I know Mack from the Mensa program."

"Good, glad to hear it. Did Hyun-woo have any intel?" Jordan asked.

"No." She quickly repeated her brief conversation with the North Korean. "I'm not sure where to go next. DC is a big area, if there truly is a bomb stashed somewhere, it would have to be brought within shooting distance of the White House."

"I've been thinking that it could have come by boat," Jordan mused. "It's the most accessible way to sneak into the city."

They'd searched numerous warehouses along the shoreline back when Jordan and Diana's daughter Bryn had been kidnapped. She didn't relish the thought of doing that again. "Okay, I'll try to come up with something. Oh, and we've run into a few problems as well."

"Like what?" Jordan was instantly on alert.

She filled him in on her Jeep explosion and the alleged danger, but she didn't mention her safe house since that had been done on her own dime. "We suspect the regime is tracking me down and that they're looking for my mother."

"A credible threat?" Jordan asked. "Maybe you should go into hiding, we can have Remington work the nuke case."

"No need, I'll handle it." She could take care of herself, as Jordan well knew. "I promise to let you know if things change."

"Okay, I'm going to hold you to that," Jordan said in warning. "And if Remington gives you any problems, let me know."

"Later." Sun disconnected from the call, thinking that Mack was already giving her problems. She'd gone from being glad to see him, to suspicious about him, to being glad to have him covering her back, to being suspicious of him once again.

This yo-yo of emotions had to stop.

It would be easier if she hadn't cared about him. More than she should. The way he'd claimed to trust her more than anyone had surprised her.

"My story checked out?" Mack asked.

"Yeah."

"You didn't mention the safe house," Mack noted.

She narrowed her gaze. "Because it isn't part of Security Specialists, Incorporated."

"I see." Mack eyed her thoughtfully. "But the attack there could have been from the regime."

"Maybe." She yawned. "We need to get some sleep, we'll need to start searching for the nuke at dawn."

"Okay, sounds good." He gestured toward the bathroom. "Do you want to go first?"

"No, you go ahead."

He shrugged, then headed into the small bathroom. The minute the door closed, she punched in the number she'd memorized years ago. Holding her breath, she waited for the answering service to pick up.

The familiar voice invited her to leave a message, but Sun wasn't sure that was the right move. There was no message from her mother, and she couldn't be sure this method of communication hadn't been compromised.

Sun shut down the disposable phone and tried to quell a flash of fear. Even if she wanted to fly off to meet with her mother, she had no idea where to go.

Hana had told her in no uncertain terms to call the answering service only as a last resort. That they were both safer if they never met in person.

What did it mean that her mother didn't leave a message for Sun?

Sun broke into a cold sweat. She shivered and hugged her arms across her body.

Had the regime already found and killed her mother?

JANUARY 19 – 1:01 a.m. – Chicago, IL

Despite Geoff's kind hospitality, Jarek had trouble relaxing enough to sleep. It wasn't just the wind causing the old home to creak and groan. In his mind's eye, he could still see the Asian's anger as he'd been wheeled out of the airport.

The man would not stand around wringing his hands at

how Jarek had gotten away. No, he'd have a plan B. Maybe even a plan C.

Was he crazy to think about borrowing Geoff's passport to fly to Geneva? What if he couldn't find Hana once he got there?

One thing was for certain, the woman he'd once loved was in trouble. The only reason the Asian would follow him was in an attempt to find Hana.

If only she'd come to him before now. He'd told her how he'd always stay in Chicago at the address he'd forced her to memorize. That he'd be waiting for her if she should ever need him.

Yet thirty years was a long time.

For all he knew, Hana had forgotten all about him by now.

His heart didn't want to believe it, but his brain reminded him that holding on to young love was incredibly foolish. Hana was stunningly beautiful. She could have anyone she wanted.

Plenty of men who were not in their late-fifties working as a boring professor of English literature.

A loud noise made him suck in a harsh breath, his heart jackhammering in his chest. If this kept up, he'd have a heart attack for real.

He slipped from the bed, glad he'd remained dressed in his clothes. The guest bedroom had an adjoining bath and a large walk-in closet. Neither offered a good hiding spot. Both areas would be the first place to look for him.

Easing the door open, he listened intently. The upper level of the house had a total of four bedrooms. The master, which Geoff was using, and three guest rooms. Jarek had been there enough to know that the lower level housed a living room, kitchen, dining room, and study.

What Geoff did with all this living space was beyond him. As a single guy, his condo was almost too big.

Stepping carefully, Jarek entered the hallway and closed the guest door softly behind him. For the first time in his entire life, he wished he owned a gun. Oh, and it would be nice to know how to shoot it too.

Not that he was capable of killing another human being.

The face of the Asian flashed in his mind. Okay, maybe if someone was going to shoot him, he'd be able to fire in self-defense.

Stupid to philosophize about gun control now. He made his way toward the door leading to the master bedroom. He turned the handle, wincing at the slight click.

The room was dark, blinds covering the windows so that no ambient light from the moon or early morning sunlight would show through. He could just make out the lumpy form of Geoff sleeping in the center of the king-sized bed. Jarek slipped into the bedroom, closing the door behind him, before making his way over to Geoff's bedside. He'd have to wake him while forcing his friend to remain silent.

He froze when he heard another creaking sound.

The stairs! Someone was coming up the stairs to the second level!

The Asian? Or someone else?

Jarek had no idea what to do. If he woke Geoff, his colleague might do or say something to draw the intruder's attention. Instead, he felt for the bed, then dropped to his knees beside it.

There was just enough room for him to slide beneath the frame. Without thinking through his actions, he went down on his stomach and crawled beneath it, shivering like a six-year-old boy afraid of monsters.

What kind of coward was he?

Before he could rethink his position, he heard the sound of the bedroom door opening. Every muscle in his body froze, he didn't dare breathe, as he heard the padded footsteps enter the room.

Then he heard it. A gunshot, but not very loud, muffled as if the barrel of the gun had been covered by a pillow.

No! It couldn't be! Not Geoff! The horror was too much to comprehend.

Still frozen, he listened as the footsteps retreated. There wasn't a moment to lose.

Wriggling out from beneath the bed, he kept his gaze averted from Geoff Webber's inert body and crept to the door. His heart was beating so loud he couldn't hear what the gunman was doing.

He opened the door, saw that the hallway was empty, and left the master suite. The only advantage he had was that he knew the house and the surrounding area extremely well, whereas the intruder likely didn't.

When he reached the bottom of the stairs, another muffled gunshot rang out, but he didn't dare stop.

Within seconds, Jarek was out the door and running for his life.

CHAPTER FIVE

January 19 – 1:18 a.m. – Washington, DC

The ringing phone pulled him from sleep. He scowled at the number on the screen, sensing he wasn't about to receive good news. "What?"

"We lost her."

He locked his jaw to stop himself from raining angry epithets down on the idiot's head. "How?"

"She has help. Some guy. And her car blew, too, without her in it." There was a pause before he added, "She shot me. Thankfully, it's just a flesh wound."

His fingers tightened on the cell. "I don't care if you're injured or half dead! I need you to find her and finish the job I hired you to do, understand? This is critical to my mission. We don't have much time."

"Yes, sir." The wounded idiot disconnected from the call.

Fury made it impossible to get back to sleep. He'd needed this guy to take out one tiny little woman. How difficult could it be?

Oh, he knew Sun Yin was well trained, he'd put his

sources to good use, hearing about this elite company called Security Specialists, Incorporated. But he'd come up with a surefire plan to kill her. First by planting the car bomb, and if that didn't work, by staking out her so-called safe house. It had been a stroke of luck that his man had followed her there a month earlier and knew to hide there to find her.

It was the perfect setup. And should not have resulted in failure.

But somehow she'd stayed one step ahead of him.

How had she escaped? And who was this man who was helping her?

He didn't like surprises. Especially ones that threatened his carefully thought-out plans. This had to work, or he and his cohorts would not get what they wanted.

Everyone thought the president had the most power.

Oh, but how wrong they were. It was those who survived and thrived in chaos that possessed power and control.

Soon, very soon, he'd have everything he needed.

At least, once he'd eliminated the one tiny, frustrating, pesky woman who dared to stand in his way.

JANUARY 19 – 1:26 a.m. – Geneva, Switzerland

Hana spent several minutes in the women's restroom at the Geneva station changing her appearance to match the photo on her fake passport.

Ignoring the tremor in her hands, she added the molded plastic to the upper ridge of her mouth to change her facial features. When she was satisfied that her face looked rounder and puffier, she used makeup to add to the slant of her eyes and deep creases to her face, which managed to add several years to her current age of fifty-three.

Disguises were her specialty and had kept her alive for this long. She hoped and prayed it would help her now.

The cold January weather was useful. She wrapped a long woven scarf over her head, crossing the ends around her neck, in an effort to cover most of her hair. Lastly, she added the bulky sweater beneath her jacket, adding the illusion of several pounds to her normally lean frame.

When she emerged from the restroom, she took on the air of an older woman, walking slower and slightly bent at the waist. There hadn't been enough room in the locker for a cane, so she leaned on the wall when the opportunity presented itself as she slowly made her way to the counter to purchase a bus ticket.

After boarding a bus for the airport, she dropped heavily into her seat, making a soft groan as if her old bones ached. But her mind was elsewhere, anticipating what the weather would be like in Chicago this time of year. Much colder, she knew, than what they experienced here in Switzerland, along with the chance of snow. Any snow that fell in Switzerland tended not to stick around for very long.

She tried not to imagine Jarek's reaction to her arriving on his doorstep after all this time. Especially because she desperately needed his help. She'd traveled the world but had only spent six months in the United States. Thirty years since they'd been together, although they had spoken on a rare occasion, but not recently. As much as she'd missed him, she'd done what had been in his best interest.

The only thing she knew for certain was that he was still alive and living in Chicago. The city where they'd met and fallen in love. She didn't think he'd married or had children but mentally braced herself for that news in case she was wrong.

Just because he'd claimed to love her didn't mean he

hadn't moved on with someone else. She would never blame him if he had. In fact, she'd told him to move on without her.

As she walked into the airport, she found herself hesitating, wondering if she was making a mistake. What if she brought danger to Jarek's doorstep? Despite her disguise and traveling under the name of Mi-Cha Kung, she couldn't be absolutely certain the regime hadn't found a way to follow her.

Hana leaned heavily against the counter as she purchased a one-way ticket to Chicago using cash, ignoring the raised eyebrows of the woman standing behind her. Normally, the airlines didn't allow you to travel without purchasing your ticket online, but slipping extra cash while murmuring about an abusive ex-husband seeking revenge was enough to convince the clerk to break the rules for an older Asian lady.

Her flight didn't leave for several hours, but that was okay. She planned to sit in a corner, keeping a wary eye out for anyone who looked as if they didn't belong.

At least Chicago was a city large enough to get lost in. If she didn't find Jarek, or he was married with a family, then she would find a way to locate Sun on her own.

Praying the regime didn't find her first.

JANUARY 19 – 1:48 *a.m.* – *Clarksville, MD*

Mack couldn't shut off his brain, a common problem when he was knee-deep in a case. If there really was a small nuclear bomb hidden in DC, their hopes of finding it before the inauguration at noon on January 20 was slim to none.

But bringing the bomb in via the water was an intriguing idea. If he'd planned something so outrageous, where would he hide such a device? Many of these bombs were small enough to be carried by one man, yet bulky enough to draw attention.

"You're thinking too loud," Sun complained.

He smiled in the darkness. "Sorry."

"No you're not." He glimpsed her shadow sitting up and reaching for the light. He squinted in the sudden brightness. Sun frowned at him. "Let's talk it out."

"Okay." Better to talk about a nuke than notice how beautiful she was. Her silky hair was cut chin length, making her look even more like the teenager she'd once been. She'd been like a younger sister, yet somehow after breaking up with Abigail, his feelings for Sun had morphed into something more. Unrequited feelings, as he knew she considered him to be the annoying big brother she'd never had.

Enough, this line of thought wasn't going to help. He dragged his attention back to the important matter at hand. "What kind of nuke are we talking about? A backpack device that a single man could use while walking into a crowd? Or something that would be shot out from the back of an SUV?"

"You think North Korea made a new and improved version of the Davy Crockett?" Sun's eyes widened with concern.

"The old Davy Crocketts weren't all that small," he pointed out. "They shoved enough uranium and plutonium to yield twenty tons of explosives in a container that was still too heavy for one man to use without being noticed."

Sun's expression turned thoughtful. "It's interesting, though, isn't it? I mean, Kim Jong-un made a big deal out of testing large nuclear rockets not small nukes. Almost as if he were testing his ability to strike the US from his homeland. I never would have thought he'd create a new smaller device that could be sneaked into the country."

"You have a point," Mack agreed. "And Kim Jong-un also signed the nuclear bomb treaty with South Korea last year, giving at least the appearance of not wanting to go to war."

There was a moment of silence before Sun spoke. "Well, Kim Jong-un isn't known for keeping his word, so I'm not sure that means much. Trust me, his regime is extremely corrupt. I wouldn't be at all surprised if he'd managed to create a small nuclear bomb."

"Unless it's all a figment of someone's overactive imagination." The weight of responsibility was staggering. At first, he hadn't really believed in the nuke's existence. But now? He had to admit the possibility was all too real. And they couldn't forget about the North Korean threat to Sun personally. Which was likely related to their case. "If there really is a device here, we need to find it as soon as possible."

"I know, but where?" She spread her hands helplessly. "The only theory, if you want to call it that, is that someone brought it in via boat. And even if that's true, it's not enough. Do you have any idea how many warehouses and boarded-up buildings there are near the shoreline? I spent more hours than I care to remember searching for a missing child in those warehouses, and we barely scratched the surface of what's out there. Not to mention, anyone with a truck could bring that device in from a pier located just about anywhere—Virginia, Maryland, Connecticut . . ." She shook her head. "Anywhere."

She was right, the possibilities of a hiding place for this thing were endless. "We need Hyun-woo. He must know more than what he's told you."

Sun looked thoughtful. "I don't know, Mack. He was

deeply afraid, and I assumed his emotion stemmed from the overwhelming power of the regime. It's something my mother spoke about often and hard to imagine unless you lived through it." She shrugged. "But you could be right, it's possible I didn't ask the right questions."

"Any idea where we can find him?"

There was a slight hesitation before she admitted, "I followed him after our meeting."

He stared, doing his best to keep a lid on a flash of anger because she hadn't mentioned that small fact earlier. What else was Sun holding back from him? He managed to keep his tone level with an effort. "Really?"

"Yes, so I know where he was staying at least as of yesterday. He could have moved, but maybe not since we met in a neutral location." She shrugged. "I guess it can't hurt to pin him down to press for more information."

"Let's go," he said tersely. The sense of urgency was impossible to ignore.

The North Korean defector was their only potential lead. And if they didn't find Hyun-woo and get something more out of him, they were right back at square one.

If the bomb was here, he couldn't begin to fathom what life would be like after a nuclear explosion took out a group of politicians, including the incumbent President of the United States.

Unimaginable mass chaos.

JANUARY 19 – 2:06 a.m. – Chicago, IL

Jarek felt certain God was watching over him. He'd stopped his mad rush deep in the park and had hidden behind a trio of trees when he caught a glimpse of a taxi slowing down at the intersection. Lunging forward from the woods, waving his arms like a mad man, he almost wept when the driver lowered his driver's side window, eyeing him with suspicion. "Where you headed?"

For a moment, his mind went blank. He had no idea where to go other than away. Far, far away. "Do you know where I can get a cheap motel room?"

"Sure, there's a Motel 8 about ten minutes from here. Hop in."

Jarek gratefully pulled open the back passenger door and slid into the taxi, glancing over his shoulder to be sure the gunman hadn't managed to follow him. If not for knowing his way through the park, Jarek didn't think he'd have made it without being shot or worse. He relaxed against the seat, every muscle in his body wailing in pain. He hadn't sprinted for that long of a distance since his college days of running track.

Clearly he needed to make better use of the gym in his condo. If the gunman had caught him—he shivered and dragged his hands over his face.

Geoff was dead! Because of him. His dear friend, shot in his bed, and for what? Inviting Jarek in? Being kind to a colleague? What kind of monster did such a thing? Had he been followed to Geoff's home? If so, how?

Or was it possible the Asian knew who his friends were prior to all of this? The same way they'd known he'd purchased a plane ticket to Geneva, Switzerland.

Who was this man? Why did he kill people without blinking an eye?

Why, Lord, why?

"You okay, buddy?"

The driver's question helped him get a grip on his spiraling emotions. He couldn't fall apart, not yet. Not until he was safe. He met the guy's gaze in the rearview mirror.

"Yes, I'm fine, thanks for asking. But would you mind finding a different cheap motel? Something farther away perhaps?"

The driver shrugged. "Hey, it's your money."

"Thank you." Jarek swallowed hard and stared out the window at the various homes they passed along the way.

Obviously, after this, he didn't dare call any of his other friends or colleagues. Any contact from him would place a giant target on their backs. In fact, it may even be too late. A gunman could show up at their homes at any time, killing senselessly while searching desperately for him.

Another shiver rippled over him, and he almost threw up right there in the back of the taxi. Despite the chilly January air, he was sweating beneath his clothes. He took several deep breaths in an attempt to calm himself, but he couldn't escape the horrific memories flashing through his mind.

Geoff Webber was dead, and it was only by God's grace that he hadn't been killed too.

And the worst thing about this entire situation was that he knew without a doubt that his meddling had put Hana in danger. In fact, he couldn't seem to shake the sense of keen desolation that she may already be dead.

His chest tightened painfully to the point he thought this is what it felt like to have a real heart attack. He bowed his head and squeezed his eyes shut tightly to prevent unmanly tears from streaking down his cheeks.

Forgive me, Hana, my love. Please, forgive me.

JANUARY 19 – 2:19 *a.m.* – *Washington, DC*

Sun didn't mind driving in the middle of the night, far

less traffic compared to the congestion that made getting around DC impossible in the daytime.

But despite her exhaustion, she was keenly aware of Mack's large presence beside her. He wore some kind of woodsy aftershave that was driving her batty.

"Where exactly is this place?" Mack asked.

She pulled her wayward thoughts together with an effort. "It's an apartment building that looks like it should be condemned." She glanced at him. "I'm planning to leave the car someplace safe, then hailing a taxi to get to his place."

Mack nodded. "The only problem with that idea is that it makes it difficult for us to leave in a hurry if something goes south."

"I know." She'd already considered that possibility. "I can park it somewhat close, but I don't want this vehicle to be compromised in any way." Bad enough her safe house had been found, she didn't want to give up her only vehicle.

"Your call." Mack's affable agreement made her frown. It wasn't like him to give in so easily.

Then again, their reunion hadn't been anything like she'd imagined.

Of course, Mack hadn't come to see her for personal reasons. Well, other than he'd been attacked and had discovered that she and her mother were in danger.

But that wasn't the same as finding her because they'd been friends and had often spent holidays together while other boarding school kids went home to their families. They'd bonded over their similar situations and bickered over everything else.

And he preferred pretty blonde's like Abigail rather than her.

Whatever. All of that was in the past. She wasn't interested in starting something with Mack, even if that was a possibility. Most of the time she found him incredibly annoying.

"What's the address of the apartment building?" Mack glanced up from the smartphone in his hand.

She gave it to him, and he quickly punched the information into the phone.

"There's a drugstore that's open twenty-four seven less than two miles from that area," he said. "If we leave the car there, we can easily run back to that location if something goes wrong."

It irked her to admit he had a point. "Okay, fine. We'll park the Chevy in the drugstore lot and walk over from there."

"Do you know where the drugstore is, or should I turn on the GPS?"

She mentally visualized the area, irritated that she hadn't thought of doing that herself. "I know where it is, thanks."

"No need to get testy," Mack said, slipping his phone back into his pocket.

"I'm not testy." Although she knew her voice sounded like she was. "I have the same eidetic memory you do."

"Then why didn't you think of going to the drugstore?"

She tightened her grip on the steering wheel so she wouldn't give in to the urge to punch him in the arm. After exiting the interstate, she drove down toward the drugstore. "Listen, when we get to the apartment, I want you to back me up outside while I go to talk to Hyun-woo."

"You're not going in alone." Mack's voice was firm.

Oh, for pity's sake! "Are you going to argue every step of the way? I've already met with Hyun-woo, he clearly knows me. He won't talk to you."

Mack scowled. "You've already mentioned it's a lousy neighborhood."

"Yeah, but I've been there before and know how to take care of myself."

Another long moment of silence, up ahead she saw the lights of the drugstore sign. When she pulled in and parked, she turned toward him. But before she could say anything, he surprised her. "Fine, I'll stay out of sight in the hallway."

Taking the compromise, she nodded. "Let's go."

As it turned out, they didn't see a single taxi as they made their way down toward the dilapidated apartment building where Hyun-woo lived. It burned her to admit Mack had offered the better option, but she didn't plan to tell him that.

His ego was already too big for his head.

The apartment building looked worse in the dead of night, and a shiver of apprehension slid down her spine. She whispered, "He's in apartment 2B, which is on the second floor to the right."

"Got it," Mack replied.

The door to the apartment building had a broken lock, no surprise there. The stairs creaked loudly as they took them to the second floor. Upon hitting the landing, she stopped abruptly when she saw the door to apartment 2B hanging open.

Not good.

She glanced at Mack. He had his weapon in his hand and clearly wasn't going to stay in the hall. And maybe that was okay. This was one of those times it was nice to have backup, even though she was armed too.

Giving the door a push, she gagged at the horrific smell that wafted toward her. And she knew in an instant what she'd find inside.

Two steps into the room confirmed her suspicions. Hyun-woo's dead body was sprawled on the floor, blood congealing around the deep slice in his throat that stretched from ear to ear.

The North Korean defector had been murdered.

CHAPTER SIX

January 19 – 2:38 a.m. – Geneva, Switzerland

Hana kept her head down while keeping a wary eye on the people milling about the airport terminal.

When she caught a glimpse of two men of North Korean descent, her blood ran cold. She held her breath, keeping her gaze down at the book in her lap. She'd decided to purchase one to give herself something to do and to help with her disguise.

Now she feared her disguise was useless. If these men found her here, she'd be dead before she had a chance to board the plane heading to London and then on to Chicago.

Only an hour had passed since she'd purchased her ticket, and there was still another hour to wait until it was time to board.

Too long.

She concentrated on slowly turning the pages of her book as if she were deeply engrossed in the story, rather than using every one of her five senses to keep tabs on the two men. How had they replaced the man she'd taken out of commission so quickly?

Because the regime had hundreds of men who would jump to do Kim Jong-un's bidding. No matter the cost.

Each one of them knew they'd be dead regardless. Not following orders would get you killed, and if you died in the line of duty, then at least your death brought honor to your family.

How messed up was that?

After what seemed like forever, but was only fifteen minutes, the two North Korean's moved on.

Still, there was no time to rejoice. The Geneva airport was large, but there were likely more men searching for her now than the two-man team that had staked out her apartment building.

The sick feeling in her stomach intensified. They'd be back. Oh yes, they would be back.

She needed to be on board the plane before they discovered her true identity.

JANUARY 19 – 2:53 *a.m.* – *Washington, DC*

"Sun? Let's get out of here!" Mack clamped a hand on Sun's arm, not liking this turn of events one bit.

Sun nodded and turned away from the gruesome sight. He was mentally kicking himself for not coming to question Hyun-woo sooner, before he'd been taken out.

As he headed to the door, a man darted out from the shadows. He reacted instinctively, kicking out at the gun in the guy's hand. The weapon clattered to the floor, and from the corner of his eye, he noticed Sun kicking it farther out of reach.

He struck again, hearing his sensei in his head. Strike, block, strike!

The man backed up but didn't go down despite the

power in Mack's kick. He had to give the guy credit, most men would have been on the floor by now.

Sun joined the fight, kicking the guy's head as Mack struck him in the chest. The duel assault made the guy stagger backward all the way through the doorway and slam into the hallway wall.

In the back of his mind, Mack knew they couldn't stay long. Hand-to-hand was less alarming than gunfire, a sentiment Sun obviously shared as she hadn't pulled her weapon, but this amount of noise was still bound to raise an alarm. Someone would eventually call the police, and while he had his creds, he wasn't so sure Sun would be as protected as an employee of a private security firm.

Sun kicked the guy again, in the chest, and the man groaned and then threw up. Mack figured he'd probably had enough and lifted a hand to stop Sun from coming at him again. He crouched next to the man, who appeared dazed and confused.

"Who sent you?" Mack hissed in a low voice.

The man wore a full face mask covering his features, and his head lolled to the side as if the man didn't have enough strength to keep himself upright. Mack reached over to yank the mask off but stopped when he heard someone yelling through a door at the end of the hall.

"The police are on the way!"

He pulled off the mask. The guy's face was swollen from where their combined kicks had connected with his cheekbone.

The assailant was a stranger. And also not of North Korean descent.

"Come on, Mack. We need to get out of here," Sun urged.

She was right, but he went through the guy's pockets

anyway. He found cash, a disposable phone, and nothing else.

He pocketed the cash and the phone before rising to his feet. Once again, Sun led the way out of the apartment building while he covered her.

The wail of sirens proved the resident of the nearby apartment hadn't been lying about calling the cops. Which was somewhat interesting as the police weren't often viewed as trustworthy in neighborhoods like this.

At least, that was his experience in New York. Could be that DC was different.

When the sirens grew louder, he looped his arm over Sun's shoulders and pulled her close to his side. Lowering his head, he spoke directly into her ear. "We may need a place to hide out for a bit."

"Not yet, let's keep walking. Acting as a romantic couple hopefully won't attract attention."

As much as he enjoyed playing the role of being romantically involved, he didn't agree with her logic. "Unless the person who called it in saw the two of us through their peephole."

She blew out an annoyed breath. "Fine, have it your way."

"This way." Taking a page from her earlier playbook, he drew her through the front yard of a residence and through to the next street. From there, he went one more block, then crouched in the shadows.

Bright red and blue flashing lights lit up the sky from the very direction they'd come. Two squads from what he could tell.

And the minute they found the dead body, there would be dozens of officers fanned out and searching the area.

"Time to run," he whispered.

Sun's response was to jump up and sprint out of their hiding spot.

The woman was fast, no doubt about it. It took him longer than he cared to admit to catch up with her, but when he finally did, he stayed a step behind mostly so he could continue to cover her back.

It wasn't unusual for Mack to put his life on the line for his country, but covering Sun was personal.

He'd do whatever was necessary to keep her safe.

Sun didn't slow her pace until they were about a block from the drugstore. They slowed to a walk so as not to attract undue attention. Once again, Mack put his arm around Sun's slim shoulders, keeping her close, but it wasn't easy to remain nonchalant. He kept expecting the police to show up to arrest them at any moment.

When they reached the car, he dropped his arm from Sun's shoulders, but he still didn't draw a breath of relief. Sun backed out of their parking space and drove sedately back toward the highway.

"You think the drugstore has cameras?" He hadn't seen any but felt certain most drugstores, especially those in this type of neighborhood, would have them. Narcotics would always be a target.

"Maybe, but didn't you notice how I muddied the license plates?" Sun glanced at him. "I might not work for NSA, but I'm not a rookie either."

"I never said you were." He let out a soundless sigh. "We just lost our best lead."

"I know." Sun's expression turned grim. "And it's my fault."

That surprised him. "No, it's not. I should have mentioned going to confront him sooner."

"Only because I didn't get enough information from

him the first time," Sun countered. She lightly smacked her hand on the steering wheel. "What is going on here? Did you notice the assailant wasn't Korean?"

"Yeah, I noticed. What about the guy at the safe house? Think they're one and the same?"

Sun slowly shook her head. "The man we just left behind at the apartment building wasn't injured, and I know my shot hit the guy at the house. I heard him cry out in pain."

"So there're two of them," Mack surmised.

"Or more."

Great, wasn't that just peachy? Two different factions trying to kill them? Or did all roads lead to one guy in charge of the whole shebang?

He wished he knew. As it was, they were fighting blind, trying to find a nuke that could be just about anywhere.

Talk about being set up for failure.

It would take a minor miracle for them to pull this off in time. And these days? He didn't believe in them.

JANUARY 19 – 3:03 *a.m.* – *Chicago, IL*

Jarek would have preferred to drive in the taxi for what was left of the night, but he sensed his driver becoming impatient. He finally settled on a low-budget motel that was located to the north of the city.

He paid the man well, but he noticed his stash of cash was beginning to dwindle. He'd purposefully stocked up with cash for his trip, which had thankfully come in handy. Still, he couldn't keep doing this, running from one place to the next like a scared rabbit.

What he needed was some sort of plan. But it was difficult to think clearly after witnessing the callous murder of your closest friend.

Pasting a benign smile on his face, he approached the desk clerk, a young kid with a bad case of acne. "Good evening. My car broke down a few miles from here, would you happen to have a room available? I hope to call my brother for assistance come daylight."

The kid shrugged. "Yeah, I gotta room. Didn't you see the vacancy sign?"

Of course he had, so much for his attempt to be polite. "Thank you. How much?" He pulled out his cash clip.

"Gotta have a credit card." The kid stared at him as if he was a numbskull. "That's the rule, in case of damage to the room."

"Well, you see, I don't have a credit card, but would an extra hundred suffice?" He slid the money across the counter. "Perhaps you'd like to put this toward your college fund?"

The kid eyed the money suspiciously, then snatched it up. "Okay, room's fifty-eight bucks, and you gotta be out by eleven."

"Thank you." He gave the kid a fake name, praying he wouldn't ask to see an ID. Thankfully, he didn't, likely swayed by the hundred-dollar bill that was already stashed deep in his jeans pocket.

Jarek took the key to room seven and turned to go back outside. He walked down the sidewalk, glancing over his shoulder before using the key to enter his room. The interior was dim and reeked of stale cigarette smoke, mold, and some heavy air freshener that didn't come close to masking the obnoxious odors. The accommodations were sorely lacking, but he told himself that it was better to suffer the awful smell than deal with a gunman intent on killing him.

He shot the dead bolt home and added the chain lock too. After another peek outside, he pulled the curtains closed. Lastly, he dragged a heavy chair across the room, placing it in front of the door.

Yet he still didn't feel safe.

And worse, this was only a pathetic and temporary haven. He had no idea what his plan might be when checkout time rolled around.

JANUARY 19 – 3:12 a.m. – Washington, DC

Sun couldn't erase the image of the dead North Korean defector from her mind. A common problem when you had an eidetic memory.

Every gory detail remained imprinted in her brain, forever.

She glanced at Mack, knowing he was likely suffering the same way. Their Mensa brains, complete with photographic memories, had been their bond when they were young.

Now they were partners in a deadly game. One in which they had no clue who the players were or why they'd come after her. The regime, she understood, but this latest attack? Very strange.

And she desperately needed to get in touch with her mother. But how?

"Where are we headed?" Mack asked.

"Another motel." Thankfully, her previous work with Jordan provided several potential places they could use in a pinch.

"I think we need to stay close to DC," Mack said. "After all, that's where the nuke is supposed to be."

"Yeah, okay. There's a place just outside of DC we can

use." She glanced at her watch. "I'll need to call Jordan in a few hours; we could use more cash."

"We're okay for now." Mack waved his hand. "I came prepared, and what I took off the assailant helps too."

She supposed stealing from a man who'd tried to kill them didn't count as a real crime, although it still made her uncomfortable. "I don't understand why a non-North Korean would have killed Hyun-woo."

"Why does the nationality of the assassin matter?"

She flushed. "It doesn't, except that we've been dealing with North Korean bad guys until now. The Korean culture is such that outsiders are not trusted. Especially Americans."

"You're the expert on Korean culture, so I can't argue that. And we already established the guy at the apartment building wasn't the same one you injured outside the safe house."

"One thing the North Koreans have is manpower. Lots and lots of obedient soldiers who will do anything to make their commander happy." The stories relayed by her mother painted a grim picture of her mother's homeland. Sun knew she was half American and half Korean, yet she preferred to think she had more American blood running through her veins.

Her mother had refused to give her any information related to her biological father, claiming the truth was too dangerous to those who support the regime.

The fear in her mother's eyes had been so real that Sun had clamped a lid on her innate curiosity. What did it matter who her father was? If she couldn't have any sort of relationship with the man, there was no point in wondering about him.

"We need to plot the most likely places in the city that

could be used as a launch point for the bomb," Mack said, interrupting her thoughts.

"Do you really think that's easier than searching for the hiding spot?" She let out a harsh laugh. "Come on, there are millions of places around DC where this thing could be launched. The whole point is that it's a nuclear bomb. Even a small one can do a considerable amount of damage to the city."

"Okay, then what's your idea?" He sounded tired, which she knew from experience made him cranky. "We need to do something, we can't just sit in a motel room somewhere and twiddle our thumbs."

"What about that phone you took off the assailant? You're the hacker, there must be something you can do with it."

He pulled the device from his pocket. "Maybe. Although finding out who hired the assailant may not get us anywhere near the location of the bomb."

"It's the only lead we have at the moment. I mean, sure, we can wander around DC looking for the perfect launch site, but we could get to it too late. We know the North Koreans are involved somehow. At least according to the chatter transcript Jordan sent me."

"I'd like to hear that transcript for myself," Mack said.

"Don't trust me?" She inwardly winced at how defensive she sounded.

"Of course I trust you, but sometimes two people can hear subtle differences and nuances in speech patterns."

"That's a poor use of resources when you have the assailant's phone in your hand."

"Not much I can do without a computer."

He was right. "Yeah, okay. I'll get Jordan to supply us with a sat computer."

Neither of them spoke as she drove to the motel. As before, she went in to secure the room while Mack waited in the Chevy.

Once they were settled in the motel room, Mack began playing with the assailant's phone. Curious, she crossed over to sit beside him to watch.

"Are you trying to break the passcode?"

"Yes." His fingers flew over the buttons.

She frowned. "Is there a specific method to do that?"

"Not really, but I'm a patient man. One of these will work."

Sun couldn't believe he was really going to try every possible number sequence to get into the device. That would take hours, although really, she wasn't sure what else they could do. Poking through warehouses along the shoreline seemed even more of a long shot than Mack's attempt to break into the assailant's phone.

Moving away from where Mack was working, she used her own disposable cell to call Jordan about their need for a satellite computer and more cash.

"Okay, I can get you what you need. Where do you want to meet?"

Sun thought for a moment. "Remember the motel near the freeway exit ramp? The one where we ended up exchanging gunfire? We're at the same place."

"I remember it very well," Jordan said dryly. "See you soon."

"Thanks." She glanced at Mack, who was still working the phone. "Don't break your fingers, Jordan will be here shortly with a satellite computer and more cash."

"Got it," Mack announced with glee, a wide grin slicing his features.

"No way." Sun was impressed with his tenacity.

"Always helps when they start with a low number," Mack said modestly. "I usually pick a number in the middle followed by a high number and a low number. Makes it harder to crack."

She didn't want to admit she never considered a hacker's perspective when creating her own passcodes. Sliding close, she leaned over to see the flip phone. "Now what? Is there a way to track incoming calls?"

"Yes, but just know there could easily be another disposable phone on the other end, which makes this less likely to be helpful." She watched as Mack found the menu screen. "See here? These are all the calls coming in and going out, and they have Washington, DC, area codes."

"Not surprising, why wouldn't they pick up phones here in the city?"

"Oh, I've had the gamut. Some people buy them from cities they're not working in as a way to cover their trail." He looked up. "There are only two different numbers here, and not that many calls to each of them."

"And that means what?"

He shrugged. "In my humble opinion? Means the guy in charge is keeping a tight rein on his hired help."

"Are you going to call the numbers?"

"Yes, but don't get your hopes up. This likely won't yield much."

"It's more than we have now," Sun pointed out.

Mack punched in the first series of numbers, the last call the assailant had made. She leaned close to hear better.

"Is it done?" a deep voice asked.

"Yes, but there was a complication," Mack said in a clipped tone. She was impressed there was no hint of his New York accent.

There was only the slightest hesitation before the call

abruptly ended. When Mack tried the number again, there was no response. Then he tried the second number, but that call went unanswered.

"You're right," she said in disgust. "That wasn't much."

"On the contrary, we learned two things," Mack said. "One, the job is likely to kill you."

"We already kinda knew that." She furrowed her brow. "What's the other thing?"

"The guy in charge didn't recognize my voice and quickly aborted the call."

She threw up her hands. "That's nothing!"

"We might find out more when Jordan brings the computer. I may even be able to hack into the cell tower database to find out where the disposable phone he was using on his end was last located."

Might? Maybe? Not encouraging.

Then again, Mack had surprised her by getting into the phone in the first place. Maybe she was selling him short.

It was both humbling and annoying to realize how much she needed his help working this case.

Maybe he could even help find her mother.

CHAPTER SEVEN

January 19 – 3:24 a.m. – Geneva, Switzerland

Hana slowly made her way over to stand in the boarding line, making sure she moved like an old woman with severe arthritis. A sweet man gestured for her to cut in front of him, and she gave him a nod.

"Thank you, kind sir." She kept her voice low, knowing that her disguise didn't cover the nuances of her voice. It was the most difficult thing to change, which is why voice recognition had become so important in solving crimes.

"You're welcome." The man hesitated, then said, "If you'd like to sit, I can save this spot for you."

As much as she appreciated his concern, a humbling if rare thing to experience in the midst of running from men trying to kill her, she shook her head. "No, thank you. I'll be sitting long enough on the flight."

"Yes, I'm sure we all will."

She fell silent, shuffling forward a foot at a time as passengers boarded the plane. She'd left her book behind in order to keep her hands free in case she was attacked. Despite how badly she wanted to turn and search the area for the Koreans, she purposefully kept her eyes facing forward.

Moving stiffly wasn't a problem, she was so tense it felt as if her joints were rusted in place like the tin man in the *Wizard of Oz*. Any moment she expected to feel a hand on her shoulder, two men flanking her as they attempted to force her from the line.

Time seemed to stand still, but eventually the people in front of her moved enough that she was next up to board. When it was her turn, she scanned her boarding pass and was waved through.

Still, she didn't dare increase her speed, needing to stay in character until she was safely on US soil. At that point, she might feel safe enough to shed her disguise.

She found her window seat in the middle area of the plane. Edging into the spot, she sat with a soft groan. The tightness of her chest eased, and she risked a quick glance around at her fellow passengers.

So far, so good.

For a moment, she rested her forehead against the glass window, looking out at the city she'd used as her home base over the past few weeks. Ridiculous to feel sad about leaving when she'd really never had a place to call home.

The closest she'd come were those months in Chicago with Jarek thirty years ago.

Yet this was the life she'd chosen. Making the best out of an impossible situation. And even knowing what she did now, she couldn't necessarily say she wouldn't have made the same decisions again.

If she'd saved at least one life by her actions, it was worth it.

Shaking off the maudlin thoughts, she tried to think about what she would do once she landed in Chicago. Oh, it would be hours yet, but still, she needed to think of some way to get in touch with Jarek.

Thinking of the man she'd once loved made her smile. She lifted her gaze, then froze, the smile seemingly a horrific caricature on her face.

One of the North Koreans was walking down the center aisle of the plane!

Her heart thudded painfully, fear gripping her by the throat. No! It couldn't be! They couldn't have found her on this flight.

Or were they just walking through each plane, searching for her? But who would let them do such a thing? With all the security in place, you couldn't get onto a plane without a boarding pass.

She forced herself to lower her gaze, reaching forward casually to pick up the magazine from the seat pocket. Sitting there calmly reading was the hardest thing she'd ever done.

From the corner of her eye, she saw the Korean move past her, disappearing from view.

He didn't leave the plane either. Within ten minutes, the flight attendants closed the doors and did their final preflight check.

She was stuck with the Korean, at least until they landed in London.

There had to be a way to lose him in England. No matter what happened, she couldn't allow him to follow her all the way to Chicago.

She'd rather die than allow harm to come to those she loved.

JANUARY 19 – *3:51 a.m.* – *Washington, DC*

Mack eyed Jordan Rashid curiously as he set the satellite computer on the desk in their room.

"Jordan, this is Macklin Remington. Mack, my boss, Jordan Rashid."

He'd nodded in response to Sun's brief introduction. He had to remind himself there was no reason to be jealous of the guy. After all, Jordan was married with a daughter and a baby on the way. Mack forced a smile. "Nice to meet you. Have you spoken to Yates recently?"

"No, why? You have something I need to report?"

He glanced briefly at Sun, then shrugged. "No, but we need more intel to go on or this mission will be a complete bust. There must be more chatter out there about this alleged nuke."

"Mack's right," Sun added. "My only contact, the North Korean defector named Hyun-woo, has been murdered." She went on to explain how they'd disarmed the assailant and escaped.

Jordan blew out a heavy sigh. "That's not good."

"No, and without a lead, we're spitting in the wind." Mack gestured to the computer. "I'm going to try to hack into the assailant's disposable phone carrier in an attempt to trace the number, but if that doesn't turn up something good, we're stuck."

"You can do that? Hack into the phone account to trace a number?" Jordan looked impressed.

"I can try," he admitted modestly.

"Mack started his career with NSA as a hacker," Sun added helpfully. "If anyone can do it, he can."

He was touched by how quickly Sun defended his skills, especially since she hadn't seen them in action. His feelings toward her vacillated between wanting to throttle her and kiss the daylights out of her.

If he tried the latter, he felt certain she'd clip him under the chin in response. The thought made him grin.

"Would you send the transcript of the earlier chatter?" Sun asked. "Mack wants to listen in as well."

Jordan raised a brow. "You think that's necessary?"

"It can't hurt," Mack retorted.

Jordan's gaze shifted between the two of them. "It's interesting you both share that same ability. I couldn't believe it when Sun began to speak Arabic."

Mack grinned and winked at Sun. "It came in handy when we were young and wanted to talk about stuff we didn't want anyone else to know."

Sun elbowed him in the ribs. "Don't tell him that. We should have been more inclusive."

"Hey, we were the odd ones out, remember?" Mack had protected Sun more than once from kids who'd called her all sorts of derogatory names because of her Korean heritage. And they'd both had the lack of family in common. Mack's parents had passed away in a horrible car crash, leaving him with an inheritance and a chip on his shoulder, while Sun's mother had dropped her off and never returned except for two occasions that he knew of.

"Okay, let me log in and I'll send you the transcript." Jordan opened the sat computer and waited for the device to find a signal before logging in. "Hmm, that's weird."

"What is?" Sun leaned over his shoulder to peer at the screen.

"The file won't open." Jordan turned to look at Mack "You wanna try?"

"Sure." Jordan moved away so he could take over. Sun stayed where she was, resting her hand lightly on his shoulder. The warmth of her palm and the hint of citrus that clung to her skin was distracting, and he focused on the screen with an effort. He made several attempts to open the file but without success. "Looks like the file is corrupt." He frowned and glanced at Jordan. "Who sent this to you?"

"One of Yates's agents, guy by the name of Ian Chandler."

"Sun, see if you can get at it from your email." He moved aside, missing her touch when she dropped into the seat.

After several attempts to access her file, she looked up at him. "Mine's corrupt too. But I don't understand how this could happen."

Mack grimaced. "The file must have had some sort of self-destruct command built into it. That's why I asked who sent it to you. The Feds don't usually do that kind of thing."

"Then who did?" Jordan asked.

It was a good question. Unfortunately, Mack didn't have a good answer.

"Someone who's trying to sabotage our attempt to find this nuke." Mack glanced between Sun and Jordan. "And from what I see here, it must be a person with access to federal government files, likely a government employee."

JANUARY 19 – 4:05 *a.m.* – *Washington, DC*

He'd done nothing but pace the room since receiving the call from the stranger who must have gotten ahold of his fixer's disposable phone.

It had been difficult not to call the number back, demanding to know whom he was speaking to. Stupid idea, since he knew the strange voice wasn't going to admit anything.

Now what? He needed a backup plan, someone competent that would take care of this mess once and for all.

But he was hesitant to make the call. Once he made contact with the guy, there would be no going back. And such a move would also put his own life on the line, forging a bond that would never be broken.

He knew these types of people were used only as a last resort. A deal with the devil always was. He should know as he'd done this before. Maybe not to this extent, yet he hadn't gotten to where he was today without crawling over the backs of those who weren't as determined as he.

But timing was everything, and he couldn't let this opportunity go. Not now. Not when the next inauguration was four years away.

Besides, the current political environment was perfect. There would never be a better time.

He needed to act now.

A wave of dread hit hard as he picked up the disposable phone and punched in the number he'd memorized. Ironically, making the necessary arrangements didn't take as long as he'd expected. Half the money to be wired now, and half when the job was complete.

Without hesitation, he logged into his laptop and sent the cash as directed.

When he'd finished hitting the send button, he sat motionless for a moment staring at the screen. Then he abruptly stood and bolted to the bathroom, losing the contents of his stomach in the toilet.

Too late to back out now.

It was done.

JANUARY 19 – 4:11 a.m. – Chicago, IL

A muffled thud woke Jarek, sending his pulse into triple digits as he swept his gaze over the darkened room. He must have fallen asleep, exhaustion combined with his physical exertion catching up to him.

But he was wide awake now.

Crawling from the bed, he inched toward the window, wondering what he would do if the Asian had found him here. After all, there was nowhere to run. The only windows in the hotel faced the front and the parking lot, which is where the sound originated. Hiding in the bathroom would be of no use.

He was trapped in the room like a mouse who'd tried to steal the cheese.

And wasn't that what he'd done? Tried to steal a piece of his past? Reunite with the woman he still loved? The cancer scare had turned out to be nothing, but he'd decided then and there to live what was left of his life to the fullest.

Starting with finding Hana.

Selfish. How could he have been so stupid? Hana had told him she would be in danger from the regime; he should have listened to her. In his defense, he hadn't considered his trying to find her thirty years later would cause this surreal sequence of events.

The Asian showing up at the airport. The gunman, maybe the same Asian man, finding him at Geoff's home and killing Geoff in his sleep. Then shooting at Jarek, chasing him through the streets.

Why? None of it made any sense.

He strained to listen but didn't hear anything. Had he imagined the thudding noise? Or was the gunman right now stationed on the other side of the door, waiting for the right time to burst in? The Asian may have already killed the pimply kid behind the lobby desk and was making his way here with a key to the room.

He felt himself begin to hyperventilate. This level of

paranoia would be the death of him. How much more of this could he take? Maybe he'd be better off if the Asian would just shoot him and be done with it.

Surprisingly, the will to live was too strong to be ignored. Jarek wasn't going to give up without a fight. With infinite slowness, he lifted a hand and parted the curtain a fraction of an inch. The red light from the vacancy sign illuminated the parking lot in an eerie crimson glow.

It made him think of blood.

Swallowing hard, he moved the curtain a little more to get a wide-angle view of the exterior. There was nothing to see. No new car parked in front of his room, or anywhere else for that matter. There had only been one vehicle parked in front of room two when he'd arrived, and that was the only car out there.

Reluctantly, he moved back and pulled the edges of the curtain together. Skirting the chair he'd placed in front of the door, he made his way back to the bed.

He tried to relax, to slow his racing heart. This hotel had no ties to his past. There's no way the Asian could find him here. Not without checking every single low-budget motel in all of the metro Chicago area. An insurmountable task.

As he began to drift back to sleep, it occurred to him that his best chance of surviving this was to be armed with a weapon. Unfortunately, he'd never owned a gun.

He shot bolt upright in the bed. What about his condo neighbor, William Kratz? William had a handgun, and maybe, just maybe, Jarek could convince the guy to sell it to him.

Along with some ammunition.

As plans went, it wasn't the best he'd ever come up with. It required him to return to his condo complex, something he was loath to do, especially since he felt certain the Asian knew where he lived. Yet knowing his address and knowing Kratz had a gun were two different things. He didn't want to be responsible for another death.

But as he huddled in the darkness, the idea—outlandish as it might be—wouldn't leave him alone.

Anything was better than sitting here, waiting for death to strike.

JANUARY 19 – 4:23 a.m. – Washington, DC

After Jordan left the motel, Sun was acutely aware of being alone with Mack once again. She wasn't sure why she was so in tune to the guy. They were childhood friends, nothing more. She refused to be foolish enough to dream of anything else.

Too bad her hormones hadn't quite gotten the message.

Resting her chin in her hand, she watched as Mack began to hack into the disposable phone company's records. His fingers flew over the keys, typing commands she'd never seen before in her life. She had to admit, Mack was so far above her level of expertise he may as well have been standing on top of the Washington Monument.

Her thoughts skirted to her mother and the need to warn her of the danger. But without contact through the answering service, she wasn't sure what to do. Was she crazy to be sitting here in a vain attempt to find a potential nuke?

Could she live with herself if she didn't and the stupid thing went off?

She tried to focus on Mack, but her interest began to wane. It was hard to watch someone else work, especially when she didn't understand most of what he was doing. She rubbed her bleary eyes, thinking they'd need to catch a few hours of sleep very soon.

Her chin slipped off her hand, startling her.

"Why don't you stretch out and catch a few z's?" Mack must have noticed her nodding off, despite the way his eyes seemed glued to the screen.

She straightened in her seat, trying to blink away the fog. "What if you find something?"

He grinned, and her stupid heart thumped wildly for a moment. What was wrong with her? It must be her bone-weary exhaustion causing her to be so aware of him and his woodsy scent. After he'd broken her heart, she'd found it easier to think of him as a friend.

Which is all she wanted from him. The last thing she wanted was to ruin the only close friendship she had. After Abigail had gone out with Mack, despite knowing Sun's feelings toward him, she hadn't cultivated friendships easily. Well, other than the relationships she now had with Sloan, Natalia, Jordan, Diana, and even Bryn.

Thanks to the Mensa program, Mack had been her friend for years, the longest connection she had with anyone except maybe her mother.

And how sad was it that she'd seen far more of Mack over the years than of her mother.

To think that she'd given up all contact only to have her mother be in danger now was disheartening.

There was no denying the regime may have already found her.

"I promise you'll be the first to know." Mack's statement jarred her from her thoughts. He gestured to the bed. "Go, before you fall over."

Since the thought of his having to carry her was completely unacceptable, she decided he was right. "Okay."

She stood, grabbed the duffel, which they'd managed to keep with them, then frowned at him. "You need to get some sleep too, Mack. We won't be able to fight the enemy if we're not well rested and on top of our game."

His gaze captured hers for a poignant moment. She was very fortunate to have him as her partner in this. Jordan and Sloan were great, but Mack was doing extremely well. "I know, Sun. If I don't find something soon, I'll crash for a bit too. I won't do anything that puts you at risk of being hurt."

"Both of us are at risk, Mack." And it bothered her that he was in danger because of her.

"Mostly you," he corrected.

She was too tired to argue. A wide yawn caught her off guard. Rubbing her eyes, she staggered to the bathroom, brushed her teeth and combed her hair, then headed toward the bed, climbing in fully clothed. Mostly because Mack was there, and also because it was important to be ready for a quick getaway.

A trick that had served her well in the past.

She sank into the mattress, every muscle in her body relaxed, but her brain refused to shut down. Images of the times she spent with Mack rotated through her mind, their formative years, then as teenagers.

The time they'd been sparring and had almost kissed.

Almost.

"Sun?"

His deep husky voice echoed in her mind, and she could almost imagine him lowering his head to kiss her . . .

"Sun? Wake up!"

The dream shattered, and she awoke with a start, raking her gaze over the room, searching for the threat. "What?"

"I found the location."

She blinked, then understanding dawned. "You found

the location of the man who sent the assailant to our informant's apartment?"

"The general location, not a specific place, but it's in the heart of Washington, DC." There was no mistaking the gleam of anticipation in Mack's eyes.

Her hopes deflated like a punctured balloon. "That's not much help."

"The location is on the eastern side of Capitol Hill," Mack continued as if she hadn't rained on his parade. "Is that a coincidence or what?"

"Well, yes, but that's a stretch, Mack. I mean, a ton of rich people live in Capitol Hill, too, not just members of Congress and other federal employees."

"It coincides with my theory that someone with connections in the federal government corrupted the chatter transcripts." His expression went solemn. "We need Jordan to tell us exactly who might be involved in this, because one of them must be trying their best to sabotage our ability to find the nuke."

She tucked a strand of hair behind her ear, wondering if he was right. It wouldn't be the first time someone from within the federal government turned out to be a bad guy interested in money or power—and it wouldn't be the last.

Making their job that much more difficult to accomplish.

CHAPTER EIGHT

January 19 – 5:01 a.m. – London, England

Hana was required to disembark the plane in London in order to catch her connecting flight to Chicago. As she followed the passengers in front of her, still maintaining her disguise, she felt certain the North Korean was staring at her back, watching her every move.

It took every ounce of willpower she possessed not to turn around and look for him.

Swallowing hard, she stayed within the crowd, fearful of being alone and mentally bracing herself for the moment the Korean made his move. Surely he must have guessed she was the one he sought, despite her disguise. She felt vulnerable, knowing she still had to get through customs.

Then again, so did he.

A glance at her watch confirmed her flight to Chicago was scheduled to leave in an hour and forty-five minutes. Barely enough time to get through customs and across the international airport to the correct terminal.

Even less when trying to lose a tail.

She continued moving through the airport, trying to

mesh with the crowd. By some miracle, she found herself next to the kind man who'd urged her to go ahead of him while boarding in Geneva. She purposefully bumped into him, then looked up to apologize.

"Oh, it's you." The kind man smiled as he recognized her.

"I'm sorry to stumble into you like that, guess I'm not too steady on my feet after sitting so long." She'd learned chatting with strangers was a good way to avoid suspicion.

"No problem." He smiled, and she was surprised when he slowed his pace to match hers. "Must not be easy traveling alone."

"No, it's not." She prayed the North Korean would assume they were traveling together. If only she could stay at the kind stranger's side all the way through customs and to the other side of the terminal. "But I appreciate your consideration toward a weary old woman."

"My mother suffered from arthritis," he confided. "Let me know if you need a helping hand."

"Thank you." His unexpected kindness once again made tears prick her eyes. Here was a complete stranger being nice to her, believing her to be near his mother's age, while the North Korean was back there somewhere, waiting to kill her.

As she followed the kind stranger to customs, a moment of indecision struck hard. Should she leave the airport and head into the city in an effort to lose the Korean?

Or continue through the airport to the terminal that would take her to the United States? No, she absolutely needed to get to the United States.

Even if that meant she'd die trying.

. . .

JANUARY 19 – 5:18 *a.m.* – *Washington, DC*

Mack tried not to notice how adorable Sun looked with her sleep-tousled hair and heavy-lidded eyes. They were trying to find a nuclear weapon, this was hardly the time to be thinking about kissing her.

Although he'd thought of little else since she'd kicked him in the chest outside her home. The memory still made him grin.

He gave himself a mental shake. This was what happened when you didn't get enough sleep, your brain short-circuited to things better left unimagined.

Sun had disappeared into the bathroom, leaving him yawning and struggling to keep his own eyes open. He should have taken his own advice and gotten some sleep too. He hadn't slept since napping on the flight between New York and DC. Not a long flight by any means.

When Sun emerged, she looked fresh and wide awake. More so than he did.

"Let's take a drive and check out the Capitol Hill area." He wanted to head to the high-end residential area for himself, and he hoped she'd be more enthusiastic about what he'd uncovered.

The sense of urgency grew stronger. If someone within the federal government, maybe even someone as high up as a congressman, was working against them, there wasn't a second to waste.

"Now?" Sun's expression was skeptical.

"If traffic here is anything like New York, the earlier the better."

She blew out a sigh. "It's already too late, rush hour starts early here, but that's fine. We may as well go. Do you need time to get ready?"

"Yeah." He hoped a shower would refresh him the way it obviously had for her.

When he emerged ten minutes later, she was peering at the screen of the sat computer. He lifted a brow. "Find anything I missed?"

"No. Other than the cell phone tower covers a significant area."

"I know." He packed up the computer and followed her outside. When she slid behind the wheel of the rusty Chevy, he reminded himself that she knew the area better than he did. He didn't necessarily like riding shotgun, but he opened the computer on his lap and zoomed in on the map. "You know how to get to Capitol Hill?"

"Yes." She gave him a look that made him feel foolish for questioning her. "Everyone knows where Capitol Hill is, even those who don't live here."

"I don't, it's my first trip to DC." He shrugged. "How long will it take to get there?"

"Not sure, traffic will grow more congested the closer we get to the downtown area." She glanced at him. "You mentioned your boss, Ken Tramall at the NSA. How do you know he's not the one involved in setting up this bomb threat?"

He frowned. It was a fair question. "I guess I don't know for sure, other than I've been working for him for the past five years without any hint of his being anything but a good agent." He shrugged. "What about Yates?"

"I completely trust Yates," Sun said without hesitation. "He's uncovered moles working on his team in the past and has always been there for Security Specialists, Incorporated. We wouldn't be nearly as successful without his support."

"There's always a first time to turn traitor," Mack pointed out.

"Not Yates." Sun's tone was firm. "I'm telling you, Jordan and Sloan both trust Yates with their lives and those of their families. They wouldn't do that if there was even a tiny sliver of doubt about him."

"Okay, I'll agree with you on that. But keep in mind Yates also trusts Tramall. That has to count for something."

"Maybe, but no guarantee." Her stubborn tone made him want to sigh. He knew part of his crankiness was due to lack of sleep, which wasn't Sun's fault.

He glanced at her. "What about Ian Chandler, the guy who sent you the chatter transcript that ended up being corrupted? What do you know about him?"

"Not a lot," Sun admitted. "But I doubt he's the one who corrupted the file. Don't you think someone on the technical end of things is the real culprit?"

He thought about that for a long moment. "Yeah, actually, you're probably right. It would be easier for someone with hacking skills to accomplish that."

"Look up Ian Chandler on the computer," she suggested. "Let's see if we can find out more about him. Could be he has better tech skills than we're giving him credit for."

After ten minutes, he found himself staring at a professional photo of Ian Chandler. The guy looked to be in his early forties, but he had degrees from some very prestigious schools, including an MBA from Harvard. "He could have the skills, but no way to know for sure." He turned the computer screen so she could see him. "Does he look familiar?"

Sun glanced at the photograph, and he knew she was imprinting Chandler's face in her mind, the same way he had. "No, unfortunately, but it's good to know what he looks like." She brightened. "Hey, since we're on the road, maybe we should set up a meeting with him about the corrupted files."

"That's a good idea." One he was miffed he hadn't thought of for himself. He decided to blame the lapse on lack of sleep.

At least they had a plan moving forward. Especially if this idea of his turned out to be nothing but another dead end.

He stared down at the location of the cell tower signal they were slowly approaching. Dawn hadn't come close to arriving yet and wouldn't for at least another ninety minutes.

Plenty of time to explore the area before they could even begin to make plans to meet with Chandler.

And as they approached the location where the disposable phone signal had originated, he wondered if Sun was right to be wary of Tramall.

Their lives could very well depend on who they decided to be trustworthy.

At the moment, he wasn't inclined to grant that privilege to anyone.

Except Sun.

JANUARY 19 – 5:47 a.m. – Washington, DC

Sun slowly navigated the DC traffic, thinking about the potential meeting with Chandler. It seemed too obvious that the guy would have corrupted the files he'd forwarded to them, anyone with half a brain would try to make it look as if the deed had been done by someone else.

Which meant that Chandler was the likely patsy in this.

"Over there," Mack said, interrupting her thoughts.

She glanced in the direction he indicated with a frown. "The Ironshore condo building?"

"Yes." His tone sounded excited. "The disposable phone I took off the assailant pinged off the cell tower located just behind the condo."

"But that tower covers a wide area, doesn't it?"

"Yeah, but I still think we need to find a place to park. I want to walk the area, check things out."

"Park?" She scoffed. "In Capitol Hill? You're joking, right?"

"A paid structure is fine, and it's early enough we should find something." Now he sounded impatient. "I just want to get a feel for the place."

"It's ritzy, no doubt about it." And frankly her rusty Chevy stood out like a wart on a beauty queen. "There's parking up ahead, and I'm sure it will cost a small fortune if we can get in at all."

"I have plenty of cash and prepaid credit cards."

It didn't take long to pay for parking and to find an empty spot to leave the vehicle. With a sweeping gaze, she memorized where they'd left the car. "Let's take the stairs down," she suggested.

Slinging the computer bag over his shoulder, Mack nodded, apparently having the same aversion to small enclosed spaces that made fighting for your life more difficult, and followed her down the six floors to the ground level.

"Going up won't be nearly as fun," Mack muttered.

His grousing made her smile. "Bet you a buck I'll beat you when it's time to head up."

"You're on. I'll win even with carrying the computer."

He turned and walked toward the Ironshore condos. "There must be a coffee place around here somewhere."

She silently agreed with the plan of ingesting caffeine. The brief nap at the motel had only made her more tired. "Over there, a few blocks down, see it?"

"Yeah. Let's go." He cupped his hand beneath her elbow, keeping a hold on her as she dodged pedestrians who were also up at this crazy early hour. As they walked past the condo, she noticed a guy dressed in a business suit coming out through the front door, staring at his phone while he walked.

Of course, he didn't look familiar, and why would he? There were thousands of government employees, and this jaunt wasn't likely to yield anything useful.

But since they couldn't even arrange a meeting with Ian Chandler yet, there was no harm in hanging out at the coffee shop for a bit. She'd call Jordan to see if he could smooth the way to getting a sit-down with Chandler.

Jordan was better at cutting through political red tape than she was. And after his recent success in foiling a terrorist attack back in September, he was very connected within the bureau. Yates raved about their work, which helped them get more jobs. However, none quite as frustrating as this one.

Her thoughts spiraled right back to the North Korean regime and the threat against her mother that Mack had learned about.

Sun wished there was a way to track down her mother and keep her safe. Should she try the phone number again? There was no guarantee her mother was in Geneva any longer. Her mother never stayed in one place for long.

Could she leave Jordan and Yates while there was a nuclear threat here in DC?

No. Despite the fact that she was half Korean, she was also a citizen of the United States.

There was no way could she turn her back on her country. Especially when she had no way of knowing where to find her mother. She could be anywhere. It was maddening to feel so helpless.

Mack held the door of the coffee shop open for her. The blast of warm air was a welcome relief from the frigid temperatures.

"Still drink your coffee with cream and sugar?" Mack asked as he led the way to a small table overlooking the street.

"Yes." She slid onto the high stool and took the computer case from his hand. "Thanks."

Mack returned a few minutes later with two large coffees. He dropped small containers of creamer on the table, along with several packets of sugar. She knew he preferred his coffee black and had no idea how he managed to drink the stuff without doctoring it up.

"How much longer before we can ask Jordan to set up something with Chandler?" Mack asked, taking a cautious sip of the steaming brew.

"It's just six in the morning," she pointed out. "This little foray to Capitol Hill was your idea, remember?"

"I'm aware," he responded dryly. "And I still think that the phone pinging off this tower is a good lead."

"Half of Congress along with judges and other rich people live here, so the only thing we know for sure is that whoever hired the assailant is connected to people in power." She sent Jordan a text, asking for a call when he had time.

The coffee shop had a fair amount of pedestrian traffic, and almost everyone wore business attire. She and Mack stood out among them, which probably wasn't good. At least they had their winter coats, but the jeans and fleece she wore beneath was a sure sign she wasn't heading off to work at the Capitol or the courthouse.

"We should move to a new location rather than hanging out here for too long," she said in a low voice.

"Feeling underdressed?" Mack drained the rest of his coffee. "Okay, let me use the restroom first."

Her phone buzzed with an incoming text. Jordan, telling her to call him. "Hey, Jordan, thanks for getting in touch."

"Made any progress?"

She grimaced, eyeing the customers coming and going from the café. "Nothing other than the disposable cell pinged off a tower located in Capitol Hill."

There was a brief pause. "Isn't that interesting?"

She rolled her eyes. "Yes, but not helpful. I need you to set up a meeting with Chandler."

Another pause. "You think that's necessary?"

"I don't have any better ideas, do you?" She watched Mack make his way through the crowd toward her. "We're grasping at straws here, Jordan. The sooner we can meet with Chandler the better."

"Okay." He sighed. "I'll see what I can do."

"Thanks." She disconnected from the call, grabbed the computer case, and rose to meet Mack. "That was Jordan. He thinks the lead connecting the disposable phone to this tower is interesting and is working on setting up a meeting with Chandler."

"Good. Let's go." Mack rested his hand in the small of her back, urging her out of the café.

"What is it?" she asked when they were safely outside and away from the others.

Mack darted a look over his shoulder. "A guy uttered a phrase in North Korean as he entered the men's room."

Her jaw dropped. "What?"

"He stopped talking when he saw me, but I know what I heard." Mack glanced at her. "He was clearly upset, but what was even more interesting was that he didn't look North Korean, he looked American."

American? That was definitely unusual. Most Americans didn't speak North Korean, and those who were fluent in another language gravitated toward Spanish, French, Italian, and even Russian.

Not a dialect from North Korea.

"And you're sure about that," she said, trying to wrap her mind around the information.

"Yeah." He shrugged. "Could be a coincidence."

"You know it's not." Sun didn't believe in them. Especially not an American who could speak North Korean. Who could it be?

Mack could, but he was part of the Mensa program, picking up languages without breaking a sweat, while she'd learned initially from her mother years ago.

The phone call pinging off the cell tower here was a key to the puzzle.

Too bad she had no idea where to go from here.

JANUARY 19 – 6:22 a.m. – *London, England*

Hana huddled near a group of young people as they left the TSA checkpoint and walked to the gate where her connecting flight would take her to Chicago.

She'd caught a glimpse of the North Korean in one of the lines going through customs, but then lost him. Since he wasn't a tall man, she found it difficult to keep him in sight.

Of course, her slight stature worked in her favor too. Especially as she walked hunched over. She'd inwardly debated on changing her appearance again but knew that such a plan would make it more difficult for her to get through customs in Chicago. Her current and expertly altered face matched that of her fake passport.

No, far better to keep the current disguise intact. The Heathrow Airport was large and had lots of people. Difficult to believe she'd been followed all the way to her gate.

Yet it was all she could do to keep the panic fluttering beneath the surface from showing on her features. She'd lost her kind stranger to a different flight, and she desperately searched for another lone traveler she could possibly chat with.

Anything to make her appear as if she were traveling with a companion rather than alone.

She dropped heavily into the empty seat next to a middle-aged couple. Minutes later, she heard the announcement that her flight was preparing to board.

"That was close," she said, glancing at the woman beside her. "You'd think they'd give us more time to get through customs."

"That's exactly what I told my husband, George." The woman elbowed the potbellied man beside her. "It was worth all the aggravation, though, our cruise was amazing."

Oh good, a chatty Cathy. Hana smiled. "How nice! Where did you go?"

The woman went into a long discussion of the countries they'd visited in the northern Baltic, including St. Petersburg, Russia. Hana feigned interest even as she subtly scanned the area searching for the North Korean. "Oh my, that sounds wonderful," she gushed when the woman finished.

"Come on, Sue, time to board." The potbellied man stood and offered his arm. Sue took it, and Hana rose to her feet as well, following them as they went over to stand in line.

There was no sign of the North Korean, but that didn't mean he wasn't nearby. It could be that he felt it was better to attack once she'd reached her final destination than risk being caught by TSA security within an airport.

The boarding process was arduous, but finally she was in her seat, once again at the window.

She continued searching for the Korean, but the plane was huge, one of those jumbo jets, and there was no way to keep track of everyone coming on board.

Yet the prickly feeling continued to nag at her.

Had she made the right decision to go to Chicago? Or should she have gone straight to the source of the problem?

Hana closed her eyes and silently prayed.

Please, God, please keep me and Sun safe from harm!

CHAPTER NINE

January 19 – 6:43 a.m. – Washington, DC

As they walked away from the coffee shop, Mack's eidetic memory replayed the fragment of North Korean he'd heard while in the restroom.

Je sigan-e oji anh-eumyeon bobog halge.

Which roughly translated meant something along the lines of *Be on time or I'll retaliate.*

Be on time for what? And who had the American been talking to?

Like Sun, he didn't believe in coincidences. Now that they were safe in the crowd of people, he glanced around, trying to identify the American he'd overheard speaking in North Korean.

Picking up on his intent, Sun asked in a low voice, "Do you see him?"

"No." He'd wanted to get out of the coffee shop so they wouldn't be recognized, but now he thought that may have been a mistake. Following the guy might give them something to go on. Then he caught a glimpse of the familiar features. "There, guy with blond hair wearing a dark suit, navy blue tie, and wearing a black trench coat. He just left the café and is headed in the opposite direction. See him?"

"Yes. Let's split up and follow from different angles." As soon as she'd spoken, Sun veered off and crossed the road so she could follow from that side. Which left Mack to tail the guy from directly behind him.

Without earpieces and radios to communicate, he and Sun would have to rely on hand signals. Keeping his gaze focused on the blond head while dodging the other pedestrians on the sidewalk wasn't easy. He risked a glance at Sun who waved her index finger toward the right, meaning their target had turned right at the next intersection.

Mack quickened his pace in an attempt to keep up. Sun was still on the opposite side of the street, so it would take her longer to do the same.

He soon realized the blond was headed toward the Capitol. Which meant he was likely a congressman or a state representative or a state senator.

None of those possibilities was remotely reassuring.

Without missing a beat, Mack continued to discretely follow the blond, wishing he'd gotten a better look at his face. But as the blond had been talking on the phone, the glimpse he'd gotten wasn't enough to form a super clear picture in his head.

Although he might be able to pick him out of a photo array. If the guy was indeed a member of Congress and not some aide.

Sun was closing the gap from the other side of the street. He frowned, not liking the fact that she was getting so close to the guy, then realized she wanted to get a look at his face too. In fact, she got close enough to touch him, but of course, she didn't. Instead, she passed him up, then quickly glanced over her shoulder.

From there, she pulled out her phone and turned away from the blond man. Mack couldn't hear anything, so he wasn't sure if the call was real or something she'd made up to avoid going all the way up and into the Capitol.

The blond guy disappeared inside the building. Mack hastened to reach Sun. She had already put the phone back in her coat pocket. "Did you get a good look at him?" Mack asked.

"Yes, but I didn't recognize him." She turned and walked toward the street. "Jordan called, we have a meeting with Chandler at eight thirty."

So the phone call was real. "That's good. Where are we going to meet with him?"

"Jordan suggested neutral territory, so I figured we'd meet at the coffee shop."

Mack frowned. "The one we just left?"

"Yes, why?"

"I don't know . . ." He wasn't sure how to articulate his concern. It wasn't as if the coffee shop was some hot bed of North Koreans looking to bomb the US. Other than the American blond guy who spoke the language, there had been nothing suspicious about the place.

"We can pick another meeting location," Sun said. "I know we don't want to stay in one place for long. It just popped into my head when Jordan asked."

He shook his head. "No, it's fine. I'm being ridiculously paranoid, that's all."

Sun lightly rested her hand on his arm. "After everything we've been through, you're entitled to a bit of paranoia."

He wanted to pull her into his arms and crush her close, which was completely inappropriate. Just because he'd allowed himself to become emotionally involved with her didn't mean Sun felt the same way.

In fact, he'd always gotten the impression she'd rather fight and spar with him than share anything as intimate as an embrace.

"Mack?" Sun's melodic voice saying his name was not helping.

"What?" His hoarse voice betrayed his awareness.

"Are you sure you're okay with returning to the coffee shop?" Sun eyed him curiously as if trying to understand what was going on in his mind.

Better she not realize where his thoughts had gone. "No, let's find a new place, there seem to be plenty of them around. We can go back closer to the meeting time. I'm anxious to see if we can pick the blond out among the members of Congress."

"Good plan," Sun agreed. They stopped at a coffee shop that was only six blocks from their previous one.

The new place was busy, too, so they had to wait several minutes before a table opened up. And even then, Mack had to rush to grab it before someone else could.

While Sun booted up the sat computer, he went back to order more coffee and a couple of breakfast sandwiches. May as well eat while they were there.

With food and coffee in hand, he slid onto the stool across from Sun. "Find anything yet?" he asked, handing her a coffee and sandwich.

She looked up with a grimace. "Not yet, I'm a third of the way through everyone on the Congress.gov website."

He took a bite of his sandwich. "Take a break to eat something. The website will still be there, and it shouldn't take long to get through the photos."

"I'm looking at all of them, just in case the guy dyed his

hair or something." She shrugged and pushed the computer aside to reach for her sandwich. "Thanks for breakfast."

"You're welcome."

She was silent for several moments before saying, "We need a list of questions to ask Chandler when he gets here."

"Okay, I can work on that from a tech perspective while you search for our Korean-speaking dude."

Sun finished her meal and took a sip of coffee. "I hope we're on the right track here."

He nodded. "Me too. But it's all we have to go on for the moment."

"I know." With grim resolve, she pulled the computer close and began clicking through the photos.

He watched her for a moment before formulating a list of questions in his head. They desperately needed something more to go on, and soon.

Or they'd never find the nuclear bomb in time to prevent another world war.

JANUARY 19 – 7:19 a.m. – Chicago, IL

Jarek abruptly woke to the slam of a door and the sound of someone talking loudly on a cell phone somewhere outside his room. For several moments he lay frozen, his heart beating rapidly in his chest. Then the sensation eased. Now that a hint of daylight could be seen around the edges of the grimy hotel room curtain, he didn't feel as afraid as he'd been the first time a noise had awoken him.

Or maybe it was just sheer exhaustion that made it impossible for him to feel anything. A man could only take so much. He hadn't gone this long without sleep since his college days, and he was far too old to be pulling all-nighters now.

Moving stiffly, as if he'd aged twelve years in the past twelve hours, he tried to straighten his wrinkled clothes as he made his way into the bathroom. His stomach was growling, and his head ached, likely from lack of sleep and caffeine.

In the bright light of day, his idea of buying a gun from his neighbor seemed ludicrous. If he showed up looking the way he did now, his neighbor would likely call the police and have him arrested.

He needed food, coffee, and clean clothes to wear. Oh, and a vehicle of some sort would be nice. But he didn't dare return to the airport for his car, so once again using a taxi service would have to do.

After a long hot shower, he felt marginally more human. Checking the closet, he was surprised to find an iron and board stored inside. Gratefully, he began to iron the wrinkles out of his clothing. As he worked, he considered paying for another night's stay. Being here in the anonymous hotel room was the safest he'd felt in what seemed like forever, and he truly didn't want to head out into the real world.

One in which a stranger brutally killed his friend.

Jarek ruthlessly shoved the image away. Staying here would only provide a false sense of security. He clearly couldn't live in the motel forever. What if the Asian showed up? As distasteful as it was, he needed a weapon.

And the only place he could imagine getting one was from his neighbor.

When he'd finished ironing, he dressed, then eyed the family restaurant across the street. Walking over to eat breakfast shouldn't cause anyone to look at him with suspicion. Isn't that why restaurants were located next to hotels? To provide guests convenient access to meals?

From there, he could call a taxi to head back to his

condo. The thought of approaching the place he called home filled him with a dark sense of foreboding.

A quick stop, he promised himself. In and out before anyone knew he'd been there. Was such a feat even possible? Jarek wouldn't know until he tried.

But first, breakfast.

Jarek pulled the heavy chair away from the front of the door and slowly unlocked the chain and dead bolt. Drawing a deep breath, he cracked the door open, looking around cautiously before stepping outside.

He could see his breath in the cold air, but the frigid temperature didn't register, every nerve in his body stretched to the breaking point as he searched for the Asian.

Leaving his key behind, he closed the door and began walking to the restaurant. When he reached the building unscathed, he relaxed and requested a seat in the back of the dining room.

So far, so good.

Yet Jarek knew the real test of his courage was yet to come.

One he felt woefully unprepared for.

JANUARY 19 – 7:36 a.m. – Washington, DC

Sun pushed the computer away with an aggravated sigh. "I can't find him on the Congress website."

Mack frowned. "I guess he must be an aide of some sort."

"If so, it won't be easy to find his identity. I don't think there's a general listing of aides anywhere on the internet. The only reason they list senators and representatives is because they're elected officials and must be accessible to all."

"Do you mind if I take a look?" Mack asked.

She lifted a brow. "You think I missed something?"

"No, but I'm curious when the website was last updated. It's possible the newly elected officials haven't been updated in the system yet."

She felt foolish for not thinking of that for herself. She pushed the computer toward him and finished her coffee.

At the moment she felt as if they were chasing ghosts.

"The site was last updated before the November elections," Mack said with satisfaction. "Our guy might be new to the political scene."

"And he just happens to speak North Korean?" She couldn't hide the doubt in her tone. "I find that highly unlikely."

"Okay, maybe not new to the political scene," Mack amended. "Could be he lost his seat a couple of years ago and ran again to gain it back."

She was forced to admit his theory had merit. "Okay, I guess we can run a search on congressmen who've been re-elected after losing a previous term in office. There can't be that many of them."

Mack was already typing in the search command. After several long minutes, he sighed. "There is only one, and he's not our guy."

Disappointment stabbed deep. "So either our blond is a freshman in Congress or he's one of the aides. Not helpful."

"I know." Mack pushed the computer back toward her. "It was worth a shot. Do you have any other ideas?"

"I wish I did." She stared morosely at the computer screen, then pulled it close and began typing.

"What are you doing?" Mack asked.

"Going state by state to see who was newly elected." She keyed in Alabama. "Starting at the top of the alphabet and working my way down." She met his gaze. "Unless you have a better idea?"

"Nope." He glanced at his watch. "We should finish up though. We need to meet Chandler soon."

"I know." Sun did her best not to lose hope, but it wasn't easy. This case had more holes than a teenager's jeans. What made it worse was that she had no way of contacting her mother to put her on notice of the danger.

Sun had never felt so helpless in her entire life. Not even the day her mother sent her off to Mensa school, then allowing years to pass by before coming back to see her.

JANUARY 19 – 7:59 *a.m.* – *Somewhere over the Atlantic Ocean*

Hana was doing the math in her head, estimating the time she'd land in Chicago's O'Hare airport. London was six hours ahead, and the flight was roughly eight hours, so she figured they'd land around eight forty-five in the morning.

How long to get through customs and out of the airport? Probably the same amount of time as it had taken in London, maybe a little less. The good news was that she had no baggage with her, so a luggage search wouldn't slow her down.

And what if she saw the North Korean? She tried not to borrow trouble, to put her worries in God's hands, but it wasn't easy.

A hint of a smile creased her features. Jarek had been the one to teach her his Christian faith. It was easy enough to turn her back on the religion her family had taught since they were dictators who thrived on power and violence.

God and prayer had helped keep her sane over the

years. She would be forever grateful for Jarek showing her the way.

She wondered again what Jarek might think of her showing up after all these years. Would he be upset? Angry? Or happy to see her? Was she making a mistake taking this detour rather than going straight on to DC?

Her smile faded as she caught movement out of the corner of her eye. A man was walking slowly down the narrow pathway on the other side of the plane. A glimpse of dark straight hair and slanted eyes made her stomach tense.

No, it couldn't be. The Korean couldn't have followed her onto this flight. What were the chances?

She didn't dare lift her gaze to get a better look. Instead, she tucked the pillow against the headrest so that her features were obscured from his view.

How many people were on this jet? At least 350, maybe more. There weren't any empty seats that she could see, and the pamphlet claimed a total of 400 passengers could be accommodated.

Three fifty to four hundred people. The dark-haired man could be anyone. There was no reason to panic.

Still, Hana planned to keep her face buried against the pillow for the remainder of the flight.

JANUARY 19 – 8:13 *a.m.* – *Pyongyang, North Korea*

He didn't want to face the Supreme Leader, but he had little choice as the men on either side would drag him by force if he didn't walk under his own power.

"Have you found the traitor?"

He swallowed hard, staring at the floor. "We only know she is flying to the United States. Our source has indicated she is using yet another alias, and we believe she will land in Chicago soon. We will be ready."

There was a long pause. He didn't move, not even to breathe.

"Return with news of her capture or die."

He remained in a submissive position, his heart hammering with fear. From the corner of his eye, the Supreme Leader made a gesture, indicating he should be removed from the room.

Again, there was something off about the encounter, but there wasn't time to think it through at the moment. Getting the results the Supreme Leader expected him to deliver was all that mattered.

JANUARY 19 – 8:19 a.m. – Washington, DC

They'd returned to the coffee shop that was their designated meeting spot, and Chandler would be there soon. Mack watched the steady stream of pedestrian traffic pass the coffee shop window. "You might want to take a break from the computer and help me watch for Chandler."

Sun had been methodically working through the states in what he now believed was a hopeless effort to find their blond North Korean–speaking guy. She blinked at him, her eyes glassy. "Huh?"

"Take a break," he repeated, concerned about Sun's ability to keep going in her current state.

And frankly, his wasn't much better. Going without sleep was one thing, but trying to do something sedate like reading names on a computer while being up for more than twenty-four hours was nearly impossible.

"I don't have that much further to go." Her slender fingers flew across the keyboard. He ground his teeth over her stubborn streak and glanced back at the people milling about outside. It was a little surprising to see so many walking around despite the cold January weather.

Then again, it could be that the impending presidential inauguration had brought a renewed energy to Capitol Hill.

He could only hope that the energy wouldn't be transformed into something as horrible as a nuclear bomb being detonated.

"How much further?" he asked.

"I'm on the V's, so almost finished." She stubbornly continued her task. "Although I'm not finding anything even closely resembling our guy."

"Another dead end." He was beginning to think this entire case was hopeless. Unless Chandler pulled some kind of rabbit out of his hat, they'd be back to having nothing.

Other than an exploded Jeep, a man with a gun who shot at them at Sun's so-called safe house, and a dead informant.

Clearly something was going on, but what? And how was this all connected to the chatter about the nuke?

Mack caught a glimpse of a man walking slowly toward the coffee shop. He raked his gaze over him, easily recognizing the federal agent.

"Sun? He's here." He tipped his chin toward the window. "Coming in from the west."

She swiveled in her seat to see for herself. She shut the computer and stood so she could move to the stool in the corner. "You have your list of questions?"

He tapped his temple with a lean finger. "Right here."

She rolled her eyes.

Mack was tracking Chandler's progress when suddenly a man brushed against him, causing Chandler to stumble and clutch at his side. The hair on the back of Mack's neck lifted in warning.

"He's hurt!" Mack leaped to his feet, staring in horror.

Bright red blood pooled on the ground beneath Chandler, where the man lay motionless on the sidewalk. People clustered around the fallen man. He could hear Sun calling 911, but he bolted to the door, trying to find the guy who'd obviously stabbed Chandler.

He caught a glimpse of a man wearing a dark coat and a black knit hat moving swiftly through the crowd and took off after him.

CHAPTER TEN

January 19 – 8:37 a.m. – Washington, DC

After calling 911, Sun shouldered the satellite computer and rushed outside several seconds behind Mack. She didn't join the chase but pushed her way through the crowd to kneel beside the injured Chandler.

"What happened? Ian? Can you hear me?" The amount of bright red blood oozing from his side indicated an artery within his liver had been hit. She quickly pulled up the bottom part of his trench coat, balling it up and shoving the fabric against the jagged knife wound along his right side, putting as much pressure against the injury as she could.

Ian Chandler's gaze was wide with fear as he looked up at her. "I—I . . ."

"Do you know who did this?" She needed to get something from Ian. Anything. "Did you see the man who hurt you?"

"No." The word was barely a whisper. His eyes slid closed, but she gave him a shake.

"Ian, stay with me. Did you realize the chatter transcript had a self-destruct command embedded in it?"

He looked so pale, as if he'd lost half his blood volume right there on the sidewalk. And maybe he had. Sun began to feel desperate.

"Ian, please. Tell me who sent the transcript to you."

He stared blankly for a moment, then whispered, "Allan."

"Allan who? Do you have a last name?" She felt bad for pressing so hard for information, but she had a sick feeling Ian Chandler wasn't going to make it. In the distance, she could hear sirens and prayed the ambulance was on its way. "Do you hear the sirens, Ian? You need to stay with me, help will be here soon. Tell me who sent the transcript, Allan who?"

His gaze clung to hers for a long moment, but then his eyes drifted shut again. Sun shook him, but his entire body went limp.

Chandler had fallen unconscious. She glanced around at the pedestrians gathered around, gawking. "I'm with the FBI," she fibbed. "Did anyone see what happened?"

Several people shook their head no, and others commented about how they had noticed Ian stumbling but not the attack itself. It was about what she'd expected, but frustrating just the same.

While continuing to put pressure against Ian's wound, she subtly checked his pockets to see what, if anything, he may have brought with him. When her fingers closed around a USB drive, she felt a surge of hope. As inconspicuously as possible, she palmed the drive and removed it from Chandler's pocket, placing it into her own.

"Ian? Come on, stay with me." She put her fingers against his neck but couldn't feel a pulse.

The sirens were louder now, but she knew they would be too late. Ian Chandler had already lost too much blood. Of course there was always a chance, but she felt certain whoever had stabbed him had known exactly what he was doing. Striking deep into his liver hadn't been an accident.

The clear intent had been to kill him. To keep Chandler from sharing whatever he might have known about the transcript.

Who on earth could have done this? Had Chandler mentioned the meeting to someone? Or was his phone tapped? It had to be one of those things because the only people other than her and Mack who knew about this meeting was Jordan, Yates, and Chandler himself.

Still, even with a bugged phone, how had he been ambushed so quickly?

The USB drive was burning a hole in her pocket. Glancing up, she could see the ambulance, followed by two Capitol Hill police cars, heading toward them. Several of the bystanders were moving away, so Sun went along with them carrying the computer, deciding it was best to slip away to avoid being interviewed by the cops.

When she was several blocks away, she called Jordan. "Someone got to Chandler before the meeting."

"How?" Jordan asked incredulously.

"I don't know, but he's lost so much blood I don't think he's going to make it." She hesitated, then added, "You better let Yates know since Chandler is with the Bureau. The cops are going to jump all over that. I left the scene to avoid being questioned, just in case you hear something about an Asian woman being there too."

Jordan sighed heavily. "Okay. Did he tell you anything?"

Sun kept walking, putting more distance between

herself and the crime scene. It disturbed her to know she still had Ian's blood on her hands and glanced around for a place with a restroom. "Only that someone named Allan sent the transcript to him, although truthfully, I don't know how with it he was. And I also don't know if Allan is a first or last name. Mack took off after the guy, but I'm not sure if he's caught up to him or not."

"Maybe Mack will learn something."

"Maybe." She could only hope. "I need you to see if Yates can verify if someone named Allan works in the cyber security department?"

"Yes, right away. And Sun? Be careful. This job is getting more dangerous by the minute. Especially since there seems to be multiple threats."

"I will." She appreciated Jordan's concern; frankly, it mirrored her own.

The way Chandler had been brutally silenced mere minutes before their meeting was deeply troubling. And what was worse is that they didn't have much to go on.

Other than the USB drive.

Another quick glance around revealed no sign of Mack. She did, however, see yet another café, one that served breakfast and lunch. She went inside to use the restroom, hoping Mack would call soon.

She could use Mack's expertise to view whatever was on the USB drive.

And she desperately wanted to know Mack was safe.

JANUARY 19 – 9:01 a.m. – Washington, DC

He'd lost him.

Mack wasn't sure how, one minute he had the guy with the black knit cap in his sights, the next he was gone. Mack had thought he'd left the street level to catch the Metro, but when he'd headed down to check, there had been no sign of the assailant.

Inwardly railing at himself, he returned to the street and began making his way back toward the coffee shop where he'd left Sun. He was somewhat surprised she hadn't followed him, she was fast enough to have caught up without a problem.

But knowing Sun, she'd likely stayed back to check on Chandler.

His phone rang, and he grinned, recognizing the number of Sun's disposable phone. "How's Chandler?"

"Dead. What about you? Did you catch the guy who knifed him?"

"Unfortunately, I lost him. I thought he went onto the Metro, but I couldn't find him anywhere." He hated admitting failure. "I'm sorry, Sun. We lost our best lead."

"Not entirely," she said, surprising him. "I found a USB drive in Chandler's pocket. Where are you right now?"

"Um, good question." He glanced at the street sign and brought up the map of Capitol Hill in his memory. "I'm probably fifteen minutes from the coffee shop."

"I'm not at the coffee shop, I'm at a breakfast café." She gave him the name and street. "I'll wait here for you."

"I'd rather we meet back at the Chevy." After the way Chandler had been stabbed so close to their meeting location, he felt certain they weren't safe in this area.

"Not yet. See you soon." Sun disconnected from the call.

Battling a wave of frustration at Sun's stubborn streak, he quickened his pace. It wasn't until he'd caught sight of the breakfast café that the tension in Mack's chest eased a bit. When he entered the restaurant and saw Sun unharmed and sitting in a booth near the kitchen, his muscles relaxed.

His annoyance had masked his fear of Sun being hurt or killed as quickly and easily as Chandler had been.

As he wove through the crowded tables to join her, he realized how much he cared about her.

Far more than he wanted to admit.

JANUARY 19 – *9:11 a.m.* – *Chicago, IL*

Jarek had lingered over his breakfast, dreading the task before him. Which had resulted in his taxi being stuck in bumper-to-bumper traffic.

As the taxi crept closer to his condo, his stomach twisted painfully. Was he crazy to return here? How on earth would he convince his neighbor, William Kratz, to sell him his gun?

When the driver stopped at yet another red light, Jarek figured they were close enough. He leaned forward to capture the driver's attention.

"Sir? Would you mind letting me out here?"

"Sure." The driver punched the button to display the fare.

"Thank you." Jarek paid in cash from his dwindling reserves, adding a nice tip, then pushed open the passenger side door and climbed out. The cold wind made him shiver.

Or maybe it was the wild idea he'd decided to undertake.

Jarek knew he couldn't simply walk up to his brown brick condo building and stroll inside. First, he needed to figure out if the Asian man he'd seen at the airport was hiding nearby.

Not as easy to slink around in the bright light of day, for either of them.

At least Jarek knew the area as he'd been living here for over thirty years.

Hunching his shoulders against the wind, he made his way down one of the side streets, one that paralleled the condo building. His busy gaze flicked from one potential hiding spot to the next.

Praying this wasn't another giant mistake.

JANUARY 19 – 9:16 a.m. – Chicago, IL

Hana lost sight of the dark-haired North Korean after getting through customs, which had taken less time than she'd anticipated. She'd played her role as an older woman so well that an airline employee had approached with a wheelchair, offering to take her through.

"Thank you," Hana said as she sat heavily in the chair. Being pushed by the employee was a risk, but at this point, speed was more important than remaining hidden.

The Chicago airport was large, similar to London's. Being whisked through the airport by the female employee had felt liberating. As if she might be able to get away without being caught by the North Korean after all.

Who knew? Maybe she'd been mistaken about seeing him on the plane. For all she knew, the North Korean was still in London searching for her.

At least that's what she sincerely hoped for.

By the time they'd reached the baggage claim, Hana was ready to make her move. She lifted a hand. "Miss? I'd like to use the restroom if you don't mind."

"Oh, of course." The female employee instantly veered

off in a different direction, pushing her toward the women's room.

"Thanks again." Hana stood with more agility than she'd displayed earlier, smiling broadly at the employee. "You've been so kind, but I think I can manage by myself from here."

"Are you sure?"

"Positive, but thank you again." Hana had taken a few moments to convert her Euros to American dollars after getting through customs, so she gave the woman a five-dollar tip.

"Thank you and have a wonderful day." The female employee turned away, taking the wheelchair with her.

Hana quickly slipped into the restroom and began shedding her disguise. Without a change of clothes, there wasn't much she could do, but removing the molded plastic from her mouth, getting rid of the makeup, and taking down the scarf changed her outward appearance enough that she felt confident leaving the airport and standing in line for a taxi.

Standing outside with her large handbag over her shoulder made her feel a bit vulnerable, but her turn came quickly, and she slid gratefully into the taxi. "Where to, lady?" the driver asked.

"A condo at 2701 Wilton Avenue." She still remembered Jarek's address and could hardly believe she was actually here in Chicago.

"Okay." He started the meter and pulled into traffic.

As the airport grew smaller behind her, she let out a deep breath. She'd made it into the United States for the first time in thirty years.

Now she only had to worry about Jarek's reaction to seeing her after all this time.

. . .

JANUARY 19 – 9:33 a.m. – Washington, DC

Sun tried to ignore Mack's woodsy scent as he crowded next to her in the booth so that they could both see the computer screen.

They'd ordered fruit and yogurt for breakfast to keep up appearances. Sun wasn't at all hungry, still seeing the bright red blood surrounding Chandler's body, but Mack had made quick work of both of their meals before opening the sat computer and inserting the USB drive into the port.

The problem was that Chandler had password-protected the drive, so Mack was doing his best to hack into it without ruining any of the data.

"What do you think is on here?" Sun whispered.

Mack glanced at her. "I'm hoping the original transcripts of the chatter mentioning the nuke."

She scoffed. "I'm hoping for more than that. I already went through those transcripts, and we need additional information to help find this thing."

"Anything is possible," Mack admitted as his fingers flew over the keys. The screen looked like a bunch of gibberish to her, and she was once again grateful to have Mack partnering with her on this case.

For more than just his superior computer skills.

Her phone rang, and she recognized Jordan's number. "Did you find something on our Allan?"

"There are three possibilities. Karen Allan, Allan Stokes, and Sean Allen." He went on to give her the spelling of each name. "Apparently, they are all employed in our information technology area."

"Okay, I guess it's better to have three than none," Sun said with a sigh. "Thanks, Jordan. Anything else on Chandler?"

"He was declared DOA, which you already suspected.

Yates is fielding calls about him and hasn't mentioned the planned meeting with you and Mack." Jordan paused, then added, "I'm worried about this alleged bomb. With the way people are dying, I think the threat is very real."

"I know, me too." Sun watched as Mack continued working the computer. No way would she have the patience to hack into a computer program. "Jordan, you didn't mention the USB drive to Yates, did you?"

"No. I figure there's time for that at some point when you find out what information is on it. I take it Remington hasn't gotten into it yet?"

"No, but he will." She didn't have to force confidence into her tone, she believed wholeheartedly in Mack's skills. "We'll keep you posted on what we find."

"Please do. Stay safe, Sun."

"That's the plan. Later." She pushed the end button and tucked the phone back into her pocket. She stared at the computer screen. "How much longer?"

"As long as it takes." Mack's calm tone set her teeth on edge.

Sun took a sip of her water and tried to be patient as the three names Jordan gave her swirled in her head. Karen Allan, Allan Stokes, and Sean Allen.

Which one had Chandler meant to implicate?

JANUARY 19 – 9:52 a.m. – Chicago, IL

Jarek had remained hidden behind the brown brick building housing his condo but hadn't seen any sign of the Asian. Or anyone else that appeared to be watching the place.

But the sick feeling in his stomach hadn't lessened one bit. If anything, the knots had only gotten worse.

How long should he stay out here? It seemed as if he'd been watching forever, but he knew it had been just over thirty-five minutes.

Was there some protocol for this kind of thing?

No, he was being ridiculous. He hadn't come all this way to stand beneath a tree. He needed to head inside and buzz William's unit. The man was retired from his career as a banker and had confided in Jarek of his plan to trace his roots. Apparently he spent hours on those ancestry sites running down genealogy leads.

Jarek took a deep breath and tried to shake off the impending sense of doom. He'd get in and out before the Asian could catch him.

He hoped.

Still, he waited another agonizing fifteen minutes before forcing himself to leave the shelter of the tree. He went up to the front of the building with his key in hand. His back felt exposed as he used the key to access the building. Once inside, he pressed the buzzer for William Kratz's unit.

"Yes?"

The sound of his neighbor's voice was like a balm to his ragged nerves. "Will? It's Jarek Zeman. I need to see you. It's a matter of life and death."

"Life and death?" Will echoed in alarm. "Well then, I guess you'd better come up."

"Thank you." Jarek took the stairs to the second level. His and Will's condos were located across the hall from each other, and he slowed, approaching Will's door with apprehension.

What if the Asian was in there right now, holding William at gunpoint waiting for Jarek to arrive? He tried not to be so paranoid, but his footsteps dragged as if an unseen force was holding him back.

Rather than going to William's door, he went across the hall to his unit. Twisting the door handle, he expected it to be locked the way he'd left it, but the knob turned without a problem.

Every instinct in his body went on red alert. Whirling away, he silently left the way he'd come. Calling himself every kind of coward, he burst outside just as a taxi pulled up.

Run! He picked up his pace but then gaped when he saw Hana emerge from the taxi.

Hana? Here? His mind whirled, and then he rushed forward. "Get back in the taxi." He barely acknowledged her but pushed her back into the seat.

"Why? What's going on?" Hana asked.

A gunshot rang out. He ducked into the taxi. "Go, go!"

The driver hit the accelerator, and the taxi leaped forward. A quick glance behind him confirmed the Asian was there, watching them drive away.

CHAPTER ELEVEN

January 19 – 10:12 a.m. – Chicago, IL

"Get out of my taxi!" The driver fumbled with his phone. Sensing he was about to call 911, Hana plucked it from his grasp.

"I'm sorry, sir, but you must take us far away from here." Her voice was kind yet underlined with steel.

"Hana? W-what are you doing here?" Jarek's voice was full of confusion.

"Looking for you." Despite the dire circumstances, she smiled. "It's been a long time, Jarek."

"I want you people out of my taxi!" The driver was swerving all over the road as he kept glancing at them over his shoulder.

"Take us a few kilometers more please, then we'll get out," Hana promised.

"I—am I dreaming?" Jarek stared at her in a way that made her think he might be in shock.

Then she saw the dark stain on the sleeve of his jacket. "You've been hit?"

"Huh?" For an English professor, he seemed to be at a

loss for words. He reached up and touched his sleeve, then frowned at the blood stain. "I don't feel anything."

She took a moment to examine the wound more closely, relieved to note it wasn't deep. The bullet had grazed along the edge of his arm, causing only a flesh wound.

It could have been so much worse.

"I'm sorry, Jarek." Hana couldn't help but wonder if the North Korean had already known her destination and had somehow beaten her to it. She'd gotten only a brief glimpse of the man with the gun, but he'd definitely been from the country of her birth. "You being in danger is my fault."

"No, it's the other way around. I'm the one who put you in danger." Jarek wiped the blood from his fingers with a tissue. "The gunman had been aiming at me."

With an abrupt move, the taxi driver pulled over and hit the brakes, hard. "Get out!"

Hana huffed. "Fine, but if that man catches up with us, our blood will be on your hands."

"Now!" The taxi driver was not taking no for an answer.

Hana paid the man in cash, providing a tip despite his behavior. After all, it wasn't entirely his fault. Most taxi drivers would be upset over being shot at.

"Better for us to find a new ride anyway," Jarek said, pushing his door open. Cold air filled the vehicle.

The moment she and Jarek were out of the car, the taxi driver took off, barely giving her time to shut the door. She grimaced, looped her bag over her shoulder, and took Jarek's arm. "Come, we must keep moving."

"I can't believe you're here." Jarek still seemed stunned by her presence. "After all this time, you're really here."

"Yes. Now please, we must find another taxi." As they were still in a residential area, she wasn't sure hailing another taxi was even possible. "Do you have a number to call?"

Jarek shook his head. "I ditched my phone after the gunman found me the first time. Not that it's helped much."

The first time? She glanced up at him as they continued walking briskly down the street. She had her disposable phone, but without a number for the taxi service, it wouldn't help them. At the next intersection, she followed when he turned right. Her recent work must have been what started this cascade of events. "How many attempts have there been, Jarek?"

He shook his head and placed his hand over hers where it rested in the crook of his elbow. "Later. Let's focus on finding another taxi."

Hana knew he was right, the North Korean was likely already hot on their tail. But if the gunman wasn't the same man who'd followed her from Geneva, which is what Jarek implied, then who was he?

Another comrade from the regime? If so, how many? How many people had the regime sent to kill her and those she loved? Her attempt to do good things, to right the wrongs, had backfired in a big way.

She swallowed hard and huddled close to Jarek. At the next intersection, he turned left. A taxi was at the stoplight, and he waved his uninjured arm to flag the driver. The taxi idled for a moment as they both climbed in.

"Take us to Union Station please," Jarek said.

The driver nodded and pulled into traffic. Hana glanced through the back window, searching for a sign of the gunman.

She didn't see him but sensed he was out there, somewhere. Ready for the perfect opportunity to pounce.

Jarek was wrong, the danger was all about his association with her, not the other way around.

Depressing to realize that if something bad happened to Jarek Zeman, she only had herself to blame.

JANUARY 19 – 10:19 a.m. – Washington, DC

"I'm in." Mack looked at Sun with a surge of satisfaction. She was sitting with her chin in her hand, her eyes closed as if sleeping. "Sun? You hear me? I'm in!"

"Huh?" She pried her eyes open. "I'm awake."

"Hardly." He smiled at how adorable she looked, not that she'd want to hear it. "I can access the files on the USB drive."

She straightened as the implication sank deep. "That's great. What did Chandler have on there?"

Good question. "I've only started to check them out. There's a large audio file that I believe might be the original transcript, but there are other documents uploaded as well. It's going to take some time to review them."

Sun glanced around the restaurant. The breakfast crowd had waned, and it was too early for those looking for lunch. "We need to find another place to hang out for a while. We've already been here too long."

"I was thinking the same thing." He clicked on the keyboard. "Give me a moment to finish transferring the data from the drive to the computer."

"I'm glad you're working with me on this," Sun admitted softly. "I'd be dead in the water on this case without your hacking skills."

Her praise warmed his heart and made him think once again about kissing her. Which was becoming a bad habit.

Staying focused was important if they were going to find and abort the nuke.

He stared at the screen, mentally urging the computer files to transfer more quickly. When the last file was complete, he quickly ejected the USB drive and shut down the computer. "Okay, let's go."

"Back to the Chevy?" Sun asked as she left cash for the server.

"Yes." So far his instincts had been right on. Capitol Hill had not only been the area where the disposable phone had pinged off the tower but where Chandler had been murdered, not to mention his overhearing the American speaking North Korean.

But now they needed time to review their new intel. To see if they could get another lead that would reveal the location of the nuke.

"This way." Sun turned in the opposite direction from where the parking structure was located, but he understood her plan was to avoid being followed. He covered Sun's back as they made their way down one street, then another.

He didn't see any sign of the man with the black knit cap or the blond who'd disappeared into the Capitol building. But that didn't mean there wasn't someone else watching from afar.

Their trip to the parking structure took twice as long as it should have. Sun glanced at him with a cheeky grin. "Don't forget our bet."

She took off up the stairs, leaving him little choice but to follow. Sun won, but they were both breathing hard as they reached the sixth level. Sun headed toward the rusted vehicle, but he stopped her with a hand on her arm.

"Let me check it out first. Just in case."

She blew out a breath and nodded. "All right, give me the computer."

He handed the computer case to her, then cautiously approached the Chevy. He wanted to believe the car was safe, but the way things had been unraveling around them, he couldn't afford to assume anything.

Not when their safety was at risk.

He ran his hand along the underside of the bumper but didn't feel anything. He stretched out on the ground to peer underneath, wishing he had a flashlight to see better. The gloomy day, along with the dark interior of the structure, made it difficult to see something as small as a GPS tracker.

Smart of Sun to pick an older vehicle, one without fancy GPS devices built in, as her backup vehicle.

"Allow me," Sun said, dropping down beside him. "I'm smaller."

He reluctantly moved out of the way so she could examine the undercarriage. After what seemed like forever, she scooted out. He frowned. "Find anything?"

"Other than this thing is leaking oil? No." Sun dabbed at a spot of oil that had dropped onto her cheek. "I think we're good to go."

"Okay, you want to drive? Or review the files?"

"I'll drive, but only because I know the area." Sun glanced at him as he picked up the computer case. "But I'm curious to what Chandler thought was important enough to put on the USB drive."

"Me too." Mack slid into the passenger seat with the computer at his feet.

"Play the audio file," Sun suggested as she left the structure and eased into traffic. "It's going to take us a while to get out of the city proper."

He lifted the computer to his lap. "Maybe we should stick close."

She shook her head. "Not if we want to find a cheap motel that takes cash."

It was a good point. He opened the computer, then began the audio file, listening intently to the North Korean phrases being spoken in a female voice.

There was the usual rhetoric about hating the American government because of the sanctions that had been taken against them. For a while there was nothing but compliments about the current regime and the all-powerful commander. But then he heard what Sun had mentioned. The translation went something along the lines of: *Very soon they will receive a small demonstration of what we are capable of. And those who take us lightly shall learn the truth. We are many, and we are strong.*

"We are many, and we are strong," Mack repeated. He glanced at Sun. "Does he mean people or bombs?"

"I took it to mean people." She glanced at him. "I mean, how many nuclear bombs could they really have?"

"More than they should," Mack said with a sigh. He listened to the audio chatter again and again, hoping to pick up something they'd missed.

He could see why the FBI and NSA both felt that there was the possibility of a nuclear bomb, it was a logical theory based on the claim of a small demonstration to show what they are capable of. Yet it was incredibly vague as well.

He hoped the rest of Chandler's files had more to offer, or the time he'd spent breaking into the password-protected USB drive would have been nothing but a waste of time.

And time was not their friend.

. . .

JANUARY 19 – *10:41 a.m.* – *Chicago, IL*

Jarek knew it was a risk, but he changed his mind about Union Station and directed their second taxi driver to return to the small motel he'd left earlier that morning.

Frankly, it was the only place he could think of that felt safe.

"We need bandages for your arm," Hana said softly. "Every time you move, the wound bleeds again."

"I'm fine." He still had trouble believing Hana was really here in Chicago. Thirty years had passed, but she was still as beautiful to him as the day they'd first met. She'd been a graduate student and he a brand-new young English professor. She hadn't been in any of his classes, but relationships between professors and students had been frowned upon.

Yet that hadn't stopped them from seeing each other. Jarek had been infatuated with Hana, not just her beauty but the world from which she'd come, so different from his Chicago roots.

They'd spent every moment of their spare time together. Looking at her now, he felt the same yearning he'd experienced thirty years ago.

A soul mate, if one believed in such things. He did.

"A hotel, Jarek?" Hana sounded a bit uncertain.

Immediately, he felt contrite. "Just for an hour or so until we can decide where to go from here." He glanced at the taxi driver who didn't appear to be listening to their conversation. Still, he lowered his voice to a mere whisper. "I don't think we can ride along in a taxi forever."

"You are right, yes. A place to plan is a good idea." Her voice was so quiet he could barely hear her. She twisted her hands in her lap, a gesture that reminded him of their initial encounters all those years ago.

"Hana." A taxi wasn't the ideal place to pour his heart out, but he wanted, needed to let her know how much he still cared. "I've thought of you often and can't tell you how wonderful it is to see you again."

A smile tugged at her mouth. "For me too, Jarek." She glanced at the driver. "We'll talk more privately at the hotel, yes?"

"Yes." His heart soared, and he wanted to shout from the rooftops about how much he loved her. Had always loved her.

But their reunion had been marred by gunfire and a mad escape from his condo building. The burning in his upper arm proof of their close call.

His feelings could wait. Being safe and finding a way to escape the men who'd tried to kill him had to take priority.

But now that he had Hana at his side, he didn't want to lose her ever again.

JANUARY 19 – 10:49 a.m. – *Washington, DC*

"We believe they may have the original transcript."

He stood in the corner of the office, eyeing the door warily. The owner of said office would be back any minute. "How could you let that happen? You disposed of the target, correct?"

"Yes, but I couldn't linger. It was broad daylight in Capitol Hill, and there were plenty of people around. As it was, I was lucky to escape the man who followed me."

"You should have lured him close and taken him out of the equation." He muttered a harsh curse under his breath. "You've failed me."

"No, there's still time," the man said in an attempt to soothe his ire. "I have a plan, a man with skills that will report to me where they're headed next. I will take care of this."

"You better. Time is running out. Get the job done or I'll find someone who will." He disconnected from the call just as the office door opened.

He pasted a smile on his face and moved forward to pick up the boring routine business at hand as if the phone call hadn't taken place.

But he kept a wary eye on the clock, hoping for better news sooner rather than later.

The wheels of the plan had been put into play. He'd enlisted help from the devil himself to prevent it from being derailed by a couple of amateurs.

Yin-lee and Remington had to die. It was as simple as that.

JANUARY 19 – 11:06 a.m. – Washington, DC

"Traffic is worse than usual," Sun said on a weary sigh. Pushing the overwhelming exhaustion away wasn't easy, especially since they were moving at a snail's pace. "It's going to take forever to get out of here."

"It will be worse tomorrow," Mack predicted. "Which makes me think they'll be working to get the nuke in place sometime during the night."

"But where?" She stared morosely out the windshield, then glanced at Mack. "Maybe you should start going through Chandler's documents. Maybe there are notes that will help us make sense of all this."

Mack didn't move to bring the computer back out of its case. As soon as they'd finished listening to the audio file, he'd packed the computer up. "I don't like this. It feels like we're exposed being stuck in traffic like this."

"We agreed it was time to get out of the restaurant," she reminded him testily.

"I know, but I think it was the wrong decision." Mack rubbed the back of his neck. "I keep going back to the self-destruct command that was embedded in the transcript."

"What about it?"

"It takes someone with technical skills to do that. Technical skills that are above and beyond your average fed."

"We already know that." She did her best to control her fraying temper. "Just spit it out already."

"I was thinking of how quickly Chandler was found and taken out. And how we keep getting found. I have to assume Washington, DC, is much like New York with traffic cameras everywhere."

"Probably more so," Sun was forced to admit. Realization dawned. "Are you thinking that whoever has the nuclear bomb is going to try to mess with the cameras before the inauguration?"

"It's possible."

Her breath caught in her throat. "That would not be good. What if they have access now too?"

"They might have only sporadic access since there hasn't been an attack on us here in Capitol Hill. But it might explain how they found your super secure safe house." Mack grimaced as she pushed on the brake, bringing the Chevy to a stop just in time to prevent them from slamming into the SUV in front of them.

"So much for obliterating the license plates," Sun muttered. She turned to look at the side streets where traffic was moving slightly faster. Cranking the wheel, she took a narrow road sandwiched between large buildings. "I wish you'd have told me about your traffic camera theory sooner. Now we're stuck."

"I know, I'm sorry. We're both exhausted, Sun. It's a miracle we're holding it together as well as we are."

His calm tone didn't do much to soothe her nerves, although his apology helped. She blew out a breath. "Okay, but we still need a plan to get out of here."

"We may want to find a place to ditch the car."

She let out a harsh laugh. "Like where? I can barely move from one street to the next."

"I think there's a store coming up on the right-hand side of the road." Mack was using the map application on his phone. "Just a few more blocks."

The side streets were as bogged down as the main thoroughfares. Deciding Mack was right about getting off the street, even if that meant going to some stupid store, she turned left and went back to the main road.

After another slow progress through two more intersections, she could see the grocery store was just up ahead.

Crack! *Crack!*

The rear window of the Chevy shattered into dozens of pieces.

"Gun fire! Keep your head down!" Mack shouted.

She crouched as low as possible while still keeping her eyes on the road. They were almost to the store parking lot, but then what?

Where could they go from here?

CHAPTER TWELVE

January 19 – 11:34 a.m. – Washington, DC

Mack swiveled in his seat in an attempt to identify where the shooter was located. The sound of gunshots had already caused chaos, people were running and ducking for cover.

Both shots had come through the back window, which meant the shooter was behind them. With a scope? He had to believe so.

Sun wrenched the steering wheel to the right, sending the Chevy bouncing up and over the curb.

"Shots came from directly behind us so find a spot on the farthest side of the building," Mack said urgently. "We'll need to ditch the Chevy."

"I know." Sun's tone was incredibly calm considering they were in the middle of the city and far from anything that could be considered a shelter.

The gunfire had stopped, but people were still screaming and running wildly. Mack understood their panic, but it wasn't helping them one bit as cars abruptly stopped in the middle of roads, blocking traffic.

Sun parked the car and glanced at him. "Grab the computer. There's a Metro stop not far from here."

Smart to head down to the subway where the shooter couldn't follow their progress with his scope. They ran from the car, the computer bag slung over his back, as they dashed around the grocery store to the street behind it.

Sun set a quick pace as if she ran marathons on a daily basis. Maybe she did? It was harder than he wanted to admit to keep up with her as she dodged pedestrians, the computer case thumping against him with every step.

The map of DC etched in his mind helped keep him on course even in those brief moments when he lost track of Sun's shiny dark hair.

When he glimpsed the sign for the Metro, a wave of relief washed over him. They were going to make it!

Sun darted down the stairs leading to the lower-level station, and he put on a burst of speed to catch up. They wasted precious seconds paying in cash at the machine but soon passed the turnstiles to melt into the crowds.

"The train should be here in a few minutes," Sun said in a low voice.

He was vexed that she wasn't breathing heavily and did his best to do the same. "Any chance Jordan can provide us with another set of wheels?" He knew how to hot-wire a car, but he didn't like the thought of stealing. It would be a last resort, and only if they were in a life-and-death situation.

Kinda like the one they were currently facing. He swept his gaze over the area, looking for anything suspicious. So far, it seemed like these goons coming after them were long on manpower.

For all he knew, there were dozens of men fanned out across the area searching for them.

The seconds ticked by slowly. Standing below ground

and waiting for a train contradicted the urge to keep moving.

Finally, the roar of the train could be heard as it approached. Keeping Sun in front of him, he waited impatiently for travelers to get off the train so they could get on.

Sun slipped through the doors. He followed as she made her way to the rear section of the subway. It was standing room only, but that was okay. He kept Sun positioned in front of him so that no one could get to her without going through him.

They were partners in this case, but he'd readily sacrifice himself to protect her.

No matter what.

JANUARY 19 – 11:51 a.m. – Chicago, IL

Hana followed Jarek into the motel, unfazed by the musty smell lingering in the air. She'd been in worse places. Being safe was all that mattered.

"I need to apologize." Jarek dropped heavily into the desk chair, leaving her to sink down onto the edge of the bed. "This is all my fault."

"No, Jarek, it is not." Hana offered a weary smile. Between running from gunmen and jet lag, she could have used a nap. "I told you years ago how the regime deals with defectors. They hunt them like wolves and kill them." She stared down at her hands for a long moment. "It is my fault that you are in danger." She hesitated, not wanting to admit she had basically been spying on the regime.

"You don't understand." He leaned forward and rested his large warm hand on hers. "I began searching for you, Hana, which is what began this whole chain reaction."

This was surprising news. She met his gaze curiously. "Searched how?"

He flushed and momentarily closed his eyes. "I hired a private investigator, and he found you in Geneva, Switzerland."

"I see." She had used a different name when she'd gone back to North Korea this last time and knew now that going back to Geneva was a mistake. In more ways than one. "What is this investigator's name?"

"Charles Emmerson." He grimaced. "I know it was wrong, but it had been so long, Hana. I felt certain that it was safe to be together by now."

It would never be safe, but she didn't tell him that. It was curious, though, that this Charles Emmerson had been able to find her.

Was it possible the regime had been tipped off by Jarek's search? Maybe, but it was far more likely that her undercover activities had raised their suspicions. None of which mattered at this point.

"Hana, please forgive me." Jarek's tone was ravaged.

"Of course I forgive you, Jarek." She smiled gently. "You must know that the danger follows me, regardless of where I go."

"We'll disappear together, Hana. Go someplace where no one will ever find us."

She sighed. "I'm not certain such a place exists, but it's a lovely dream." She'd done enough in trying to bring down the regime, wasn't it time for her to live her own life? Did she deserve that? Maybe, but not yet. She hesitated, then asked, "You're not married?"

"No!" He looked shocked at the suggestion. "Never. Why—are you?"

Hana shook her head. "No, there has been no one else

for me, Jarek. But I begged you to create a life without me, so why didn't you?"

"There's no one for me either." Jarek's tone was firm. "I've always loved you, Hana. Always."

Tears misted her eyes, but she blinked them away with an effort. Would Jarek still love her once he learned the truth? Was this the right time to tell him?

"I understand if you don't feel the same way," he said in a halting voice. "Thirty years is a long time."

"Seems like just yesterday," she murmured, thinking of how young they once were. How carefree. She met his gaze head-on. "There is something you need to know, Jarek. And I hope you will forgive me for the secret I have kept from you all these years."

"Secret?" His brow furrowed. "About your family?"

That too, but that wasn't what she needed to explain. At least, not yet. One thing at a time. "About our daughter, Sun Yin-lee."

The blood drained from his face. "Daughter? You . . . I have a daughter?"

"Yes." He took his hand from hers and rose shakily to his feet. She braced herself for his anger over this betrayal.

"I . . . don't understand." He began to pace the short length of the room. "You had our daughter? Without telling me?"

"I did, yes." She twisted her fingers together. "I kept Sun's presence a secret, Jarek, not to hurt you but in an attempt to shield her from the regime. My blood flows through her veins, and if those in power knew—" She couldn't finish.

"Sun." Jarek's voice had softened. "She sounds beautiful."

More tears pricked her eyes, and she subtly wiped them

away. "She is beautiful and very, very smart. But I'm worried about her, Jarek. Things have escalated in the past twenty-four hours. I fear the regime will find out about Sun." She hesitated, then added, "I came here to see you because I need your help."

There was only a moment's pause before he nodded and returned to his chair. She was humbled by the love shining from his eyes. Love she didn't deserve. "Of course, Hana. We shall go to Sun and help keep her safe." His voice grew thick. "I would like the chance to meet my daughter."

"Oh, Jarek." She wanted so badly to throw herself into his arms. "I know Sun will be very happy to meet you too."

"Does she . . . know about me?"

Hana's smile faded, and she shook her head. "No. I was vague about you, but only for your protection, Jarek. The fact that there was a gunman at your home means the truth has already come out. But I want you to know I never spoke poorly of you."

"The fact that Sun grew up without me in her life speaks poorly enough," Jarek said with a heavy sigh. "I really wish I could have been there for you, Hana. And for Sun. But that is in the past, right now we must find her. Do you have any idea where she is?"

Hana nodded slowly. "She is in Washington, DC. And we need to get there as soon as possible."

JANUARY 19 – 12:06 p.m. – Washington, DC

Sun checked the subway stops, trying to figure out which one would provide the best coverage from anyone attempting to follow them.

"Where are we headed?" Mack asked.

"We'll get off at Metro Center." The stop would not

only be densely populated but offered additional Metro trains they could jump on to head out of the downtown area. "I'll call Jordan, and we'll set up a meeting then."

"Okay." Mack was so close she could feel his warm breath against her hair. She wasn't one for being overly emotional, but after all that had transpired, she wanted nothing more than to rest her head on his chest to soak up his strength.

Normally she was cool under pressure. But not now. She knew that her lack of sleep was wreaking havoc with her mind, and these adrenaline surges after each incident, Chandler's murder followed closely by getting caught in sniper fire, wasn't helping.

The train abruptly slowed, sending her off balance. Mack easily caught and held her close. She reveled in his brief embrace, warmly surrounded by his pine scent.

She thought she felt the brush of his lips against her temple, but the sensation was gone so fast she thought she dreamed it.

Being chased like this through DC was growing weary. How was it that they kept getting found? What types of resources did these men have anyway?

"Sun? Isn't this our stop coming up?" Mack's low voice whispered in her ear.

She pulled herself together with an effort. This was not the time to start thinking about how Mack had changed—for the better. Or about how much she liked this new and improved version. He hadn't teased her once by singing the song, *Do your ears hang low, do they wobble to and fro* . . .

"Yes." She straightened and began threading through the crowd to get closer to the doorway. Mack remained close behind.

At this time of the day, the crowds were horrendous.

Sun only hoped that the crush of people helped keep them hidden from sight.

When they reached the street, she called Jordan, sending up a silent prayer of relief when he answered. "Jordan, someone shot through the back window of the car while we were trying to get out of Capitol Hill. We're at Metro Center now, we need to meet up to get a replacement vehicle."

"Okay, Sloan and I can make that work." She heard him tapping on the keyboard. "Listen, there's a hotel a little over a mile from the Brookland CUA station." He gave her the name, and she knew it was low enough on the budget scale to take cash. "We'll meet you there in about an hour."

"Okay, thanks." She disconnected and quickly checked the Metro map. If they hurried, they should be able to catch the red line. She gestured for Mack to follow as she made her way back down to the main terminal.

"An hour?" Mack sounded disappointed. "All this running around is wasting time. We have less than twenty-four hours until the inauguration ceremony."

"I know." They skated onto the subway in the nick of time. "But what else can we do? Whoever is tracking us is doing a good job of keeping us from investigating the case."

"We need to go on offense," Mack muttered.

She rolled her eyes at his football reference. "I'm frustrated too."

"Maybe the documents will reveal a clue," Mack said.

"They better." She grasped the pole as the train increased speed. "Otherwise we'll for sure be too late."

JANUARY 19 – 12:17 p.m. – Washington, DC
"We lost them."

"Again?" He couldn't believe the incompetence of these two men. "How is that even remotely possible? You promised to have an insider view of exactly where they were located, and you still lost them?"

There was nothing but silence on the other end of the connection.

He controlled his temper with an effort. "Find them, or I will take care of you." He paused, then added, "Permanently."

More silence. Anger simmered as he realized his point man had disconnected without saying a word. It was all he could do not to throw the phone against the mirror, shattering it into tiny pieces.

The door opened, revealing a smiling familiar face. One that had no clue about what was going on. "Are you ready?"

He pulled himself together and smiled. "Of course." He was more than ready for what awaited, but it would all be for nothing if things didn't go as planned.

The men had better get their act together, and soon. He was working two different angles here, one a deal with the devil himself, yet neither angle had come close to providing the desired results.

Strolling through the hallowed halls of the Capitol, he told himself he'd give the two idiots one more chance before finding replacements.

They would do the job or die.

It was as simple as that.

JANUARY 19 – 12:21 *p.m.* – *Chicago, IL*
He had a daughter.

Jarek was still coming to grips with the astounding news. The flash of anger toward Hana had surprised him, but he'd done his best to move beyond it. Why waste time being angry over the past? What was done, was done. Better now to focus on the future.

Yet it hurt to know his daughter knew nothing about him. Not his name, or his career, or anything else about his life.

A life, he hated to admit, that had not been lived to its fullest.

All these years pining for Hana had made him soft in the head. What was wrong with him? Jarek should have been at the top of his profession. Should have won accolades for his work or at least helped others to do something great.

He should have written the novel tugging at the back of his mind rather than sitting around and talking to Geoff about his work in progress.

Geoff's novel would never be completed now.

Remembering the brutal murder of his old friend brought a pang of guilt. His fault that Geoff was dead. His friend would never have been in any danger if Jarek hadn't gone there after leaving the hospital.

Hana emerged from the bathroom, looking even more beautiful than before. It was as if the hot water washed away her fatigue along with the travel grime, leaving an unblemished rose in its place.

She surprised him by walking forward and slipping her arms around his waist as if they'd never been apart for the past thirty years. "Have you forgiven me?"

"Of course." He smiled and pressed a chaste kiss to her forehead.

She pulled back enough to look deeply into his eyes. "Jarek, there is no *of course* about it. I know how unfair it was to keep Sun's existence a secret from you all these years. I promise I didn't take such a step lightly. The regime . . ."

"Would kill you both, I know." He smiled reassuringly. "I can't lie to you, Hana. I am devastated having missed so much time being with our daughter. I would have loved nothing more than to have been there for you when she was born, to assist in raising her." He swallowed hard. "But I think I understand better now the extent the regime will go to eliminate you as a potential threat." The Asian stalking him at the airport, chasing him from Geoff's, and shooting at them from his condo was proof enough.

"I wish things could have been different for us." Hana rested her forehead against his chest. He gathered her close, reveling in the fact that she was actually here with him.

There was so much to do. They had to find a way to acquire a vehicle without leaving a paper trail, then hit the road to drive east to Washington, DC. A long drive, over ten hours maybe longer depending on traffic, unless they could come up with another method of travel.

But he didn't move. Instead he held Hana close, not wanting to let her go.

Now that she'd come to find him, he refused to live another day without her.

Even if this journey they were about to embark upon ended badly, he would be grateful for every hour they had together.

JANUARY 19 – 12:48 p.m. – Washington, DC

There weren't very many people exiting the subway at the Brookland CUA station. The stop was located at ground level, so Mack followed Sun directly into the daylight.

"The hotel is almost one and a half miles from here." Mack hitched the computer higher onto his shoulder. "We may want to jog or we might be late for the meeting with Jordan and Sloan."

"We'll be fine, they'll be stuck in traffic for a while I'm sure." After they crossed the street, Sun paused and scanned the subway station they'd just left.

He did the same. There didn't seem to be anyone following them.

"Okay, we can go." Sun set out at a brisk pace.

After crossing a couple of streets, a feeling of unease trickled down his spine. He cast another furtive glance over his shoulder but didn't see anything out of the ordinary.

As they neared a tree-covered area about a half mile from the hotel, a man dressed in black with a knit hat covering his head leaped out from behind a bush.

Sun immediately dropped into a defensive stance, quickly defending herself against the knife-wielding attacker. She hadn't pulled her gun, no doubt hoping to keep him alive to get information from him. Mack was about to join her when he felt someone behind him.

Two men. Mack whirled as the knife blade slashed across the computer case. With his back up against Sun's, he faced his assailant.

He didn't want to kill them outright. Having two attackers armed with knives wasn't the worst situation he'd been in, but knowing Sun was fighting for her life brought this to a whole new level. He would not fail her.

He welcomed the anger, striking out again and again with well-placed punches and kicks. Listening to Sun defend herself was unnerving. He forced himself to stay focused on taking this guy out so that he could better help her.

When the knife flew from the attacker's hand, he didn't hesitate but closed in, striking the man's temple in a devastating blow, harder than he'd intended. The guy instantly crumpled to the ground, and he added a quick pressure point to keep him there before turning to assist Sun with taking out her assailant.

Seeing the bright red blood staining the sidewalk nearly sent him to his knees.

Sun was injured!

CHAPTER THIRTEEN

January 19 – 1:03 p.m. – Washington, DC

Sun fought with lethal precision, the way her sensei had taught her, but the assailant was also very well trained and had the added element of surprise. His knife had cut through the fabric of her jacket sleeve, but she'd struck back hard, ignoring the pain.

The assailant recoiled as she struck his wrist with enough force to break the bones. The knife dropped to the ground, and she quickly pressed her advantage.

"Who sent you?" Sun demanded.

The assailant didn't answer.

"Who sent you?" Mack repeated, bending over him.

Still nothing. Giving up, she and Mack knocked out the assailant.

"You're bleeding." The panicked expression in Mack's eyes seemed odd as the two of them had often sparred with enough force to cause bruises.

"I know." She quickly frisked the unconscious assailant, pulling cash and yet another disposable phone from the man's pocket. "Thanks for having my back," she added.

Mack surprised her by hauling her close and kissing her. For a moment, she felt as if the earth had stopped moving. His kiss was hot and hungry but ended far too soon.

"Let's get out of here." Mack pulled away, then urged her forward. She blinked away the impact of Mack's kiss, realizing their scuffle had already drawn attention from gapers, and she felt certain one of the innocent bystanders had notified the police.

Just what they didn't need.

Although it was reassuring to know Sloan and Jordan would be there soon.

How had these men found them anyway? They were both either eastern European or Americans, which struck her as odd. Why hadn't the regime sent North Koreans?

She couldn't begin to fathom.

They jogged the rest of the way to the hotel. Sun did her best to staunch the bleeding from her left arm so as not to leave a blood trail.

"Go into the restroom," Mack urged in a low voice. "I'll get us a room."

She nodded and did as he suggested, knowing that evidence of a crime would make it less likely they'd be provided a room, even with a cash bribe.

Stripping off her jacket, she surveyed the damage. From what she could tell, the tip of the assailant's knife had sliced her radial artery. A wad of paper towels and pressure helped staunch the bleeding, but probably not for long.

Stitches would work, but they couldn't risk going to a hospital. Not for an injury this minor. At least he hadn't punctured her brachial artery, which would be more difficult to manage without medical intervention.

For now, holding pressure would have to do.

When she left the sanctuary of the restroom, Mack was

standing just outside the door. "We can't stay here after all, we need to move."

The sound of police sirens was enough of an explanation. "Okay, any idea which way we should go?"

"There isn't a lot of cover in this neighborhood," Mack said, taking her out through a side door of the hotel. "Call Jordan, see if he's close."

It was a good idea. She let go of her injured wrist and made the call as they took shelter behind the hotel. It was shaped like a U, and the rear of the building couldn't be seen from the road.

But there was a residential neighborhood with who knew how many nosy people watching out their windows.

Jordan answered almost immediately. "Sun? I hear sirens, what's going on?"

"We were assaulted by two men with knives. We fought back without using guns to try and get information but were unsuccessful. We managed to escape, but the hotel is too close to the scene of the attack. And there were more than enough people likely calling 911. Where are you?"

"About three blocks from the hotel. There's a gas station about two blocks to the north, head there and we'll meet you."

"Okay." Sun glanced at Mack. "We'll meet them at the gas station."

"This way." Mack turned north, and she admired how calm and cool he was under pressure.

Having him standing at her back, fighting their enemies, had been reassuring. It had occurred to her that it had been a long time since she'd trusted someone to have her back while in hand-to-hand combat.

She certainly trusted the Security Specialists, Incorporated team, after all, they were paying her well for her language and investigative skills. But having Mack at her back was different.

Not just because they'd grown up in the Mensa program together.

But because she knew he'd fight to the death alongside her if needed.

And, of course, the way he'd kissed her as if he were starving for more hadn't hurt. A reaction to her being injured? Maybe. She told herself not to read too much into a simple kiss.

Even though, for her, there had been nothing simple about it.

They reached the gas station just as two black SUVs pulled in. Sloan and Natalia Dreyer were in one of them; Jordan alone was behind the wheel of the second.

Jordan quickly jumped out and tossed the keys at her. "You and Mack take this one, I'll go with Sloan and Natalia."

There wasn't time to argue, although she wouldn't have minded asking Natalia to take a look at her wrist. Natalia was a registered nurse and had been working in critical care when Sloan met her.

Mack slid into the passenger seat, leaving her to take the wheel. As she followed Sloan's SUV into traffic, she handed Mack her phone. "Call Jordan and find out if they have a new plan."

Mack made the call, holding the phone so she could hear. "We found a second hotel, one on the other side of the city."

"Okay, what's the address?" Mack asked.

Jordan relayed the information. Sun kept a wary eye on the rearview mirror as she drove, half expecting the two assailants to show up to finish what they'd started.

"Don't worry." Mack must have noticed her concern. "We didn't kill them, but I'm fairly certain they were out long enough for us to get away and the police to arrive."

She blew out a breath. "I just don't understand why they keep popping up wherever we are. I can't imagine how they're tracking us."

"I have a theory on that," Mack said grimly.

She shot him a questioning glance. "Like?"

"Street cameras, remember?" Mack scowled. "At first their tracking seemed sporadic, but now I'm wondering if they have someone working full time on this. A serious hacker with skills good enough to watch the street camera video feeds as well as subway video minute by minute."

Minute by minute? As in, right now? She glanced up to see the very small camera mounted on the light pole.

"If that's true, they'll find us at the new location."

"I know, but I might have a solution to that problem." Mack patted the satellite computer that he'd somehow managed to keep ahold of during their brief but intense fight.

She was afraid to ask what that solution entailed, but no matter how outrageous it may be, what choice did they have?

None. Not if they wanted to stay alive long enough to foil the impending nuclear explosion.

JANUARY 19 – 1:22 p.m. – Chicago, IL

Under normal circumstances, Hana would have enjoyed traveling by train, but there was nothing normal about these circumstances.

Somehow, they'd arrived at Union Station just in time to catch the train heading to Michigan City, Indiana. A ride that would take them one hour and forty-five minutes, which wasn't much faster than driving by car.

Except maybe by avoiding the crush of Chicago traffic.

Jarek's plan was to find a car in Michigan City and head out across the country to Washington, DC. A drive that would take longer than she liked. Time was of the essence.

Yet she also knew they'd both been followed to their respective airports in the past.

"Hana?" Jarek's low voice interrupted her thoughts. "Does Sun know we're coming?"

"No." She forced a smile. "Unfortunately, we aren't able to communicate regularly. I do have a disposable phone, but when I last checked the answering service, there was no message."

"I see." He looked concerned about this. "W-what about me? I'm sure having her father show up out of the blue will be a total shock."

"Maybe, but try not to worry. I truly believe Sun will be happy to meet you."

"I hope so." He lifted a hand to straighten his wrinkled jacket. "We don't necessarily need to tell her who I am right away. You know—the part about me being her father. We may want to wait for better timing."

"Are you nervous?" She rested her hand on his forearm. "There's no need to be. Sun is very bright and will likely see through any attempt to cover up the truth." She hesitated, then added, "She has your ears."

"My ears?" He raised both hands to his earlobes as if to make sure they were still attached to his head.

Her smile widened. "Yes, you have longer earlobes than I do, and Sun's are similar."

He frowned and dropped his hands. "I doubt that. I'm sure she looks just like you."

"Very similar to me." Her smile faded. "Unfortunately, that makes her even more of a target for the regime."

Jarek took her hand in his. She soaked in the warmth of his skin against hers. "You have never told me why the regime has come after you. And Sun."

She stared down at their entwined hands for a long moment. There were certain things she didn't dare say out loud on a train, even though there was no one sitting directly in front or behind them. "I believe I mentioned this before, but I defected from my country." She couldn't go into details on the spying she'd done. This would have to be enough for now. "In their view, that is a serious crime punishable by death."

"But why?" Jarek insisted. "I don't understand."

Her bleak gaze met his. "Because they must set an example in order to prevent others from doing the same." Especially since others, like her, had turned around to use their knowledge about the regime against them. Spying on North Korea had been her attempt to help quash the power of the regime.

Now, the small attempt seemed absurd.

"That's ridiculous and terrifying," Jarek sputtered.

Yes, it was. And this was the world she'd exposed him to.

His being in danger was her fault, not the other way around. It was the reason she'd sent him away thirty years ago, despite being pregnant with his daughter.

Despite how much she'd loved him.

She'd managed to stay far away, until now.

And she would never forgive herself if Jarek died because of the choices she'd made.

. . .

JANUARY 19 – 1:46 *p.m.* – *Washington, DC*

He glanced at his watch for the third time in thirty minutes. Why hadn't he heard from either of his sources? What on earth could be taking them so long? Once the deed was done, he could relax.

At least until tomorrow. A hint of a smile crossed his features. He could just imagine how the utter chaos would play out.

The only problem was these two meddlers who needed to be removed from the equation. After all, he had a team to report to as well and did not relish the idea of admitting failure yet again. Especially now that he'd joined forces with people who would just as easily kill him too.

Several high-level people were counting on him to deliver.

And he would. Going to any lengths needed to get the job done.

Finally, the disposable phone in his pocket vibrated with a text message. Subtly pulling the phone from his pocket, he kept it shielded beneath the edge of the desk, ignoring the droning voice regarding the latest political strategy as he read the message.

Injured, will need to regroup. Will be in touch soon.

He ground his teeth together in frustration as he dropped the phone back into his pocket. Injured? Regroup?

He'd show them injured! The wave of fury was difficult to suppress, but since he was surrounded by others, he did his best not to let his feelings show.

It was inconceivable that these men had once again failed to execute such a simple task. Getting rid of two people shouldn't be this difficult. Not with the resources he'd thrown at this little problem.

Time to implement plan B.

And to get rid of two utterly useless loose ends.

JANUARY 19 – 1:51 p.m. – Washington, DC

Mack emerged from the passenger side door of the SUV and regarded the members of Security Specialists, Incorporated warily. They'd parked the two vehicles side by side along the side of the hotel that was not visible from the road.

Sloan's dark hair was a direct contrast to his wife's straight blond hair. Natalia was slender, with a slightly rounded abdomen showing the early phase of her pregnancy, yet her direct gaze let him know she was no pushover.

Mack imagined that, much like Sun, Natalia was more than capable of holding her own.

Jordan also had dark hair and olive skin, reflecting his Arabic heritage. There was no sign of Jordan's wife, Diana, or their daughter, Bryn. A fact he was secretly grateful for.

As if things weren't complicated enough. He didn't want to add other innocent lives to the mess they were in.

Personally, he didn't much like the idea of exposing women to danger, especially pregnant ones, but how these men involved their wives in their business was not his concern.

Keeping Sun alive and safe from the regime while finding this dangerous nuke was.

Then again, Sun was proof that women were just as valuable in the field as men were. Maybe more so as assailants often underestimated a woman. Especially one as tiny and petite as Sun.

He still couldn't believe he'd kissed her. And that she hadn't flattened him for doing so. Maybe he should test the water by kissing her again? The thought made him smile.

"I'll secure a set of connecting rooms," Jordan offered.

"Thanks." Sun turned toward Sloan and Natalia. "Natalia, I may need you to look at a wound on my wrist. I believe the artery was nicked in the knife fight."

"Wait, what? An artery?" Mack had convinced himself that the blood on the sidewalk wasn't Sun's, but apparently he was wrong. "Let me see."

"Mack, please. Natalia is a nurse, and I'd prefer to hear her expert opinion."

Sun pulled her coat sleeve up, revealing dark red bloodstained paper towels that had been clumsily wound around her slim wrist.

"Hmm." Natalia peered closely at the wound. He stepped forward to get a better look for himself, but Sun pushed him back with her uninjured arm. "You did a good job of using a pressure dressing, but I think a few stitches are in order."

"Stitches?" He scowled. "You're not a doctor."

Natalia gazed steadily at him. "No, but I have done more than my share of patching up injuries far worse than this."

Mack rubbed the back of his neck, trying not to overreact. "What if those stitches cause a problem with the circulation in her hand?"

"There are two arteries that supply blood to the hand, the radial artery, which is what has been injured here, and the ulnar artery. I would not offer to place stitches if I thought they would cause more harm than good." Natalia shifted her gaze to Sun. "It's up to you, Sun. I travel with a very large first aid kit these days. I'm happy to apply a pressure dressing or stitches, whichever you prefer. But know if you have to fight again, the blood clot could break free of a pressure dressing and cause more bleeding."

"I trust you, Natalia." Sun sent him an irritated look. "Ignore Mack, I'm not sure what his problem is. You can stitch it up when we get into the room."

Mack scowled but didn't say anything more. Clearly, Sun had everything under control as usual. Besides, how was he supposed to know Natalia was some sort of expert trauma nurse? He hadn't liked the way she'd treated an arterial bleed as negligible, but it certainly sounded as if stitches were the way to go.

By the frown on her face, Sun must not have enjoyed their kiss as much as he had.

Jordan arrived with room keys, and they made their way across the parking lot to where their connecting rooms were located. Mack entered last, setting the satellite computer on the desk, plugging it in, and opening it.

"Sloan, will you grab the first aid kit from the SUV?" Natalia asked, holding Sun's wrist as fresh blood oozed from the wound.

"Sure." Sloan left without hesitation.

"What are you doing?" Jordan asked as he waited for the computer to find a signal.

"We have been found several times, despite taking great lengths to ditch our tail." He glanced at Jordan. "I believe there is a hacker involved in this scheme, the same one who embedded the transcript to self-destruct has also likely found a way into the street camera and subway video feed. It's the only explanation I can come up with."

Jordan whistled under his breath. "That's a level of expertise I don't have," he admitted.

"I do." He pulled out the chair and dropped into it, ignoring the various aches and pains from the blows his assailant had landed. Nothing he hadn't experienced before.

Although the deep slash in the computer case was proof that he'd been fortunate.

He glanced over to where Natalia was using soap and water to clean the wound on Sun's wrist. He wasn't squeamish by nature, but watching Sun's wound bleed made him feel a tad queasy.

Ridiculous reaction to a minor wound. He gave himself a mental shake, then turned his attention to the computer.

He'd never tried to hack into the DC street camera system, but how hard could it be? He'd hacked into plenty of other secure systems.

But first he needed to find the name of the company hosting the Washington, DC, city-wide camera system. And since this was the home of the White House, he figured the hack job would be anything but simple.

Jordan leaned close, watching as he worked. Mack tuned him out as best he could, along with the medical treatment Sun was receiving. Although out of the corner of his eye, he saw Natalia pull a needle and thread from the large first aid kit Sloan had fetched for her.

His stomach rolled, and he quickly looked away.

No way was he going to pass out in front of Sun's team.

He found the camera company and began to dig into their network. It wasn't easy starting from scratch, but soon he found the gateway he needed to enter the program.

Hacking was tedious detailed work that encompassed a lot of trial and error. After five minutes, Jordan grew bored and moved away.

"All set," Natalia said. "Three stitches, not too bad. We'll wrap it too, just in case you find yourself in another tight spot. And here are some antibiotics, three days' worth should do the trick. If you can remember to take them in all the excitement."

"Thanks, Natalia. You're the best," Sun said.

Mack was relieved to know Sun's injury had been taken care of and made a mental note to make sure Sun took the antibiotics over the next, well, less than twenty-four hours.

The shrinking timeline was sobering.

Here he was wasting time hacking into the stupid camera system when they should be looking for the stupid nuke.

His frustration only added to his determination. And soon his persistence paid off.

"Gotcha!" He felt a surge of satisfaction as he broke through the last firewall.

"You're in?" Jordan and Sun both came over to see for themselves.

"Yep." He entered a series of commands, then sat back. "It's done."

"What is?" Sun looked confused.

"I shut down the entire camera system." He exited the program and stared for a moment at the computer.

"You what?" Jordan's incredulous tone made him wince. "Isn't that illegal?"

He wasn't going to admit the obvious. "They were constantly one step ahead of us and tried to kill us. We need to be able to travel the city without being followed, so I shut the video system down using a coded virus that should take them a long time to repair." Mack glanced between Jordan and Sun. "We need to find that nuke before they're able to do that." He hesitated and added, "Or all of this will have been for nothing."

CHAPTER FOURTEEN

January 19 – 2:14 p.m. – Washington, DC

Sun was secretly impressed with Mack's idea of using a virus to shut down the cameras in the city and hoped he was right about the time it would take for them to get it back up and running. "Okay, so now what? Where do we go from here?"

There was a long moment of silence as they exchanged grim glances. "I'll start reviewing the other files on the USB drive, maybe that will give us something to go on," Mack finally said.

"What else do you need from us?" Jordan asked.

She ruefully shook her head. "I wish I knew. I appreciate the extra cash and the SUV. We already have the sat computer. If we had even a remote idea where to look for this bomb, we'd be in business."

"Natalia and I are both available if you need backup," Sloan offered. "I know we don't speak any North Korean, but we can help keep you both safe."

"Thanks, Sloan." She shrugged. "If Mack can find something in Chandler's files, I'll let you know."

Jordan and Sloan exchanged a glance, and she understood their frustration. "Doesn't seem like much to go on, does it?" Jordan groused.

"No. But Chandler was murdered for a reason. We can only hope and pray his death isn't in vain," Sloan agreed.

She snapped her fingers and met Jordan's gaze. "That reminds me of the two men who'd attacked us. Can you try to find out from the local authorities if they were picked up?"

"Yes." Jordan's dark eyes gleamed. "Knowing their names would be helpful in tracing who may have hired them."

"Exactly." Sun gestured impatiently. "Try them now."

Jordan pulled out his phone and moved to a quiet corner of the room to make his calls. She leaned over Mack's shoulder to check on his progress.

"These are all previous transcripts." He glanced up at her. "So far, it's the same type of rhetoric as the one we have."

"Nothing about the location or type of nuke?" Sun asked.

"The constant reference to the word *small* reinforces our theory of a suitcase nuke," Mack admitted. "Like this here, *big surprises come in small packages.*"

A shiver snaked down her spine. "The saddest part of this is our own government is the one who first manufactured these small nukes. Now it may be used against us by North Korea."

Mack grimaced. "True, but remember it was a different world back then. These suitcase nukes were made back in the 1960s during the Cold War. The US was fighting against Russia, which posed a very real threat."

"Exactly," Sloan agreed, coming over to join them. He

kept his arm around his wife, Natalia, who Sun knew had been born in Russia but adopted and brought to the States when she was a baby. "I can't help being surprised at the idea that North Korea has created the same technology all these years later."

"Those in power will do anything to keep it," Natalia said darkly. "We learned that lesson the hard way."

Sloan gave her a hug, and Sun had to tear her gaze away from the happiness radiating off them. Times like this it felt like something she'd never have.

"There is no doubt in my mind that the North Korean regime craves power." Sun sighed and raked her fingers through her straight hair. "Yet, if someone asked me which country would try to build a new, secret, small yet powerful nuclear bomb, I'd guess Russia over North Korea."

"Same here," Sloan agreed, and Natalia nodded.

"Russia." Mack straightened, pinning her with an incredulous look. "Sun, you might be onto something."

"I know, I'm brilliant," she teased. "But humor me anyway. Why do you think I'm onto something?"

He turned in his seat to face them. "What country meddles the most in our elections? Russia. And what's the potential target of this nuclear explosion? The presidential inauguration."

She picked up on his train of thought. "Russia designed the nuke, helped transport it into the US, specifically Washington, DC, to be used against us. Only they want to be sure North Korea gets the blame, not Russia."

Natalia sucked in a harsh breath, and Sloan's frown deepened. "And if they were successful, it's a plan that would create World War III."

"A war in which Russia would pretend to be our ally, until it was too late," Sun finished. "It's a crazy plan really."

"But it could work," Mack said.

Sun nodded slowly. "I'm afraid you're right. And thinking back to the murder of my informant, his throat was slit in a way the Russian mafia tends to use as their calling card." She swallowed hard. "Which would also explain why the assailants we've been dealing with don't look Asian. In fact, I thought the last two guys looked like they were from Eastern Europe."

"Russia," Sloan repeated. "We may be able to help you with that."

"I hope so," Sun murmured. Factoring in the Russian connection only added to the complexity of their case.

Making her feel as if they were right back to square one in finding the nuclear bomb.

JANUARY 19 – 2:39 *p.m.* – *Michigan City, IN*

Jarek kept his hand cupped beneath Hana's elbow as they made their way to the taxi station. The train ride had seemed to take forever, and he didn't relish the thought of driving all the way to Washington, DC.

"Jarek, I think we should risk flying to DC," Hana said in a low voice. "I don't think we were followed to the train station, and the sooner we get to Sun the better."

"You read my mind," Jarek admitted. "The only problem is that Michigan City only has a couple of small airports for private prop planes. To get a flight to DC, we'll need to get to South Bend, Indiana's international airport."

"And how far away is South Bend?"

"At least half an hour, maybe more with traffic." Jarek ushered her toward the waiting taxi.

"I have plenty of cash," Hana offered.

"I do too." He held the door for her and climbed in after

her. "Although I may not have enough for our plane tickets. I could use an ATM, but I am worried that will allow us to be tracked."

"No ATM," Hana agreed. "We cannot allow an electronic trail to be followed."

"Will you take us to South Bend International Airport?" Jarek asked the driver.

"That's pretty far," the guy protested.

"We'll make it worth your time," he promised.

The driver reluctantly pulled onto the highway and then nodded. "Okay, but I'll need to add an extra fee."

"I understand." Jarek sat back in the taxi, feeling safe for the first time in hours. For one thing, he felt certain they'd finally escaped the Asian tailing them.

But mostly it was because he was with Hana. It occurred to him that he would do anything for her, even uproot his life and follow her wherever she decided to live once the threat of danger was over.

And if the danger was always present? He'd live out the rest of the life God had provided to him and stay with her.

No way was he allowing Hana to leave him a second time.

Better to spend what little time he might have on earth with her than to live into his doting old age without her.

JANUARY 19 – 2:54 *p.m.* – *Washington, DC*

Mack couldn't believe they hadn't considered a possible Russian connection before now. Leaning forward, he reread the transcript through the new lens and felt certain they were onto something.

"These transcripts are transcribed in English," he said, glancing back at the rest of the Security Specialists, Inc.

team. "But I'm wondering if Chandler knew or suspected something about this bomb being potentially built and transported by Russia. It would explain why he was followed and murdered."

"Highly likely," Sloan said. He gestured to the computer. "Do you mind if I take a look?"

Mack pushed away from the desk to make room. "Have at it."

"But why did the blond guy speak North Korean?" Sun asked.

Another good question. "I'm not sure, unless it's part of the whole pretense of making this look as if the bomb was brought here and set off by North Korea. Maybe he's setting someone up to take the fall. He did say: *be on time or I'll retaliate.*"

"Be on time for the inauguration?" Sun frowned. "I think we're missing something significant."

Mack knew they were missing a lot.

There were several minutes of silence before Sloan spoke up. "There's a reference here to the initials VVP."

Mack stared at him. "What does that mean?"

"It's a nickname for Vladimir Putin. His full name is Vladimir Vladimirovich Putin."

"Interesting." Mack hadn't known that.

"Proof that we're on the right track with the Russian connection," Sun said. "Only I'm not sure how that helps us find the nuke."

"The locals claim they didn't find anyone at the location of the nine-one-one call," Jordan said, rejoining them. "They're not happy about the fact that everyone involved scattered."

"We couldn't stay, Jordan," Sun said. "Fighting caused a scene, but not as much as if we'd used our guns. By the time the locals cleared us after finding our weapons, we'd have lost most of the day, and as it is, we still don't have much to go on."

"I understand," Jordan said. "And the cameras being down are frustrating the cops as well. Although I did learn that one of the men dressed in black picked up the other and carried him off to a vehicle parked a few blocks away. At least, according to one of the witnesses, who also saw you and Mack heading to the hotel."

"Great," Mack muttered, thinking about their kiss. "I hope their descriptions were vague."

"They were. I admitted that you were working on a case," Jordan continued. "They'd like you to come in for a statement at some point."

"How about after the presidential inauguration?" Sun suggested with a hint of sarcasm. "If we're still alive to give an interview."

"We'll find a way to stop the nuke." Mack refused to consider the alternative.

"Speaking of the nuke, any ideas on where to look?" Jordan asked.

Mack quickly filled Jordan in on the initials he'd found in one of the transcripts on Chandler's computer.

"I know of two different taverns that are owned by Russians who may have some sort of inside information," Sloan said slowly. "We could start there, but I have to warn you, these places are both total dives."

Mack glanced at Sun. "I'm ready if you are."

"I'll stay here in the hotel room," Jordan volunteered. "I'm going to ask Yates for an update on our search for a person named Allan. He hasn't gotten back to me with information on Karen Allan, Allan Stokes, or Sean Allen."

"We could use that information, but in the meantime,

going to the tavern is better than sitting around here. Let's go." Sun pulled on her coat, then grimaced. "Hopefully no one notices the blood stains."

"You'll fit right in," Natalia said in a light teasing tone. "Makes you look tough. Some of the Russians here in DC still have ties to the mob, although we've broken up two of the major rings over the past few months."

Mack eyed her with interest. "Sounds like good work."

Natalia flashed a smile. "Thanks. Sloan makes an excellent partner."

"You're going to make my head swell," Sloan warned, then grinned and planted a quick kiss on her lips. "And ditto."

Mack couldn't imagine taking on a dangerous role while working with your spouse. But as he packed up the sat computer and looped the strap of the computer case over his shoulder, he realized that working with someone you cared about, the way he cared for Sun, was at the same time both easy and difficult.

He admired Sun, knew she could hold her own, yet he wanted to wrap her in Kevlar and protect her. Was that how Sloan felt toward Natalia? Sloan looked as if he didn't hesitate to walk into danger, but he had a hard time seeing his slender and pregnant wife doing the same thing.

Not his problem, he reminded himself as he and Sun followed Sloan and Natalia out to their respective SUVs. The difference with him and Sun was that they both were highly trained in martial arts as well as weapon handling.

And, of course, they weren't married. They fought more often than he cared to admit.

A fact that did not deter him from longing for something more.

. . .

JANUARY 19 – 3:14 p.m. – South Bend, IN

Hana was surprised they'd made good time in getting to the South Bend International Airport. The taxi driver had tried chatting with them, but after the first stilted ten minutes, he had fallen silent.

She didn't mind the quiet. It allowed her time to think and to keep a keen eye out for anything out of the ordinary.

From what she could tell, no one had followed them. Not to Michigan City, Indiana, or again to South Bend.

She and Jarek might actually be safe.

But they wouldn't be once they arrived in Washington, DC. She knew from her recent trip to North Korea that things were heating up in Washington, DC, and they needed to get there. Soon.

Information she had yet to fully explain to Jarek. Not that it mattered at the moment.

Maybe once they were on the airplane heading to DC, there would be time to chat in private, if the plane wasn't jam-packed. Not that there was an easy way to break the news.

They'd run from danger in Chicago but were likely heading directly back into the line of fire by going to DC.

She could only hope and pray they'd find Sun, before it was too late.

JANUARY 19 – 3:26 p.m. – Washington, DC

Sun glanced at Mack as he impatiently drummed his fingers against the dashboard. "The traffic won't go faster just because you want it to."

"I don't know why I didn't realize the traffic was as bad here as it is in New York."

"I don't know either," Sun replied. "It's not a secret."

He grinned. "You always find a way to get in the last word, don't you?"

"Another thing you should have figured out before now." Sun hit the blinker, following Sloan's SUV, which was truly no easy feat in the maze of cars she was navigating. Since she lived previously in LA, all traffic was the same to her. She never bothered to get annoyed with it.

What was the point?

"It's interesting how Sloan and Natalia work together, isn't it?"

She eyed him curiously, not the least bit fooled by his casual tone. "A better word might be insane."

"Come on, really?"

She shrugged. "You should hear them sometimes. He's constantly worried about her being in danger. Worse now that she's pregnant."

He looked surprised. "I didn't get that impression."

What was this all about anyway? She glanced at him. "That's only because there wasn't any reason for Sloan to be all paranoid while we were at the hotel. You'll find out once we reach one of these—er—fine Russian-owned establishments. Mark my words, Sloan will be all over anyone who looks at Natalia sideways."

"Have you been to either of these places before?" Mack asked.

"No." Again, she had the impression Mack was fishing for something, but what? Her wrist throbbed in conjunction with the nagging headache, a gift from one of the blows the assailant had landed, and her eyes were gritty with lack of sleep. She wasn't in the mood for playing games. "If you want to know something, just ask."

"I'm good." Mack peered out the window. "Looks like Sloan and Natalia are heading for the seedy side of town."

"And that surprises you why?" She swallowed hard at the edge to her tone. "He warned us, remember?"

"Yeah, I know. It just looks worse than the place we found Hyun-woo." Mack shifted uncomfortably in his seat. Clearly something was bugging him.

When Sloan pulled over to the side of the road, she followed suit. She got out and went up to check with him. "Is it okay to park here?"

"Hopefully it will be fine, we shouldn't be here long," Sloan answered. "It's also still early in the day, so not sure how much info we'll get out of anyone inside."

"I'm sure happy hour has begun," Sun said with a wry smile. "Can't hurt to try."

She was joined by Mack, and they followed Sloan and Natalia into the ramshackle structure with a broken sign that read Morris's Place.

Mack hovered at her back as they crossed the threshold. The interior was dark and dingy thanks to the dirt-streaked windows and several broken lights. Sun could already tell that Sloan was in his protector mode, as he had his shoulders thrown back and was eyeing the crowd as if he was ready to rumble at the slightest provocation. And he kept Natalia close at his side.

Interestingly, she heard several low conversations in coarse Russian. She wasn't as proficient as Natalia but understood enough to get the gist.

And the patrons of this place did not like seeing four strangers walk in, especially one of Asian descent. She heard a Russian slur aimed at her heritage but ignored it.

Mack heard it too, and he tensed as if preparing to join Sloan in a brawl. Why couldn't men understand that fighting wasn't the only way to obtain key information?

"What are you drinking?" the bartender asked in a heavy Russian accent.

"Vodka," was Sloan's surprising response. He laid a twenty-dollar bill on the bar, but when the bartender poured the shot, he didn't reach for it. "Is Morris around?"

The bartender stared at him for a long moment. "Who wants to know?"

Sloan didn't answer but returned his glare with one of his own. When he spoke, it was in Russian. "Morris knows me very well. You really want to risk interfering in our business?"

Sun was impressed, Sloan's use of the Russian language had improved over the past few months. Likely Natalia's influence.

The bartender slowly ambled to the door leading to a back room. While his head was turned, Sloan offered the shot to a man at the bar, who downed it in a hurry.

"Impressive," Natalia drawled in a low husky voice. Then she, too, switched to Russian. "No one can hold their drink better than a Russian, no?"

There was a murmur amongst the patrons as they realized at least two of the four strangers spoke their native language. Sun decided to join the conversation in Russian as well. "Vodka tastes much better than soju."

"How would you know? You don't drink vodka," Mack played along, also speaking Russian.

The group of bar patrons fell eerily silent, staring at them with wary respect, clearly wondering what sort of business they had with Morris.

A big bald Russian with tattoos covering almost every inch of skin came out to the main bar. The man she assumed must be Morris scowled at Sloan. "Why are you here?"

Sloan jerked his head toward the door. "We need to talk, outside."

Morris let out a series of curse words in Russian but strode through his bar to the door. The four of them followed.

"I told you to never come here," the bald man hissed. "Those men must respect me."

"Don't worry, Morris, we didn't hurt your image," Natalia said sweetly. "And we very much appreciate your time."

The big man softened when he looked at Natalia. "When you decide to leave this lug of a husband, my door is always open for you."

Sloan interrupted, "Morris, we need info about a Russian nuclear bomb being in the city."

"I don't know anything about that," Morris protested. Sun thought it was interesting that he didn't deny such a blatant accusation.

"I mean it." Sloan leaned close. "I need to know where the nuke is."

Morris glanced around furtively. "I hear things, but there's no way of knowing if what men boast about over vodka is true."

"What are they saying?" Sloan persisted.

He paused, then said, "The bomb is Russian but not the blame for setting it off."

"Okay, I get that part, but where?" Sloan persisted. "We need to find it."

Morris shrugged. "There is a Russian boat owned by Dimitri Palov. He may know."

Sun felt a fission of anticipation ripple down her spine. Finally, a lead they could act upon!

CHAPTER FIFTEEN

January 19 – 3:48 p.m. – South Bend, IN

Jarek managed to secure two seats on the next flight to Washington, DC. The flight would take just over four hours, mostly because they'd have a short layover in Charlotte, North Carolina.

Ironic to realize most of the flights from the airport here in South Bend went through Chicago before heading onward to Washington, DC. He paid extra and added the hour in order to avoid going back to the city they'd just escaped from.

"The flight doesn't leave for ninety minutes yet," he told Hana. "Why don't we get something to eat before we go through TSA security?" He'd been surprised when she'd instructed him to use a different name rather than Hana Yin-lee. She was now traveling under the name of Mi-Cha Kung.

"Of course, that sounds good." She glanced around anxiously. "I'll need to stop in the restroom first."

Jarek smiled. "Me too. We'll meet here in a few minutes."

Hana disappeared into the women's room while he made his own pit stop in the men's room. Now that they were safe from harm, he wore a goofy smile on his face. If not for the circumstances of how they'd been forced to leave Chicago, he'd treat this upcoming trip like the vacation he and Hana never had.

He stood in the hallway waiting patiently for Hana to emerge. When she finally stepped out from the restroom alcove, he didn't recognize her for a long moment. She'd covered her hair with a scarf, and her face looked rounder and seemed to have more wrinkles marring her beautiful skin than she had before.

"W-what have you done?" He gaped in surprise.

Her smile didn't reach her dark almond-shaped eyes. "These changes will ensure that my face matches that on my passport issued under the name I provided to you. I want to be sure that there is no chance I'll be stopped by TSA."

He felt foolish for not realizing the implication of her name change sooner. "I understand. You escaped Geneva by using this disguise and the fake passport."

"Yes." Her gaze was serious. "Jarek, you should know that I'm not entirely sure this identity hasn't been compromised. Going on this flight may set off alarm bells in the intricate network of the regime."

All thoughts of a possible vacation evaporated like the mist over Lake Michigan. "Maybe we should drive instead, the way we originally planned." He wished he'd never purchased the two plane tickets, especially under her fake name.

"No, that will take too long." Hana rested her hand on his arm. "I'm sure we will be okay until we reach Washington, DC."

Apprehension swirled in his gut. "What happens once we reach DC?"

Hana didn't answer for a long moment. "I will fill you in later. Just know we will need to be on alert for any trouble when we land at Reagan International. Come, let's have dinner."

Jarek's appetite had disappeared, but he obligingly walked with Hana to the nearest airport restaurant.

He reminded himself that every moment with Hana was a precious gift that he planned to enjoy to the fullest.

But he hadn't anticipated that being safe would only last until they were in Washington, DC.

Would he have a chance to meet his daughter, Sun, before danger struck again?

JANUARY 19 – 3:59 p.m. – Washington, DC

"Okay, how do we find Dimitri Palov?" Mack asked as they gathered around the satellite computer back at the hotel. They'd filled Jordan in on the lead they'd uncovered from Morris.

Sloan and Natalia glanced at each other. "I think we can try searching for boat registrations, which in turn would provide an address."

Mack didn't waste any time booting up the computer and beginning to search. Deep down, he knew this Dimitri Palov was a long shot, after all, there had to be hundreds of Russian men who owned boats.

Yet there was no denying that Morris had also overheard the scuttlebutt about the Russian nuke that had been brought into the city. Mere rumor?

Or was there a kernel of truth to the chatter that had been picked up?

"Jordan, did you find anything steering us toward the correct Allan?" Sun asked as Mack worked the keyboard. "It's the only other lead we have other than this Dimitri guy."

"Not yet," Jordan said with a scowl. "As usual, Yates has been difficult to get ahold of."

"In the meantime, Sloan and I will head over to the other Russian tavern, see if we can find anything new," Natalia said.

"I'll come with you," Sun quickly offered.

Mack's body tensed, and he glanced up from the screen. As irrational as it sounded, he didn't want Sun going off without him. Sloan and Natalia weren't helpless, but logic didn't seem to have much to do with it. He thought quickly. "What if I find something on Dimitri? You okay if I head out to investigate him on my own?"

Sun hesitated, clearly torn between wanting to be a part of both leads. Finally, she relented. "Okay, I'll stay here for now. Sloan, call the minute you learn anything that might help us."

"Will do," Sloan agreed before he and Natalia left.

Mack relaxed and went back to his search. Now that he'd managed to convince Sun to stay with him, he needed to find this Palov dude before she got another lead to follow up on.

"I don't understand why we don't know which Allen might be involved," Sun complained to Jordan. "Maybe we should just go ahead and set up meetings with each one of them."

"And what if they're followed and killed the way Chandler was?" Jordan asked.

"It's a risk, but so is a nuclear bomb," Sun retorted. "And

it's not our fault Chandler was murdered. We need to find whoever is behind all of this."

"I know, but I don't want more dead agents either," Jordan argued. "The Feds are paying us to help find this thing, not to eliminate their agents one by one."

Mack listened while he worked, somewhat reassured to hear Sun arguing with Jordan the same way she did with him. It was just her ornery nature, which he still found oddly endearing.

Maybe he was the one who was insane, rather than Sloan.

He focused on the boat registration database he'd hacked into and let out a whoop of excitement. "I found him!"

"Dimitri?" Sun rushed over to peer over his shoulder. Her hand was warm on his back, and it took a moment for him to remember what he was doing.

"Yeah." He cleared his throat, hoping she didn't notice how hoarse he sounded. "Looks like an address here in DC." He frowned, then added, "Interestingly enough, the location isn't all that far from where we found your murdered informant."

"Let's go." Sun was ready and raring to go, but he hesitated, glancing at Jordan.

"What do you think?" The idea of putting Sun in more danger didn't sit well.

"I say go and see if you can find him, or better yet, his boat," Jordan said. "If you find any evidence he's the one who brought in the nuke, we'll call the Feds to take him into custody."

"Come on, Mack," Sun said impatiently. "Traffic is getting more congested by the second."

He nodded and shut down the sat computer, unplugging it from the wall. "Let's bring this along, just in case," he suggested.

"Fine." Sun was already halfway out the door, leaving him to follow.

As she nosed the SUV into a steady stream of traffic, he tried to relax. To remind himself they were both well trained, armed, and dangerous.

Yet he felt certain the Russians were equally so and had far less scruples.

He and Sun wanted, needed information. But the Russians were just as likely to shoot first and ask questions later, if bothering to ask at all.

The image of the informant's slashed throat was etched in his mind.

Mack swallowed hard, knowing he'd just have to work twice as hard to make sure Sun was safe.

JANUARY 19 – 4:09 *p.m.* – *Washington, DC*

It had been over two hours since he'd heard from his injured contacts. With steely resolve, he made sure the office would be empty for the next ten minutes, before he reached for his throwaway phone.

A new one, since the old one had been compromised. A fact that still irked him.

"It appears I will need additional assistance," he said when the fixer answered the other end of the line. "And time is of the essence. I need this task accomplished before the end of the day."

There was a pause on the other end of the line. "That tight of a timeframe will require double the fee."

Double? He managed to hold back a spurt of anger. "Of

course. Half now, the rest when I receive proof the deed has been done."

"Fine. Who is the target?"

"Two targets, Macklin Remington and Sun Yin-lee." He paused, then added, "I want this to look as if the North Koreans took them out."

"North Koreans?" The fixer didn't sound happy to hear the additional news. "That will add a layer of difficulty."

"Just do it," he snapped, losing his temper. He was already paying a ton of money for this job, and so far he had nothing to show for it.

"Careful," the fixer warned in a low, threatening tone. "You are not in a position to make demands."

An icy finger of fear slithered down his spine. He reached up to loosen his tie, needing to breathe. "I'm sorry. It's been a long day."

Another long pause. "Apology accepted. Add ten percent to the fee for this North Korean angle and wire the money to this account." As the fixer rattled off the bank information, he hastened to write it down.

The minute the fixer disconnected from the line, he put the phone back in his pocket and fought the urge to throw up.

There would be time to take care of the fixer permanently, once Remington and Yin-lee were eliminated from the equation.

Until then, he'd continue to deal with the devil while desperately trying to avoid getting burned.

JANUARY 19 – 4:17 p.m. – Washington, DC

Sun maneuvered the SUV through bumper-to-bumper

traffic, slowly making her way to the area of the city where most people didn't go even during daylight hours.

It was all too easy to remember the last time they'd gone there, only to find their informant brutally murdered.

But the remote possibility that this Dimitri Palov had been involved in bringing the nuke into Washington, DC, made this trip absolutely essential. They desperately needed some idea of where this nuke might be located.

Or even proof that such a bomb was armed and located here in the city. With that much, they should be able to convince Yates to pull the plug on the entire inauguration ceremony.

Yet that didn't mean the bomb wouldn't still be set off at another place and time.

Her phone rang, and she handed it to Mack who quickly answered. "What's up?"

She thought she recognized Sloan's voice but couldn't be sure. "Who is it?" she whispered.

"Hey, Sloan, thanks for the information. I'll let Sun know." Mack disconnected from the call and sighed. "They didn't get anything out of the other Russian tavern. The place was boarded up, and there's no sign of the owner anywhere."

She grimaced. "Well, I'm glad we have this lead to follow up on." She glanced at Mack. "How on earth did Sloan and Natalia get there so fast?"

"Beats me." He returned his gaze to the computer. "I found something else on Palov, looks like he's done time for assault and battery."

"So? That's hardly a surprise. In fact, I'd be shocked if he didn't have a criminal rap sheet." Sun tapped the brakes as vehicles abruptly stopped in front of her. At this rate, they'd never get to Dimitri's place while it was still light out.

Not that she was afraid of the dark, in fact, it may work in their favor.

One thing about working for Security Specialists, Inc. is that they didn't necessarily have to follow the same rules as law enforcement. Not that she wanted to jeopardize a case, but if they needed to get into Dimitri's place to find the proof they needed, that's exactly what she'd do.

If they'd get through this traffic jam any time in the next century.

JANUARY 19 – 4:28 p.m. – South Bend, IN

Hana forced herself to eat, although deep down, her nerves were stretched past the breaking point.

Going through TSA security seemed an overwhelming task—a hurdle of monstrous proportions. Her fake passport had worked fine getting out of Geneva, but that seemed like days ago rather than hours.

Still, she didn't want Jarek to pick up on her nervousness, so she daintily patted her napkin against her mouth and smiled. "Shall we go?"

"I'm ready if you are." Jarek had mostly picked at his food, and she sensed he was on edge as well. After he paid the tab in cash, she stood and walked once again like the hunchbacked old woman with arthritis she was pretending to be.

She could sense Jarek's discomfort as they approached the TSA checkpoint. She held back a flash of annoyance. He wasn't the one traveling under a fake passport, so what was he worried about?

On the heels of that thought came the realization that his fear and worry was likely for her, not for himself. Because that was the kind of man Jarek was.

She didn't deserve him.

The security line was seemingly endless, which didn't help settle her nerves. Still, she managed to keep a serene expression on her face, making eye contact to avoid being viewed as suspicious.

Silently praying for God to continue guiding her, she moved forward until she and Jarek were next in line.

"Relax," she whispered. "Don't attract undue attention."

She could feel Jarek attempting to loosen his muscles as they were waved forward by the TSA agent. Hana met the man's gaze and offered a weary smile as she handed over her boarding pass and passport.

The TSA agent looked from the passport photo back to her as if checking the resemblance. Since the photo was of her in this same disguise, she wasn't concerned about that. She was more worried that her fake name had been somehow flagged in the system and half expected a slew of TSA agents to descend upon them.

The TSA agent handed her passport and boarding pass back to her, then took Jarek's passport and boarding pass. She was a bit surprised to see his passport, but then remembered he'd been about to fly to Geneva, Switzerland, to find her.

God must have been watching out for them, that they hadn't passed each other on different flights in the air.

"Have a safe trip," the TSA agent said, returning Jarek's passport and boarding pass.

Breathing a small sigh of relief, they went through the process of taking off their shoes and going through the body scanner. When they were finished, Jarek put a hand beneath her elbow and guided her down toward the gate.

"Piece of cake from here, right?" he said with a lopsided grin.

"Yes." At least, she hoped that was the case.

One thing she'd quickly learned in her undercover role was to never relax her guard.

Never.

JANUARY 19 – 4:56 p.m. – Washington, DC

"The drugstore is up ahead," Mack said, subtly wiping his damp palms on his dark jeans. Now that they'd arrived at their destination, the sense of impending doom had returned full force. "We should park there again and go the rest of the way on foot."

"We need to find a different spot to leave the SUV," Sun argued. "Don't forget, they had eyes on us through using the street cameras the last time we were here. We wouldn't want to be predictable in case they have the system up and running again."

"I don't think they could have isolated and eliminated the virus that fast," Mack said, although she had a point about being too predictable. He mentally envisioned the area. "Okay, how about the grocery store about a half mile from here?"

"Good idea." Sun turned onto the street that would take them straight to the store. "You know where Palov is from there?"

"Yes." He had the map of the area on the computer screen and turned it so she could see for herself. There was always the slim chance they might become separated. "He lives here, on the ground floor."

Sun parked the car in the grocery store lot, then turned to peer at the screen. He knew she had the location memorized the same way he did. She gave a nod and pushed open the driver's side door. "Let's go."

Mack stashed the sat computer under the seat. Even though he'd rather keep it close, he couldn't risk being encumbered with it when they might need to fight their way in or out of the place.

Granted, the computer had prevented him from being injured earlier, but it had likely slowed his response time too. Which in turn had caused Sun to be hurt.

Sun took the lead, moving quickly. He was glad to see she took an indirect route to Palov's apartment, just in case they had indeed been followed.

The grocery store parking lot was roughly a mile and a half from their destination. As they grew closer to the apartment, it occurred to him that Morris may very well have warned Dimitri of their likely arrival.

When Sun ducked behind a tree within a stone's throw of the apartment, he put a hand on her arm to stop her.

"Now what?" she hissed.

"We need to be careful, Morris could have tipped Dimitri off."

Sun's annoyance faded, and she responded with a curt nod. "Okay, but we still need to get inside, unless you have another idea."

He wished he did, but he didn't. For a long moment he stared at the apartment building, in time to notice the curtain moving at the front window.

Was Dimitri inside? If so, was he alone or with someone else?

"I'll take the front," Sun whispered. "You go around back."

He tightened his grip on her arm. "I don't like it. Someone inside was peering past the curtain."

"Well, we can't sit out here all day," Sun said in a clipped tone. "Ready?"

He didn't see much choice but to do what she'd suggested. "Give me a minute to get around and in position."

"Two minutes." Sun glanced at her watch. "Go."

He sprinted out from behind the tree and ducked around the apartment building to the rear doorway. He had almost twenty seconds left when he heard the sharp sound of gunfire.

No! Sun! He pulled his weapon and kicked through the flimsily locked back door to the building, hoping and praying that Sun was the one shooting. That Sun hadn't been hit.

Or worse, dead.

CHAPTER SIXTEEN

January 19 – 5:16 p.m. – Washington, DC

The gunshot had missed her by a fraction of an inch, but Sun didn't hesitate. She used a jumping snap kick against the apartment door that had been opened just enough for the barrel of a handgun to poke through.

There was a muffled sound as her kick hit its mark. Somersaulting through the opening, she rolled and landed on her feet in time to face the rough-looking man standing behind the door.

"Drop the gun," she said, holding her weapon steady.

For a moment he stared at her. In a heartbeat, she knew he was going to shoot, so she did another diving somersault toward his left side, his nondominant hand. Only this time, when she rolled to her feet, she lashed out with a kick perfectly aimed at his ear.

He howled in pain and tried to swing his right arm toward her to take another shot. But she was already in motion, striking his wrist with her hand and using her elbow to clip him under the chin.

She was annoyed it took two chops of her hand against

his wrist to make him drop the gun. The man was built like a tank. With a roar of rage, he lowered his head and charged her like a bull.

Easy enough to dance out of his reach, then she brought her arm down on the back of his neck, helping him to the floor. Suddenly Mack was there, joining her in pinning the angry Russian down.

"Dimitri, is this any way to greet guests?" Sun asked a bit breathlessly. She scooped his gun from the floor, then placed the nose of her weapon against the back of his head with just enough force that he'd know it was there. "Move and I'll shoot. Get off him, Mack."

"Are you hurt?" Mack shifted to the side, keeping a tight hand around Dimitri's wrist so that his arm was bent up behind his back while he raked his gaze over her.

"He missed," she assured him. "Hold the gun on him, will you?"

Keeping one hand firmly pressed against the guy's arm wrenched up behind his back, Mack used his other hand to hold his weapon against the back of Dimitri's head.

She dropped to her knees beside the guy, bending way down in order to get a good look at his face. "Tsk tsk, bested by a woman, Dimitri. What would your Russian comrades think if they discovered the truth?"

Dimitri spit out a slew of Russian epithets.

Mack added pressure to Dimitri's arm, causing the man to groan in pain. "That's no way to speak in front of a lady," he said in Russian.

"I've heard worse," Sun said, joining the conversation in Dimitri's native language. "Come now, Dimitri, we don't have a lot of time. We need to find the bomb you brought into the city via your boat."

"I don't know anything about a bomb," Dimitri protested.

"Oh dear, and here I thought you were going to cooperate," Sun said with a disapproving frown. She pinched the trigger point in his shoulder. "The bomb, Dimitri. There's no reason for us not to kill you if you won't tell us what we need to know."

It was a bluff, but a good one. Men liked Dimitri never hesitated to kill as needed and were always ready to believe the worst about others.

"I brought in a package using my boat but handed it over to someone else," Dimitri finally admitted. "I didn't know it was a bomb."

"Who did you give it to?" Sun bent close. "And don't think about lying to us or we will hunt you down and kill you like the vermin you are."

"I—only know him as Igor. He's Russian too."

Sun glanced at Mack who scowled. She understood his concern, who was to say Igor was the guy's real name? "Where can we find Igor?"

"I don't know!" Dimitri's voice took on a whiny tone. "I only did as I was told, nothing more."

"Not good enough, Dimitri." Sun increased the pressure on the trigger point. "Where did this exchange take place?"

"A truck stop between DC and Baltimore. Place called Gerry's Diner."

"You docked your boat in Baltimore?" Mack asked.

"Yes! I met up with Igor at the truck stop and that was all!" There was an edge of panic in Dimitri's tone.

Sun met Mack's gaze, silently asking if they should press for more.

"Do you have the phone you used to call Igor?" Mack asked.

"No."

Sun didn't believe him and quickly felt his pockets, pulling a disposable phone out and looking at him. "What's the passcode, Dimitri?"

He didn't answer.

"I'll break into it without a problem, so you may as well tell us," Mack said.

Dimitri rattled off the series of numbers.

"I see there are a couple of DC numbers in here," Sun said, scrolling through the call list. "Which one belongs to Igor?"

The big Russian went still. "If I tell you, he'll kill me."

"If that bomb goes off here in the city, we'll all be dead." Sun shoved the screen close to his face. "Which one?"

Dimitri closed his eyes. "The first one."

Sun wished she believed him, but there were only two numbers anyway, so it wouldn't be too difficult to check them both out.

She slipped the phone into her pocket and rose to her feet. "Thanks, Dimitri, it's been nice chatting with you."

Mack tipped his head toward the door, indicating she should leave first. She rolled her eyes at his protectiveness but headed toward the door. Glancing back over her shoulder, she saw Mack whisper something to Dimitri before he levered up and joined her.

They left the apartment building as the sound of police sirens grew close. Without speaking, they quickly retraced their circuitous path back to the grocery store where they'd left the SUV.

"What did you tell him?" Sun asked as she exited the parking lot.

There was a pause before Mack replied, "I told him that we could have killed him but didn't. And that if he or Morris lied to us, we'd come back to finish the job."

"I don't think the NSA would approve," Sun said dryly, knowing it was an empty threat. One thing she liked about Mack was that he didn't kill unless absolutely necessary.

The same way she didn't.

Mack shrugged and scrubbed his face with his hands. "I don't have a good feeling about this. These Russians tend to stick together. Dimitri could already be calling Morris, instructing him to warn Igor. If Igor goes underground, we'll never find him."

"We'll find him," Sun said grimly.

They had to.

JANUARY 19 – 5:31 *p.m.* – *Washington, DC*

He left the Capitol building and kept a wary eye out for any sign of trouble as he took the stairs down to the street level.

The worst part about making a deal with the devil was the lack of updated information. He'd heard nothing after his most recent call, and here it was, the end of the business day before the inauguration ceremony, and he still had no idea if things would take place as planned.

It was unsettling to say the least.

He tried to shake off the feeling of unease. His priority now was to meet up with the two idiots who'd failed him. Walking swiftly, he went to the Metro and swiped his card to get access to the train.

Their meeting spot was a tavern located just a few stops from Capitol Hill. The train was packed as usual for this time of the day. Very irritating that he had to put up with traveling like this, as if he was some sort of commoner, but he didn't dare take his car and driver. Too easy to be tailed that way.

He glanced at his watch and smiled as the train rolled in exactly on time. He pushed through, uncaring if he elbowed passengers along the way. He ignored the dirty glances sent his way. The train left the station, slowly gaining speed.

Soon, he'd have these loose ends taken care of.

Difficult lesson to learn, but such was life. Only the strong survive.

Which is the way it should be. He intended to be one of those who not only survived but thrived.

And he didn't care who he had to walk all over to do so.

JANUARY 19 – 5:42 p.m. – Washington, DC

With the sat computer on his lap, Mack performed a quick search for Gerry's Diner. Places like that often didn't bother with a web presence, but thankfully most restaurant-type establishments showed up on a variety of search engines regardless.

"Found it," he said with satisfaction. "It's closer to DC than to Baltimore, which is the good news."

"What's the bad news?" Sun asked.

"In this traffic, it's going to take longer than I'd like."

"I'm not sure it's worth going there anyway," Sun said on a sigh. "It's not likely anyone there is going to remember some Russian guy named Igor."

"I know." Mack pulled out the phone Sun had taken from Dimitri. "I can try calling him, but the chances of him actually answering are slim to none."

"I was thinking about that," Sun said, hitting the gas to get the SUV through a yellow traffic light. "I know you can find the cell tower closest to where the phone is located, but what about tracking down where the phone was purchased? Those two details together may help us find Igor."

"It can't hurt." Mack knew that smart people made sure to purchase their phones far from the locations where they intended to use it, but maybe Igor had picked up the phone, used it, and then headed out to meet Dimitri at the truck stop.

He worked while Sun navigated the bumper-to-bumper traffic. Since he'd already hacked into the previous cell records, it didn't take very long. "Okay, looks like he purchased the phone in East Riverdale. Hmm, what do you know, the truck stop is only about ten miles from there."

"Okay, now try to call him. If he answers, we should be able to triangulate his location using those two things as reference points."

He used the disposable phone, which he hoped meant Igor would answer, much like the guy in Capitol Hill had.

"You shouldn't use this number," a guttural voice answered in curt Russian.

"We have a problem, I need to meet you," Mack said in his best Russian accent.

"No meetings," the Russian said.

"At Gerry's Diner, it's important. There is another transport needed. Double the last fee," he said in Russian.

Mack found himself holding his breath, hoping and maybe even praying the guy on the other end of the phone was in fact Igor and would agree.

"When?" Igor asked.

He tried to estimate how long it would take them to get from this side of town out to the diner in this traffic. "Ninety minutes."

"Fine. Double the fee." The call went dead.

Mack let out a silent sigh. "I think I convinced Igor to meet us at Gerry's Diner in ninety minutes."

"I heard." Sun changed lanes, moving the SUV into a space that seemed almost too small for their SUV. "Means we need to get there in an hour or less."

"Yeah." He dug into the cell tower information and pulled up the number. "Igor's call pinged off a tower in Bladensburg."

"And there's the third point in the triangle. That's good work, Mack." Sun flashed a grin. "Dimitri was more help than I'd anticipated."

"Yeah, if he hasn't already warned Igor of what went down at his apartment."

"There's a chance he may have, but I sense Dimitri isn't smart enough to memorize the numbers on his disposable phone."

He glanced at Sun in surprise. "What makes you say that?"

"The fact that he kept it in the first place, otherwise why didn't he toss it in the garbage?"

She had a good point. Mack looked over and saw that the bandage around her left wrist was covered with blood. "You're bleeding."

"I know. I felt one of the stitches pop when I hit Dimitri's wrist to get him to drop the gun." She frowned. "Guy was built like a tank and didn't go down easily."

Frankly, Mack was surprised she'd gotten him disarmed and down to the ground at all, considering she was about a quarter of Dimitri's size.

Swallowing the bitter taste of fear as he barreled through the apartment building to find her had been one of the hardest things he'd ever done.

Yet Sun had surprised him once again. Not only had

she not been shot, but she'd basically had Dimitri under control. He'd sparred with her enough to know she was good, but somehow she had taken her skills to the next level.

Humbling to realize she might not need him nearly as much as he needed her.

JANUARY 19 – 5:56 p.m. – Somewhere over the Midwest

Hana choked and sputtered on her apple juice when she saw a dark-haired man making his way up the main aisle of the plane toward the tiny restrooms.

The North Korean?

No, it couldn't be. Unless he'd somehow tracked her via her clearly compromised identity? She put her hand on Jarek's arm, tightening her grip until he looked at her. With wide eyes, she nodded toward the man whom she could only see from the back.

Jarek frowned and stared at the man. She tightened her grip again and shook her head, indicating he shouldn't try to draw the stranger's gaze.

Jarek shifted in his seat so he was partially facing her. "Do you know him?"

"No, do you?" she whispered back. Maybe exhaustion was making her paranoid, but the fleeting glimpse had reminded her of the man she'd seen on the plane to Chicago.

The man in the aisle slowly turned as if to face them.

Hana quickly reached up and drew Jarek close for a long, intimate kiss.

JANUARY 19 – 6:38 p.m. – Washington, DC

Sun's phone rang as she finally reached the east side of

the city. Hopefully, they could make up the time they'd lost while in traffic when she reached the highway.

"Mack, will you answer this? It's Jordan."

"Hey, Jordan," Mack said, holding the phone so she could hear too. "Do you have more information for us?"

"Yates finally got back to me on the Allan search. Sounds as if Karen Allan retired earlier this year, so that leaves us with Allan Stokes and Sean Allen."

Sun tried not to roll her eyes. "Any idea which one might have ties to something like a Russian bomb being sneaked into the city and being blamed on the North Koreans?"

"Allan Stokes has only been with the department for six months," Jordan said. "Sean has been working for us for almost ten years. If I had to pick a place to start, I'd go with the newbie. Could be he got this job just to help pull off something like this."

Sun glanced at Mack who shrugged and nodded. "I have to agree. Do you have any other identifying information on the guy? Like a date of birth or driver's license number?"

"Yates sent me personal information on both of these guys. Okay if I send it along via email?"

Mack grinned. "You can just tell us, we'll remember."

Jordan sighed. "Show off. Okay, Allan Stokes twenty-eight years old as of yesterday, lives outside of DC in a small town named Hyattsville."

"Wait a minute, Hyattsville? That's not far from Bladensburg."

Sun tightened her grip on the steering wheel. "Which is where we believe Igor lives."

"Igor who?" Jordan asked.

"Later," Sun advised. "Give us the address."

Jordan rattled it off, and she committed the information to memory. "Listen, Jordan, things are heating up here. We have a lead on Igor, who is the last person we know of to take custody of the bomb. If we can connect Igor to Stokes, then we may have enough to pull an entire federal team into this thing."

"Okay, I can try, but I've learned the hard way to only trust Yates, and he's not always easy to get ahold of. The guy is juggling a million different balls every minute of every day."

"Better than being betrayed by someone on the task force," Sun pointed out.

"Yes," Jordan agreed. "But Yates will want hard-core evidence before going to the president to push off something as big as the inauguration."

"I know, and trust us, we're trying to get that for you," Sun said.

"Our pal Dimitri admitted to bringing something in via his boat but claims he didn't know the package was a bomb," Mack added. "As much as I hate to admit it, the bomb itself is still nothing but rumor and innuendo."

"Do your best, but be careful, both of you." Jordan's voice was tense. "Just hearing the phrase nuclear bomb in the same sentence as presidential inauguration is likely to send the entire city into a tailspin of chaos."

"We'll be careful," Sun said.

"And we'll stay in touch. Thanks for the information, Jordan." Mack put the phone in the cupholder between them. "I keep wondering if that's the motive here."

Sun frowned. "What? To send the city into chaos?"

Mack shrugged. "Why not?"

She thought about it for a moment, increasing her speed to stay with traffic as they cruised along the highway. "I don't think so. We talked about this before, a rumor isn't enough. Once the time of the inauguration passes without any sign of a bomb, things will very quickly get back to normal, and it will be as if nothing ever happened."

"You're probably right," Mack said, rubbing the back of his neck. "I guess there's just a part of me that doesn't want to think the goal is to take out the outgoing and incoming presidents and their respective vice presidents at the same time."

"Me either." She glanced at her watch. "We may have time to cruise past Allan Stokes's address before heading over to the diner."

"You know the traffic better than I do," Mack said.

It was a calculated risk. They'd be cutting it close if they wanted to get to the diner before Igor. Then again, if Igor was in actually in Bladensburg, he'd beat them regardless.

Pulling up Stokes's address in her mind, she headed in that direction. It wouldn't take long to check the place out. It was unlikely Stokes would even be there if he used the Metro to commute back and forth to DC every day.

Pressing on the gas, she picked up speed, passing several cars until seeing the exit sign for Hyattsville.

"You sure about this?" Mack asked as she navigated the streets to yet another rundown apartment building. Low-rent properties were a common theme with the guys they were trying to find.

"Yes, shouldn't take long." She parked along the street and slid out from behind the wheel. Mack joined her, and together they approached the apartment building.

This time, after getting no response from the buzzer, they headed to the second floor where Stokes lived. Sun pressed her ear to the door but couldn't hear anything.

Mack checked the door handle. Locked. Then he pulled

out his wallet and extracted a couple of slender tools. Sun hadn't picked a lock in a long time, not since they'd challenged each other when they were kids to see who could pick faster.

Mack had won that round, taking his buck from her with glee, but not by much.

He made short work of this one too. Staying back, he pushed the apartment door open. Immediately, the telltale scent of death hit them.

Sun put a hand over her nose and mouth as she took several steps inside. She wasn't as surprised as she should have been to find Allan Stokes lying on the kitchen floor, his throat slit in the exact same fashion Hyun-woo's had been.

And worse? His body wasn't cold, meaning they'd just missed the murderer.

CHAPTER SEVENTEEN

January 19 – 7:11 p.m. – Hyattsville, MA

Remembering what had happened the last time they'd gone into an apartment, Mack stayed in the hallway, keeping a wary eye out for a possible assailant. It wasn't easy, every molecule in his body wanted to rush in after her, to keep her from harm.

As it turned out, Sun returned from the apartment in record time, her expression grim.

Not good. "What happened?"

"Let's get out of here." She hurried back the way they'd come, and he followed close behind. It wasn't until they were back outside and in the vehicle that he said, "Are you telling me this is another dead end?"

Sun grimaced. "Yes, literally. His throat was slit like Hyun-woo's, either an act done by the Russians or made to look as if it had been done by them." She pulled away from the curb heading back toward the highway. "Do you think Igor knows we have Dimitri's phone and beat us here?"

Good question. He tried to envision the timeline. Close, but not impossible for Igor to have gotten here in time to kill

Stokes while on his way to the diner. "Maybe. And if that's the case, we should get backup to meet us at the truck stop."

Sun shook her head. "There's not enough time to get Jordan or Sloan out here. Even at this hour, traffic would make that impossible."

He battled a wave of frustration. This case was giving him a serious headache. "We could notify the local authorities. Better than just the two of us going in alone." Mack couldn't explain why he had a bad feeling about the upcoming meeting at the diner. Igor was their only lead, but he was tempted to tell Sun to turn around to head back to DC.

Not that she couldn't take care of herself. He was letting his feelings for her mess with his mind.

There was a moment of silence as Sun considered that idea. "I'd have to get Jordan on board with something like that," she finally said. "The reason our company gets involved is to get the job done without being strangled with red tape. Once the local authorities are in, we're stuck with them."

"I know." He couldn't deny that her argument had merit. Yet going into a potentially dangerous situation without backup was crazy.

Especially if the Russians had taken out Allan Stokes.

"Don't you think it's strange that we just learned his name only to find him dead?" Sun asked. "I mean, who else could have known about the guy?"

"The man who'd hired him." The implication was sobering. "It's almost as if the people behind this are anticipating our next moves and going around to tie up loose ends."

"Yeah. The attacks on us personally haven't worked, so they're taking care of all possible leads." Sun glanced at him. "Stokes's body wasn't even cold, we must have just missed the person who killed him."

Not reassuring. "If the killer is Igor, we're not far behind him. We'll have to take extra care when we reach the truck stop."

Sun nodded. "Maybe you could check the place out on the computer, see if there's a good way to get in without being seen from the road."

"I'll try." In his experience, most truck stops were right off the interstate to make it convenient for semitruck drivers to get off, gas up, eat, and get back on the road. One way in and one way out.

But it couldn't hurt. Maybe there were other establishments close by, like a motel or another restaurant or something.

It wasn't until he pulled the diner up using a three-dimensional map program that he realized that if Igor wasn't the killer, then Igor himself could very well be a loose end. For all they knew, Igor could be lying dead with his throat slit in his apartment right now rather than meeting them at Gerry's Diner.

A chill snaked down his spine.

Would the killer be waiting for them at the diner? Or would they get there only to find that no one shows up at all?

Ironic to think he'd prefer to have the killer show, otherwise they'd be at the end of the trail of clues they'd been following.

And no closer to discovering or verifying the location of a nuclear bomb.

JANUARY 19 – 7:18 p.m. – Somewhere over the Midwest

Jarek had been so startled and secretly thrilled by Hana's kiss that it had taken him several minutes to realize she hadn't exactly kissed him because she'd wanted to, but as a ploy to avoid being detected.

Much to his dismay, she'd ended the kiss the moment the dark-haired Asian-looking man had disappeared into the tiny airplane bathroom. While he'd tried to gather his scattered thoughts into something coherent, Hana had whispered to him that she was sorry to have kissed him like that.

He'd tried to shrug off her apology, but deep down it grated. Because he hadn't been sorry.

Not one little bit.

Yet this was hardly the time to be thinking of rekindling their old romance. After all, they were on a mission to save Sun. The daughter he had never met.

After a few minutes, the red light indicating the bathroom was occupied turned green. He had only a moment to prepare himself for her next embrace, although he'd been disappointed Hana didn't kiss him a second time.

Instead, she'd turned him so that they were hugging in their seats, their faces averted from the man who was moving back down the aisle, allegedly returning to his seat.

They remained close for what seemed like only a short time before Hana loosened her grip. She blushed and reached up to trail a finger down the side of his face. "Thank you, Jarek."

She was thanking him? He'd walk through fire to kiss and hold her again. But maybe she didn't feel the same. He forced himself to stay focused on the true purpose of this trip.

Staying alive long enough to meet his daughter.

"Do you really think he's from the regime?" Jarek whispered.

Hana's expression turned solemn. "I don't know. I don't recognize him, but that doesn't mean anything."

"Not to me either. Although I didn't get a very good look at him." Jarek had been too distracted by her kiss to even try to get a glimpse of the man's face.

"We will need to be prepared for when we land in Charlotte," Hana murmured.

"Okay." What that meant exactly, he wasn't sure. Likely nothing good.

Jarek silently wondered if Hana was becoming overly paranoid about the ability of the regime. Not that he blamed her for being cautious, but to think they'd been followed from his condo, to the hotel, then to Union Station, all the way to South Bend, Indiana, and onto this particular flight seemed far-fetched.

Why do all that without making another move? Especially since the Asian hadn't hesitated to kill Geoff, an innocent victim that had nothing to do with the regime.

Frankly, none of this made any sense. It was as if they'd been dropped into the middle of a horror flick.

Some of what he was thinking must have been reflected on his face because Hana took his hand in hers. "I know it seems crazy, but I believe the goal of the regime is to kill both me and Sun. It's hard to understand unless you've walked in my shoes, but the regime is all about fear and total control. Defectors must die so others will not be tempted to escape."

He leaned forward to press a chaste kiss on her temple. "I don't think you're crazy, Hana," he murmured in a soothing voice. He hated seeing her so stressed out and on edge like this. "It's best to stay alert and prepare for the worst."

"Yes." A hint of a smile creased her features. Then she

leaned forward and whispered, "I hope the next time we kiss it is because you want to."

He flushed, feeling like the young man he'd been when they'd first met. "Hana, I always want to kiss you."

Keeping her gaze on his, she leaned in for another kiss. This time the kiss wasn't a way to avoid being seen, it was something sweet and heady.

Just for the two of them.

JANUARY 19 – 7:22 p.m. – Pyongyang, North Korea

"Do you have the traitor yet?"

Sweat trickled down his back as he knelt before the Supreme Leader without any sign of his second-in-command. Which was strange, as the second-in-command was always present. And there was still something off about the leader. Something out of place.

But he wasn't going to lift his head to visually check for anything amiss. "We have reason to believe she's going to Washington, DC. We plan to meet with her there."

There was a long silence that seemed to stretch forever. He thought he was braced for the worst, but when the blow came down on the back of his head, pain exploded, followed quickly by darkness.

JANUARY 19 – 7:37 p.m. – East Riverdale, MD

Per Mack's suggestion, Sun passed the exit where Gerry's Diner was located. They'd double back and approach from the opposite direction.

"See that small outcropping of trees?" Mack gestured toward his computer screen. "We want to find a place to park at the motel and go on foot to check things out."

"Got it." Ignoring the flutter of nerves, she pulled into the motel and parked on the farthest side of the building as far away as possible from where the truck stop was located. She swallowed hard and turned to face Mack. "Okay, let's do this."

He held her gaze for a long moment. "Last chance to call in the locals."

"Not happening. We don't even know if Igor will show." When she'd touched base with Jordan, letting him know that yet another federal agent had been murdered, Jordan hadn't liked the idea of getting locals involved. But at the same time, he hadn't been thrilled about them heading to the diner to meet with Igor either. Sun had assured him they wouldn't take any unnecessary chances, and Jordan had reluctantly agreed. After all, this is why Yates had hired them.

"Try to stay behind me, then." Mack's voice was resigned as he pushed open the passenger side door.

Yeah, that wasn't happening. She was an equal partner in this mission not a damsel in distress. Granted, finding Stokes with his throat cut was an ominous sign, but she believed that God was looking out for them and couldn't function by playing the what-if game.

Mack set out toward the cluster of trees, which looked skinny and not nearly as great of a hiding place as they'd appeared on the computer. She easily caught up to him, and for once, he didn't look annoyed.

Maybe he was finally getting what it meant to be *partners*.

The sun had set almost two hours ago, but the bright lights of the truck stop parking lot and the glow from the diner windows provided more than enough light. Dropping to her knees behind the outcropping of trees, she was glad to see she and Mack were fairly well hidden in the shadows.

Mack crouched beside her, his gaze focused on the parking lot and entrance to the diner. "Won't be easy to decide which of these guys is our Igor."

"I know." Sun tried to look for anything out of the ordinary. "Our ninety minutes is almost up."

Mack was silent for a moment. "I know you're not going to like this idea, but I think I should go inside to see if Igor is in there waiting. I'm the one who spoke to him. He's expecting a man not a woman."

He was right, she didn't like it. But Mack was right, Igor would be looking for a guy who could speak Russian not a woman with Asian features.

"Okay, I'll wait out here."

Mack looked surprised, then said, "Thank you."

His gratitude was surprising, but before she could say anything more, he eased out from the trees and headed over to the where a semitruck was parked just a few yards away. Using that as cover, he went around the other side and then approached the diner entrance with a purposeful stride. She could already tell he was mentally creating himself into a fellow Russian with ill intent.

Watching Mack going into a dangerous situation all alone wasn't easy. Despite her attempts to keep him at arm's length, they'd grown close over these past twenty-four hours. In fact, the memory of his kiss still had the power to make her knees feel weak.

She couldn't bear the thought of anything bad happening to him.

Even though she hadn't been attending church as often as she should, she sent up a whispered prayer.

Please, Lord, keep Mack safe in Your care!

JANUARY 19 – 7: 49 p.m. – East Riverdale, MD

Mack held his head high and his shoulders back as he swept his gaze over the patrons seated within the diner. It was times like this that it helped to have an eidetic memory. He didn't allow his gaze to linger on any one particular person for long.

There were several potential Igors, two men each sitting alone and two men who were sharing one table. Neither of the potential candidates had tattoos that he could see, at least from this vantage point. He slid into an empty booth near the back of the diner, not far from the restrooms. Picking up the plastic menu from behind the condiments, he pretended to look for something to eat.

From the corner of his eye, he checked out two possible candidates each seated alone at a table. One guy was older and looked very much like the stereotypical truck driver, which might be a good disguise on Igor's part. The other was younger, had blond hair similar in color to his, but was much bigger physically. Imposing really, with his beefy arms and no neck.

And a very interesting red-and-black star tattoo, exactly like one he'd noticed Morris had.

Granted, Morris had far more tattoos than this guy.

He spent a brief moment checking out the two men who shared a table. They were both wearing ball caps and didn't look to be nearly as physically imposing as the blond dude with no neck.

Of course, there was always the possibility that Igor wasn't in the diner yet, but he didn't think so. Igor was there, he just needed a way to flush the guy out. In an abrupt movement, Mack pushed his menu aside, stood, and disappeared into the restroom.

It was a risk. Either of the two potential Igors could leave the diner or the two men sitting together could come in and double-team him. He mentally prepared himself for either scenario.

The seconds stretched into a full minute. Then another. He was convinced he'd lost Igor by his meager attempt to draw him out when the bathroom door opened and the large blond guy with no neck walked in.

There was no mistaking the large knife in Igor's hand. "What game is this?" Igor asked in Russian.

"No game." Mack spoke in Russian too, keeping his hands at his sides, ready to spring into self-defense mode if needed. "Dimitri has been murdered, and I believe you are next."

His comment caught Igor off guard. "Why?"

Mack shrugged. "The bomb, of course. Anyone who knows of it has been silenced—permanently. I have come to warn you, and any others who may be at risk."

Igor digested that bit of information, the knife still in his hand. So far Mack's ploy was working.

But for how long? He sensed he was about to find out.

"Yet here you stand, unharmed," Igor finally said, his light gray eyes suspicious. "Why should I believe you?"

"Don't believe me, it's your funeral." He shrugged. "I couldn't care less if the bomb goes off tomorrow at noon, it's good for Russia, yes?"

Igor's grip tightened on the knife, but then relaxed. Mack kept his expression impassive, determined to get some kind of information from Igor. "Very good as long as the blame rests with North Korea."

"Exactly." Mack offered what he hoped was a smug

grin. "Still, Russians shouldn't be murdered because of this thing. I would recommend reaching out to the others along the line to warn them of the danger."

Igor regarded him thoughtfully for another long nerve-racking moment. "Why do you care?"

Mack leaned forward, pinning Igor with his gaze. "It's one thing to do a job for good money, yes? It's another to then be murdered by the same people unwilling to do their own dirty work." He leaned closer, risking the blade coming up to be impaled beneath his chin. "It's not right. In fact, I would like to go after those responsible, to make them see the error of their ways."

Igor tensed for a moment, then nodded slowly. "You make a good argument."

Mack leaned back and tried to look nonchalant. "Warn those after you or don't. It's up to you. I would offer to help, but if you're not interested?" He shrugged and moved to the side as if to step around Igor.

"There are two others to warn," Igor said, holding up a hand to stop him. The knife disappeared into his pocket, but Mack didn't relax his guard. The Russian was big and strong, it would not be fun to spar with him, especially in a small enclosed space. Mack did better when there was room to maneuver. Big men liked to depend on their imposing strength rather than finesse. In small spaces, that strength tended to work to their advantage. "If the threat is close, we could each take one, warning of the danger."

Yes! Inwardly he was glad to have made progress, but Mack did his best to keep his expression impassive. "What about the man scheduled to set off the device?"

Igor shrugged. "I don't know who that is, just the next two in line. You can take Mikhail Yahontov. I'll check in with Kirill."

It was difficult to know for sure if Igor was being straight with him, but he played along, regardless. "Where can I find Yahontov?"

Another flash of suspicion darkened Igor's eyes. "Where did you find Dimitri?"

A bead of sweat slithered down Mack's spine, but his gaze never wavered from Igor's. He knew better than to show any hint of weakness. "Where do you think? Morris is an old friend, we go way back. Dimitri too. But as you know, I used Dimitri's phone to find you. I don't have a number for Yahontov."

The knife appeared once again in Igor's hand, but Mack was ready. He kicked Igor in the groin and chopped Igor's wrist at nearly the same time, causing the big Russian to turn a horrible shade of green as the knife clattered to the floor.

Mack kicked the knife out of reach, pulled his gun, and pressed it against the center of the Russian's chest. Still trying to breathe through his pain, the Russian went still.

"You don't want to work with me?" Mack hissed in Russian. "That's fine. But a knife across the throat is not the thanks I should receive for saving your worthless hide. Give me one good reason not to kill you?"

Igor didn't move.

With another swift move, he kicked and swept Igor's legs out from under him. Then he hit Igor on the back of his head as he went down. Mack didn't want to kill him, that wasn't why he'd come here, but he needed to keep the guy in the bathroom so he could make a clean getaway.

Igor hit the floor hard, going limp as if he'd lost consciousness. It could very well be a ruse, but Mack didn't care, he needed to get out of there, now. He risked a moment to grab Igor's phone. Then, pulling the bathroom door open, he walked back through the diner with the same sense of purpose he'd used coming in.

He swept another gaze through the interior, making a mental note of who was there, who shouldn't be, and who'd left.

The table with two men who he assumed were truckers was vacant. He didn't remember seeing any food come either.

Quickening his pace, he left the diner and retraced his steps going around the semitruck. He paused for a moment to check the outcropping of trees where he'd left Sun.

He froze, his blood running cold when he noticed the two men standing on either side of Sun, one of them holding a gun against her temple.

Apparently, Igor had brought backup.

CHAPTER EIGHTEEN

January 19 – 8:13 p.m. – East Riverdale, MD

Sun inwardly railed at herself for not hearing the two men creeping up on her in time to prevent them from grabbing her. She blamed it on the fact that she was sick with worry over what Mack was doing and hadn't anticipated two thugs coming after her.

A rookie mistake, likely brought on by her sheer exhaustion.

Still, it was mortifying to be caught like this. Especially when they'd taken her gun.

With a Russian goon on each side, one of them holding a gun at her head, she held herself still and considered her options.

The fact that they hadn't killed her instantly meant they had a plan. Likely to wait for Mack to arrive to take them both out at the same time, maybe even make it look like some sort of murder suicide.

Odd place to do such a thing, outside a truck stop, but whatever. They probably didn't care much as long as she and Mack were both dead.

A dire fate she couldn't allow to happen.

Sun knew how to appear small and fragile. As much as she detested acting like a weakling, she'd do what was necessary to gain the advantage.

When Mack arrived, she'd be ready.

"Don't hurt me," she whimpered in English, hoping they wouldn't realize she could understand their native language. She put a tremor in her voice and twisted her hands together in a way she hoped was submissive. "I'll do whatever you want, just don't hurt me."

"Where is your boyfriend?" the one with the gun hissed in her ear. He used English, and she hoped that meant he had no idea she understood Russian. "Call him."

"I—okay, I—I'll call him." There was a hint of movement behind the semitruck, and she knew Mack was there. She couldn't really call him or the sound from his phone might give his location away.

With exaggerated movements, hoping Mack would catch on, she reached into her pocket and pulled out her disposable phone. She held it up for a moment before bringing her hands together as if to make the call.

Now! Her silent urging must have been reflected on her face because in that moment Mack called out in Russian, "What is going on? Why haven't you killed her? The boyfriend is dead."

The sound of Mack's voice along with the sudden wail of police sirens in the distance was the distraction she needed. The man holding the gun glanced over in surprise and loosened his grip. In a smooth movement, she twisted toward the gunman and swept her joined hands up to push the gun upward so it wasn't pointing at her, at the same time she brought her knee sharply up into his groin. He let out a muffled oomph but didn't let go of the gun.

She hit him again, but it wasn't long before the second man grabbed her. She kicked backward, hitting him low as Mack shouted something in Russian that she was far too busy to translate. Something about the police maybe?

The two men were big and brawny, so Sun hit and kicked, aiming for as many sensitive areas as she could manage as Mack joined the fray.

With Mack taking care of disarming and flattening one of the gunman, she focused her energy and expertise on the second man. When she hit him in the chest with enough force to send him stumbling back, she moved in closer, striking and kicking again, using every bit of martial arts training she'd received over the years.

Her guy finally went down like a rock. She turned to find Mack taking the weapons, money, and phone off the gunman.

Breathing hard, her entire body thrumming with pain, she did the same, glad to have her own weapon back.

"Are you okay?" Mack asked. She could barely hear him over the loud wail of sirens. They were getting closer now, and that wasn't good.

"Fine, let's get out of here." Despite her various aches and pains, she sprinted down the road to where they'd left the SUV, Mack easily keeping pace beside her. As her feet hit the asphalt in rhythmic thumps, she prayed the vehicle hadn't been incapacitated by these guys in some way.

Thankfully, it wasn't. Yanking the driver's side open, she jumped in behind the wheel. Mack joined her. The engine roared to life, and she hit the gas, getting out of the area toward the highway.

"Easy," Mack cautioned as two police squads came roaring toward them. He leaned over and gave her a kiss on the cheek as she passed them.

The kiss short-circuited her brain in a way fighting for her life hadn't. "What was that for?"

Mack actually let out a rusty chuckle. "You're amazing, Sun. After escaping two armed Russians, you're worried about a simple kiss?"

She felt herself flush. "I'm not helpless, Mack."

All evidence of mirth drained from his features. "No, you're not. I went a little crazy when I realized they had you at gunpoint, but then I decided to put my faith in you, in us, and in God to get out of there."

"In God? Really?" She glanced at him in surprise. Mack had attended church with her on occasion when they were young, but she'd always suspected it was more to humor her than because he really believed.

"Yes." His simple response touched her heart. "And the reason for the kiss was to throw off the cops in case they happened to glance over at us."

Her flush deepened, and she hoped the darkness hid her involuntary response. Of course, Mack hadn't kissed her because he'd wanted to. It had been an act.

Although he'd kissed her earlier, after the last two men had attacked them.

She told herself not to read anything into his kisses. There wasn't time for that nonsense anyway. "Did you get anything from Igor?"

"A couple of names, Mikhail Yahontov and a Kirill, but I'm not sure they're real leads or if he was just playing me." He paused, then added, "I should have figured Igor would have backup in the diner. I'm sorry for letting you down, Sun."

"You?" She lifted a brow. "I was the one so focused on watching the diner that I didn't notice until they were close enough to grab me." She hated to admit weakness, but the truth was, they were both exhausted and not functioning at the top of their game. "I'm the one who let you down."

Mack blew out a breath. "You didn't, Sun. Let's be honest here, we've done pretty well considering the danger is coming at us from all directions. I should have pushed harder for backup."

The spike of adrenaline began to fade, leaving a crushing exhaustion in its wake. "Nothing good comes from ruminating over the past. But we need to get some sleep, Mack. Or our next encounter with the Russians, or North Koreans for that matter, may not have the same positive result."

"I know we need to sleep soon, but we still don't have anything solid on the location of the nuke."

He had a good point. They had roughly thirteen hours to find the thing. Or enough evidence that would convince the president to cancel the inauguration for the first time in history.

"Okay, we'll find a motel to stay in for a few hours while we work on getting information on Mikhail Yahontov and Kirill. The motel we used before in Mitchellville isn't too far from here."

"Sounds good. I have Igor's phone too." Mack patted the pocket of his coat. "Between Igor's phone and the devices we took off the two Russians, maybe something will break."

Sun was beginning to lose hope that they'd ever get the break they needed.

The way these Russians were constantly one step ahead of them was deeply unnerving.

JANUARY 19 – 8:48 p.m. – Charlotte, NC
Hana kept a hand on Jarek's arm as the passengers

began to deplane. Hiding her face in the crook of his neck, she whispered, "We should stay on board until takeoff."

"Whatever you think is best," Jarek agreed.

Hana wasn't sure if staying on the plane was the right thing to do. Would they appear more obvious than if they deplaned along with the others?

She kept a keen eye out for the dark-haired man. He was behind them, so if he got off the plane, they'd see him.

And if he didn't? She couldn't help but shiver.

Just because the Asian was going on to Washington, DC, the way they were didn't make him part of the regime.

But it was a possibility she could not afford to ignore.

The knot in her stomach tightened as one by one passengers left the plane. Until there were no more.

And no sign of the dark-haired Asian.

He must still be seated behind them. Waiting, obviously, the way they were for the plane to continue on to Washington, DC. As much as she wanted to turn and look, she maintained her position of leaning against Jarek.

Okay, if he was from the regime, they needed an escape plan for when they arrived at their final destination. Something that would get them safely out of the airport without being caught.

And once they were in the air, they'd have only an hour to decide on the best course of action.

Yet another astronomical hurdle standing in the way of finding Sun in time to save her and prevent a global disaster.

JANUARY 19 – 9:17 p.m. – Mitchellville, MD

Mack hauled the sat computer into the motel room. There were two double beds, and he thought again about what Sun had said about getting sleep.

She was right. The mistakes they'd made so far were likely related to sheer exhaustion. Yet he felt certain if they didn't keep pushing forward they'd lose whatever small amount of momentum they had.

It may seem as if they kept banging into brick walls, but they'd found Dimitri, Igor, and now could likely track down Mikhail Yahontov or Kirill. Each step brought them closer to the person who actually had the nuke.

Sun disappeared into the bathroom, and he stared after her for a moment, wondering if she was hurt more than she'd let on. She'd broken a stitch over her arterial injury, what if she'd opened the wound more?

Not that she'd tell him if she had.

He rested his head on folded arms while waiting for the sat computer to pick up a signal. He must have fallen asleep because the next thing he knew Sun was shaking his shoulder.

"You'll get a crick in your neck if you sleep like that," she scolded.

He lifted his head, noting he already had a crick. Peering at his watch, he realized he'd only been out fifteen minutes.

Not nearly long enough.

"You can use the bathroom," Sun went on, looking refreshed. He dropped his gaze to her left wrist.

"How's the injury?" He pushed up to his feet and was hit by a wave of dizziness.

"Fine." Sun shooed him off. "Go before you fall."

When Mack emerged from the bathroom a few minutes later, Sun was stretched out on one of the beds sound asleep. She looked beautiful as always, and he forced himself to tear his gaze away.

He fully intended to get to work on the sat computer

but somehow found himself stretching out on the empty bed.

Just a few more minutes and he'd get back to work. They needed to find Yahontov, or Kirill. And hopefully a lead to the bomb itself.

JANUARY 19 – 10:11 p.m. – Mitchellville, MD

Sun woke up to the vibration of her phone. The interior of the room was dark with only a sliver of light from the parking lot outside shining in through the slightly parted curtains.

Groping for the phone, she pulled it from her pocket and managed to croak out, "Hello?"

"Sun? Where have you been? I've been worried sick about you."

Jordan's voice made her wince. She'd fully intended to call him after the problems they'd encountered at the truck stop. "Fine, we ran into some trouble, but we're fine."

"What kind of trouble?" Jordan asked.

She rolled into a sitting position, smiling a bit as she realized Mack was still out for the count. Which was probably a good thing, he hadn't slept as much as she had. "Hang on." She eased off the bed and padded to the bathroom, hoping to let Mack sleep for a while longer. It wasn't as if forty-five minutes even counted as real sleep.

"We have a new lead, a guy known as Mikhail Yahontov and another by the name of Kirill, unsure of his last name. Ever heard of them?"

"No. What kind of trouble? Are either of you hurt?"

"We're fine, just bruised by all the fighting." Fighting that had been mostly her fault for not being aware of the guys creeping up on her.

"Where are you?"

"In Mitchellville, why?" She yawned and longed for a cup of very strong coffee.

"I have another lead. I had Yates dig into the computer of the dead guy, Allan Stokes. Seems like he's been communicating with someone within the Capitol."

She frowned, trying to follow his train of thought. "Do you have a name?"

"Not yet, but didn't Remington chase after some North Korean–speaking guy all the way up to the Capitol?"

"Yes. But I couldn't find him listed in the members of Congress. I even went state by state looking at the newly elected congressmen and women who may not have had their picture in there yet, without success." She rubbed her gritty eyes. "We feel certain he's an aide."

"We're still following the lead back to the email that bounced off a server within the Capitol and will let you know when we have one. In the meantime, there's one more possible lead."

"What kind of lead?" She hoped it was anything but chasing after another Russian thug.

"Sloan and Natalia have transcribed more Russian chatter. It appears there is an American and a North Korean who are causing trouble for the grand plan."

"Me and Mack," she said dully, even though she was an American citizen, having been born here in the US, at least according to her mother. And her passport. "That's not exactly a lead. We're living it with every step we take."

"I know, Sun. But you didn't let me finish. The grand plan is to happen from close by," Jordan continued. "They picked up the term national. At first they didn't think much about it, then remembered the National Mall is the entire area located directly across from the west side of the Capitol building."

A shiver rippled down her spine. "That area will be heavily monitored by Secret Service and the Capitol police. No way could they get a bomb in there."

"Yes, but if someone within the Capitol is involved, they'd know how to breach security," Jordan pointed out. "I think you and Mack should check it out. I'm working on getting you security clearance to be there."

"Okay, but Jordan, isn't this enough to convince the president and the Secret Service to shut the entire ceremony down?"

There was a long pause. "I tried, but Yates doesn't think so. The word national can mean many different things, it's not necessarily the location of the bomb. Even if that is the location, the area encompassing the National Mall is huge. With all the protection we have in place, as you said yourself, the idea that someone could get close enough to set off a nuclear bomb is inconceivable. It bothers me too, but they're just not ready to pull the plug."

Of course they weren't. She let out a weary sigh. "We'll keep following our Russian trail then, unless you call to send us somewhere else."

"Go ahead and keep working the Russian angle but be careful. The body count is getting pretty high."

Yeah, no kidding. Sun disconnected from the call and then ran cold water over her face. Time to wake Mack and get back to work.

If the National Mall area really is the location, the sooner they could verify the actual presence of a nuke, the sooner the entire fiasco would be over.

If the bureaucrats bothered to listen.

. . .

JANUARY 19 – 10:27 *p.m.* – *Washington, DC*

Staying in character, Hana stood hunched over in the aisle beside Jarek, using the seat rests of each row to brace herself as they disembarked the plane. If she'd had her way, they would have been first off the plane, but that hadn't been allowed.

At least going with everyone else kept them ahead of the dark-haired Asian.

The only plan she'd been able to come up with was to use the wheelchair service, the way she had in Chicago. She'd asked the flight attendant to assist with getting access. The flight attendant had agreed to get the chair, but she would not let them off the plane before the others.

"Are you sure about this?" Jarek asked, looking nervous now that they'd actually landed in Washington, DC.

She wasn't at all sure, but since the ploy had worked once before, she could only hope it would work again.

Besides, what else could they do? It wasn't as if they had firsthand knowledge of how the Reagan International Airport was laid out. She prayed the Asian behind them didn't know anything about the place either.

Ironic how airports were supposed to feel safe. As she and Jarek stepped off the plane and onto the jetway where a smiling man stood behind a wheelchair, she felt extremely vulnerable, expecting the Asian to show up at any moment.

"If you don't mind, we're in a bit of a hurry," Jarek said, playing his role. "We're meeting our daughter."

"Not a problem." The cheerful attendant obligingly turned Hana's chair and headed up the jetway ramp, easily passing those weary travelers lugging their carry-on bags.

Jarek walked quickly beside them, and she found it amazing that people actually moved to the side to make room for her. For them.

This could actually work!

The attendant automatically headed toward the baggage claim area. As they headed for the elevator, Jarek said, "Does this elevator take us to the taxi stand?"

"Yes, sir, the taxi stand is located just off the baggage claim area," the attendant said. He pushed the button to summon the elevator.

The elevator seemed to take forever, but finally the door opened. They had to wait until another man in a wheelchair and his companion came out before they could get in.

Her attendant spun her around to back her chair into the elevator. Jarek came in, too, but just as the door was closing, someone waved a hand through the opening, causing the doors to pop open.

The dark-haired Asian was standing there, a smug grin on his features. Without saying a word, he crowded onto the elevator with them, the door sliding shut behind him.

Hana's mouth went dry, and she wanted to cry out, but she couldn't move.

The regime had caught up to her!

CHAPTER NINETEEN

January 19 – 10:40 p.m. – Washington, DC

Jarek caught a glimpse of the way the Asian's fingers were curled into fists, his knuckles bruised as if being in a fight, and knew Hana had been right to be paranoid.

They were stuck on an elevator with a cold-blooded killer!

The attendant behind Hana's wheelchair was completely oblivious to what was going on right under his nose. "Are you planning to see the monuments while you're here?"

Jarek played along, pretending he didn't know they were about to be kidnapped or attacked. The Asian wasn't saying anything anyway, he just stood silently as if waiting for the best moment to strike. He forced enthusiasm into his tone. "Oh yes, I've always wanted to see the Lincoln Memorial and the Washington Monument."

"Those are the most popular," the attendant said. "But be sure to check out the others. Lots to do and see in DC."

The idle chitchat was as difficult to tolerate as nails raking across a chalkboard. There was a ding as the elevator reached the level where the baggage claim was located.

Jarek knew he had to do something to get them out of this. But faking a heart attack wasn't going to work this time.

The elevator doors opened. The Asian stepped through, then politely put his hand in the opening so they could get out, no doubt hoping to grab Hana's wheelchair from the attendant.

Jarek went first, then purposefully stumbled and fell against the Asian, using his body weight to knock him off balance. The move seemed to take the guy by surprise, and they fell to the ground, a tangle of arms and legs.

"Run, Hana!" Jarek shouted to Hana as the Asian roughly shoved him aside. Jarek grabbed onto him, holding on with every bit of strength he possessed, hoping to give Hana enough time to get away.

But did she leave? No. Out of nowhere, the footrest of the wheelchair came down on the Asian's head with a loud thwack! The man groaned and went limp.

"Hurry!" Hana grabbed Jarek's hand, helping him to his feet. The attendant stood gaping in shock as the formerly wheelchair-bound Hana ran with Jarek toward the glass sliding doors leading outside.

The attendant finally found his voice. "Hey! Call security. They assaulted this guy!"

Out in the chilly air, Jarek looked wildly around the unfamiliar surroundings. They needed to get out of here before anyone caught them! Glancing to the right, he thought he saw a dark-haired man walking toward them from the right. The taxi line was incredibly long, so he took Hana's hand and ran down the sidewalk to the left past the line of taxis waiting for their turn to pick up a fare.

At the very end of the line, he leaned down and rapped

sharply at the taxi window. "We need to get out of here, right away!"

The driver peered up at them. "I'm supposed to wait for my turn."

Jarek pulled out what was left of his cash and shoved a fifty-dollar bill at him. "Now, please? We need to go right now!"

The guy took the money and shrugged. "Okay, get in."

Jarek let Hana get in first, then quickly slid in behind her. "If you don't mind, we're going to crouch down back here, just so you don't get into any trouble for jumping the line." And to stay out of view of the possible dark-haired man.

"Works for me." The taxi driver nosed out of the line and into the long flow of traffic as Jarek crouched behind the passenger seat. Hana was curled in a ball behind the driver.

His heart was hammering so loudly he could barely think. Reaching over, he took Hana's hand in his. "We got away," he whispered.

Hana nodded. "Because of you, Jarek."

He hadn't been the one to bonk the wheelchair leg over the Asian's head, but knocking him down had given Hana the time to jump into action.

Despite their grim situation, he couldn't help but feel a surge of satisfaction.

He and Hana made a great team.

JANUARY 19 – 11:01 p.m. – Mitchellville, MD

After Sun had filled Mack in on her conversation with Jordan, he'd forced the sleep from his eyes and went back to work on the sat computer.

They had a few possible leads, the Russian Mikhail

Yahontov, some man named Kirill, and the possible bomb being hidden somewhere in the National Mall area outside the Capitol.

Flimsy leads at best, but better than nothing.

Yet so far, the lead on Mikhail was a bust. No answer on the other end of the number he'd found in Igor's phone, which made triangulation impossible. And he hadn't been able to find anything on Kirill either.

And the way Sun hovered over his shoulder wasn't helping. The only way he could think of staying awake was to kiss her.

For real, letting her know in no uncertain terms how he felt about her.

"Why don't we try something else?" she suggested, her voice dangerously close to his ear. Her citrus scent was driving him crazy. "Is there any way you can pull up the specs on all the structures encompassed within the National Mall? Maybe seeing blueprints or something like that will help us figure out where the bomb might be located."

He glanced over his shoulder, capturing her gaze. "You think it's already in place?"

She looked surprised. "Well, yeah. Why wouldn't it be? The inauguration starts in less than twelve hours, no way they can move a bomb in now. I'm thinking it's been in place for several days at least, maybe longer."

He let out a weary sigh. "Okay, then I need to call Tramall. He should be able to get me the blueprints."

"And here I thought you'd want to challenge your hacking skills," Sun teased.

"I would, except that we don't have time for that," he argued. He was secretly touched by her faith in his skills, but they needed to move quickly. "Maybe we should head back to DC now, before traffic gets crazy. By the time we get there, we'll likely have the blueprints."

Sun straightened, finally moving away from him, and nodded. "Get in touch with him now, then we'll hit the road."

His boss answered immediately, as if he'd been waiting for Mack to check in. "What's going on? Have you found anything?"

Hello to you, too, he thought sourly. "I need you to get me the blueprints for every structure encompassed within the National Mall, especially those closest to the Capitol."

"Why? Is that where the bomb is?"

Mack knew lack of sleep was making him cranky. "We don't know, but the word national was picked up in some Russian chatter about the event. It's one of the few leads we have."

Tramall was silent for a long moment. "I'd hoped you'd have more by now. This isn't enough to take to the president."

Mack ground his teeth together in an effort to hold on to his temper. "We've chased several leads and have been attacked at least four times in the past twenty-four hours. Frankly, we're lucky to be alive. We're doing our best with little to no help from the NSA, or the FBI for that matter."

"I'm sorry to hear you've been under attack," Tramall quickly backpedaled. "I'll get you the blueprints for all those structures right away. Is there anything else?"

"Not unless you have information on a Mikhail Yahontov or a man named Kirill." Doubtful, since he'd already checked the NSA database without success.

"No. Neither one is on our watch list."

Of course not. "Get the me the blueprints, we're heading back to DC."

"Okay. Keep me posted if you find something." Tramall disconnected from the call.

"Sounds like you don't like him much," Sun said.

Mack grimaced and began packing up the sat computer. "He's okay, just your typical government leader, impatiently wanting results from the safety of his office without getting his hands dirty."

"One of the reasons I like working for Security Specialists, Inc. And Yates has gotten involved in the past as needed. I have no reason to think he won't do the same now. Or will, once we have something solid to go on." Sun drew on her thin winter jacket and headed for the door.

Mack could understand the allure, although he had credentials to help open doors and get work done, whereas she didn't.

Yet Sun also had more freedom to do the job without restrictions.

He settled in the passenger seat and opened the computer. He'd keep digging for information about Mikhail Yahontov and Kirill. After all, how many Russians out there with that name could there be?

Probably more than he wanted to know.

JANUARY 19 – 11:19 p.m. – Washington, DC

Hana couldn't believe they'd managed to escape the North Korean in the elevator. If not for Jarek's quick thinking, she believed they'd already be dead.

Or maybe they'd be captured and used as bait to get to Sun.

She needed to find their daughter!

"Which hotel?" the taxi driver asked.

"How about the Hyatt Place?" Hana suggested.

The driver eyed her in the rearview mirror. "Lady, do you have a reservation? If not, I wouldn't bother. The place is booked because of the inauguration tomorrow."

Hana went still. Of course, she knew about the inauguration. After all, it was why she'd asked for Jarek's help to come to DC. To find Sun, yes, and to help prevent the attack she knew was about to take place.

And now that they were here, what could they do? No matter which hotel they tried, they likely wouldn't find anything available.

"We do have a reservation, but I don't want to wait. Would you mind dropping us off at the Lincoln Memorial?" Jarek suggested.

"It's not open this late," the driver said with a frown. "And there's bound to be barricades up since that's along the parade route."

Hana could tell he was growing suspicious. "I understand it's not open, and you can drop us off anywhere, we'll walk the rest of the way. We're meeting up with our daughter, she's the one who made our reservations at the Hyatt and will be joining us very soon."

There was a brief pause before the driver shrugged. "Okay. I'll get as close as possible."

"Thank you." Reaching over, she clutched Jarek's hand. What would they do once they reached the Lincoln Memorial? Where would they go? Where could they stay?

And more importantly, how could they find Sun before noon tomorrow and before the regime caught up to them?

JANUARY 20 – 12:05 a.m. – Washington, DC

Sun was grateful they'd made good time getting back to the city. Another plus was that Jordan had kept their previous hotel room, so they didn't have to find yet another place to stay.

"Got the blueprints," Mack said. "Took him long enough."

"It's late. I'm sure he had to jump through some hoops to get them." She glanced at Mack wondering why he'd grown sour on his NSA job.

It occurred to her that she really didn't know much about what Mack had been up to over the past five years. Other than hacking, based on his outstanding skills in that arena. Yet since he'd dropped unexpectedly back into her life, they hadn't had much time to talk about personal stuff.

Which was probably fine, except that he'd kissed her.

Twice.

She pulled into the hotel parking lot and shut off the SUV. "Okay, let's take a look at those blueprints. I guess that's about all we can do until Jordan comes through with our security clearances."

Mack nodded and carried the computer inside. Their previous keys worked, and as they entered the room, Sun felt as if they'd been gone for weeks rather than hours.

So much had happened, the constant danger overwhelming, yet they still didn't have any way of knowing if the bomb was truly hidden somewhere within the facilities of the National Mall or somewhere else entirely. And what about the North Korean threat? So far she hadn't seen anyone who might have been from the regime, but that could change at any moment. For now, she had to concentrate on the nuke.

The idea of searching the blueprints of every structure located in the National Mall area was daunting. And possibly a waste of time.

What they needed was a better idea of the potential

trajectory of this bomb. It would help them narrow their search area.

Mack dropped into the chair in front of the computer. She crossed over to join him. "Before getting started on the blueprints, check out the specs of the old Davy Crockett."

He frowned. "Why?"

"The National Mall area is huge. This thing could be fired from just about anywhere. But we know the target is the area in front of the Capitol. We need to narrow our search by understanding how close this thing needs to be."

"Good idea." He began working the keyboard.

Less than twelve hours. And she knew that the crowd would build around the Capitol starting bright and early. Sunrise was roughly seven fifteen to seven thirty in the morning.

Finding anything once the crowds had gathered would be impossible.

JANUARY 20 – 12:26 *a.m.* – *Washington, DC*

"This is as close as I can get," the taxi driver informed them. "You can see the lights from the monument over there." He gestured toward the windshield.

"Thank you." Jarek paid the man with money he'd borrowed from Hana, grimacing at his lack of funds. Hana waited until they were out of the taxi, then put her hand on his arm.

"It's fine. I have plenty of money, Jarek. But I'm not sure what good it will do. We'll never find a place to stay anywhere in this area."

"I know." The adrenaline that had fueled him getting out of the airport with Hana had drained away, leaving pure exhaustion in its place. "Maybe we can catch the subway."

"I don't think it runs all night in DC."

He bit back a groan. The subway ran twenty-four seven in Chicago, it had never occurred to him that it wouldn't run all night here. "Let's walk," he suggested. "We'll find another cab and see if we can find a hotel far enough away from the city with available rooms."

Hana nodded and huddled close to his side. He put his arm around her slim shoulders, trying to shelter her from the wind.

"Any idea on how to find Sun?" he asked as they walked.

"I can try to leave another message with the secure answering service we only use in case of emergency, but she hasn't responded to the first one," Hana admitted. "I called from the airport in South Bend."

He didn't want to consider the possibility that Sun couldn't respond because she was injured or worse. He needed to have faith, but it wasn't easy. Then he caught a glimpse of a hotel. "This way," he urged. "The hotel may not have rooms, but they'll have a way to get a taxi."

Hana pushed money at him, which he reluctantly placed in his pocket. Taking money from her felt wrong, but these were extraordinary times.

Together, they'd find Sun and warn her of the danger.

He desperately wanted the chance to meet his daughter.

JANUARY 20 – 12:44 a.m. – Washington, DC

He woke to his phone vibrating beneath his pillow. Easing silently out of bed, he took the phone and padded into the kitchen. Muttering a vicious curse under his breath, he swallowed hard and answered, "Yes?"

"Your fee has just tripled."

The deep Russian voice sent a shiver of fear down his spine, but he fought hard not to let his voice show any emotion. "And why exactly would you call me at this hour demanding I triple your fee?"

"Because you failed to mention that the two you want dead are highly trained operatives. They have remarkable skills, and as such, they have injured several of my men. One of them is still lying in the hospital in a coma. I will be compensated for the loss of my men."

He hesitated, debating the best response. The idea that one of the Russians was in the hospital was unnerving. Why hadn't he been silenced for good? Wasn't that routine for the Russians?

The last thing he wanted was to make this man angry, yet he couldn't simply let the guy demand triple the fee either. At least not without some protest. "The job has not changed. Why should I compensate you for the incompetence of your men? How hard can it be to take care of two people, one of them a mere woman?"

"Triple the fee," the Russian repeated, "or take the risk of finding someone else to do your dirty work."

Unacceptable how the Russian had backed him into a corner. And here he'd thought this little problem had been taken care of. So much for no news being good news.

"Fine, I'll triple the fee, but you better get the job done. You're running out of time."

"Wire the money to the designated account." With that, the caller disconnected.

He drew in a deep, ragged breath and crossed over to the laptop computer on the table. With trembling fingers, he sent the cash via wire transfer, then slammed the computer shut.

The money wasn't the biggest issue, there was plenty more where that had come from as he'd married well. But time was running out. He desperately needed Remington and Yin-lee eliminated from the equation.

Very soon.

JANUARY 20 – 1:09 a.m. – Washington, DC

Mack rubbed at his eyes, trying to fix his blurry vision. The hour of sleep he'd gotten wasn't nearly enough.

"Have you figured it out?" Sun had poured them both coffee made from the small pot in the room. They could use more, but the motel was stingy on conveniences such as free coffee.

He turned toward her. "Yeah, I know the trajectory, but the problem is that the nuke isn't a gun. They don't have to hit a specific target within a few inches like a sniper does. Targeting the bomb in the general location of the west lawn of the Capitol will cause the same amount of damage."

"There has to be something we can do to narrow it down." Sun looked beyond frustrated.

"Within this radius," he said, drawing a half circle with the tip of his finger. "If I were to take an educated guess? I'd say the Smithsonian or the National Gallery of Art."

"Not the Washington Monument?"

He shook his head. "Too far away and you can't take backpacks up there."

"You can't take backpacks into the Smithsonian or the National Gallery of Art without being searched either," Sun argued. "We need to remember that there is someone working this thing from inside the Capitol."

The words hit him hard. "Inside the Capitol."

Sun stared at him, realization dawning on her features. "No way."

He shivered and quickly pulled up the map of the Capitol building. "To use your words, why not? Who better to have access than someone who can go freely in and out of the place?"

"But—the place is heavily guarded, and there are metal detectors that would prevent anyone from bringing in a penknife, much less a nuke," Sun argued.

"Maybe." He knew she was right, but there had to be something they were missing. "Call Jordan, we need that security clearance ASAP. In the meantime, I'll scour the blueprints. See if I can come up with something."

Sun pulled out her phone and rose to her feet. "Jordan? How quickly can you get us those security passes?"

Mack listened to her side of the conversation with half an ear. The blueprints to the building were so large it took several minutes to load. He tried what he'd hoped was Yahontov's phone number again, still no answer.

Were they on the right track? Or should they be focusing their energy on the Smithsonian and the National Gallery of Art?

Or something else completely?

Making the wrong choice this late in the game would be deadly.

CHAPTER TWENTY

January 20 – 1:17 a.m. – Washington, DC

Hana tried not to shiver as the cold wind seeped into her bones. They'd walked briskly, but it had still taken longer than she'd anticipated to get here. She approached the bellhop standing outside the Hyatt with a gentle smile. "Good evening, I wonder if you would mind calling a taxi for us."

The bellhop frowned. "Are you a guest here, ma'am?"

"Our daughter is, but we aren't." She tried not to display any hint of anxiety on her face, even though she had no idea where they'd end up staying, if anywhere, and didn't like the idea of riding in taxis for what was left of the night. "We walked over to see the Lincoln Memorial. Even though it's not open, we were drawn by the lights. So beautiful."

She wasn't sure the bellhop was buying her story, but she doubted he'd refuse to offer any assistance, even though they normally only called taxis for guests. She was still in her disguise and hoped he'd take pity on her. He reluctantly nodded and lifted his cell phone. Within a few minutes, a taxi rolled up. The bellhop was about to reach for the door, but Jarek beat him to it.

"Thank you, sir," Hana said before sliding in.

Jarek gave the bellhop a small tip before joining her.

"Where to?" the cabbie asked.

Hana leaned forward. "Do you have any idea where we may find a hotel room?"

"On Inauguration Day?" The guy laughed. "Not anywhere close to the mall, that's for sure. Maybe in the outskirts of the city."

Hana looked down at the DC tour map she'd found on their walk to the Hyatt. She really had no idea where to start. "Any specific area more likely to have a room than another?"

The cabbie pulled away from the hotel and headed off in the only direction he could go considering the closed streets. "If it were me, I'd try someplace north of Capitol Hill. There are smaller hotels there that might have a room." Despite the suggestion, his tone was not exactly encouraging. "Unless you want to try heading back over the river toward the Arlington area."

She glanced at Jarek who shrugged. "I say we stay within DC."

"North of Capitol Hill, then." She lifted a hand to tuck her hair beneath her scarf. She'd worn it as a disguise but now appreciated the scant bit of warmth it provided. She stared out the window, hoping this wasn't a wild-goose chase. The only good thing was that traffic was light at this hour of the morning.

But that wouldn't last long. She was fairly certain that the streets would be jam-packed with people and cars within a few hours.

She'd already called the number of the answering

service in an attempt to reach Sun, but as before, she hadn't heard back.

There had to be a way to find her daughter before another North Korean found them. And before noon.

Hana bowed her head and sent up a silent prayer for God to continue watching over them.

JANUARY 20 – 1:24 a.m. – Washington, DC

Sun would have given anything for another cup of coffee. An entire pot would have been better. Jordan was working on their security clearances for the Capitol, which she still saw as a long shot, and Mack was examining the blueprints.

The Russians were a dead end, and that was disturbing.

The more she thought about the plot to shoot off a nuke during the inauguration, the crazier it sounded. It was just impossible to imagine where such a device could be used in an area teeming with security.

She plopped onto the edge of the bed and scrubbed her hands over her face. What if they were on the wrong track? What if the nuke wasn't intended to be used during the inauguration ceremony where the new president was sworn into office but at some point during the parade route?

Or maybe the inauguration wasn't the target at all?

It was all so maddening. Yet the danger as they'd worked this case was very real. Hard to imagine why someone would be so determined to kill her and Mack if there wasn't a really good reason.

She felt certain they were getting close to the truth.

"Wait a minute." Sun sprang to her feet. "What if the nuke is smaller than we originally thought?"

Mack looked at her with bloodshot eyes. "What difference does that make?"

"I don't know, but let's take the backpack theory. We know they're not allowed in any of the buildings here in DC without being searched, but they can't possibly keep every single pedestrian from carrying one." Her thoughts whirled fast. "Or maybe the backpack is hidden someplace outside so that a pedestrian can find it and pick it up once they're in the National Mall area."

Mack let out a sigh. "So we're back to scrounging around the area searching for a bomb that may or may not be there?"

He had a point. "We know someone is helping from within the Capitol, so rather than assume the bomb is inside the building, maybe it's just been cleverly hidden somewhere close by."

Mack threw up his hands in frustration. "But where? That's the key to this mess."

Her surge of excitement faded, and her shoulders drooped. "I don't know. A garbage can?"

Mack straightened in his seat. "That's a thought. If they picked one that was off in a corner somewhere, maybe camouflaged in some way, the bomb could still be there, waiting for the trigger man to pick it up and use it."

"The trigger man would be putting his life on the line to do that. It's not like he can show up wearing a gas mask."

"True, even if he was dressed as a member of the Capitol police, it would be too obvious," Mack muttered, turning back to his screen. "Let me check out a few things. See if I can find the locations of the trash cans from the sanitation department."

Sun tried not to groan. More hacking? Appreciating Mack's computer skills was one thing, but watching him work was pure torture. "I'm going to see if I can get additional packets of coffee from the front desk. We'll never make it through this without more caffeine."

"Okay." Mack barely noticed as she pulled on her thin jacket and pocketed a room key.

The cold air made her shiver but also helped slap back the overwhelming wave of fatigue. She tucked her hands into her pockets, her fingertips brushing against her phone. With a wince, she realized it had been hours since she thought of contacting her mother. She tried to think back, when was the last time she'd called the number they used only in cases of emergency? Yesterday sometime? Everything was one big blur. Maybe she should have left a message.

Pausing outside the lobby, she dialed the numbers her mother made her memorize all those years ago. A number that would be routed through an answering service. When a voice at the other end of the line informed her of two new messages, she nearly dropped her phone in shock. She listened to the most recent message first.

"Sun? I hope you get this soon, you're in terrible danger from the regime." Hearing her mother's tense voice speaking North Korean after all these years made her eyes fill with tears. "I'm here in Washington, DC, please call this disposable cell number as soon as possible."

Here? In Washington, DC? With trembling fingers, Sun dialed the number. After what seemed like forever, her mother's voice answered, again speaking in North Korean. "I'm sorry, you must have the wrong number."

Sun recognized the code they'd used in the past. "Please forgive me," she responded. Then after waiting a beat, she said, "Mom? Are you really here in DC?"

"Sun, I'm so glad you've called. We must meet, where

are you?" Her mother sounded even more tense in person than she had on her message.

"I'm at a motel." Sun gave her the name and address. "Are you close?"

Her mother let out a choked laugh. "Believe it or not, we are only five minutes away."

Five minutes? For a moment, Sun wondered if this was some sort of trick, if the regime had gotten ahold of her mother's phone and was right now holding a gun to her head. Although if that was the case, why had she used their code?

"Sun, listen to me, the danger is real." Her mother's voice went on. "I will be there soon, but the North Korean tailing me is not far behind. They've managed to follow me all the way from Geneva."

Not good news, and a complication she didn't need while trying to find the nuke. "Okay, listen, it's going to be fine. I'll be waiting for you in the lobby, okay?"

"Yes, Sunflower. I will be there soon."

The old nickname made her smile, her throat clogged with emotion. It had been so long since she'd seen her mother.

Why was her mom here now, in the middle of a potential nuclear disaster?

Sun lifted her gaze up to the sky. *Why, Lord? Why?*

JANUARY 20 – 1:55 *a.m.* – *Washington, DC*

Jarek felt a surge of anticipation intermixed with a hint of apprehension as their cabbie pulled up in front of the motel lobby. This was it. The moment he'd been waiting for.

He was about to meet his daughter for the first time.

What would Sun think of him? A fifty-seven-year-old English professor? He had nothing to offer a brilliant woman like Hana's daughter.

His daughter. After all, Hana claimed Sun had his ears.

"Ready, Jarek?" Hana asked. Her gaze searched his. "I didn't tell her about you yet. I thought maybe you'd want to get to know her a bit first."

Jarek wasn't sure if that was a good plan or not, but he didn't argue. He slid out of the taxi and offered Hana his hand to help her out. The taxi drove away and almost instantly the door to the lobby flung open, revealing a younger version of Hana.

"Get your hands off her!" Sun yelled, rushing toward them.

"No, Sun, please stop." Hana stepped around him to prevent Sun from doing something rash. "This is my friend, Jarek Zeman. He's a dear friend, Sun. Not part of the regime."

Sun came to an abrupt halt, looking embarrassed. "Sorry," she muttered. Then frowned at her mother. "You didn't mention a friend."

"I know, maybe I should have, but I was worried you'd be concerned. You must know, Sun, that I would not be standing here right now without Jarek's help. I promise you we can trust him."

Sun seemed to gather herself and smiled. "Mr. Zeman, it's nice to meet you, and I'm grateful for your assistance in bringing my mother here."

It took a second for him to find his tongue. "I was glad to help. You're very beautiful, Sun, just like your mother."

Sun arched a brow and glanced at Hana, then back at him. "So you've known my mother for how long?"

"Ah." He floundered for an answer. He waved a hand. "Years."

Sun narrowed her gaze and moved closer, peering at his facial features illuminated by the motel sign light with an intensity that made him squirm. Then she raised a hand to touch her earlobe.

"I should have known," Sun whispered, taking a step back. "I've always wondered about my big earlobes." He could feel his face flushing as he tried to come up with a plausible explanation as to why he was there. Why had they ever thought they could fool their Mensa daughter? "You're my father."

JANUARY 20 – 2:16 a.m. – *Washington, DC*

What was taking Sun so long to get coffee?

Mack rubbed his eyes, but his vision refused to clear. This is what happened when you didn't get sleep and stared at a computer screen as long as he had.

He needed a break. And now that Sun had put the idea of coffee in his head, he craved a cup.

Pacing the tiny room, he thought about the various garbage locations he'd found. More than he'd thought possible.

Four hours, maybe less before the entire area encompassing the National Mall would be packed with people. The sooner they got out there to begin searching the better.

And if they were on the wrong track?

He didn't even want to think about the dire consequences. Not just to the entire fate of their country, which was bad enough, but to him and Sun as well.

They'd be in the nuclear blast zone.

The motel room door opened, and he spun to see Sun

walking in with two people behind her. He put his hand on his gun, then gaped in surprise when he saw a woman that could only be Sun's mother, along with a distinguished-looking man standing behind her.

"Mack, this is my mother, Hana Yin-lee, and this is my —er—father, Jarek Zeman." Sun's eyes were suspiciously damp, and his heart wrenched when he realized she'd found her father after twenty-nine years.

And could very well lose him within the next several hours if they didn't find and neutralize the bomb.

"Nice to meet you both," Mack said, offering his hand in greeting to Hana and Jarek. "I'm only sorry it's under these circumstances."

"It's a blessing to finally meet my father, but the danger is very real. I explained how you were attacked in Central Park by a North Korean who mentioned me and my mother," Sun said.

"And we've been running from the North Koreans for the past several hours ourselves," Jarek added. "Now that we've found you, Sun, we need to disappear, permanently."

Disappear? Not hardly. Mack scowled and shot an accusing glare at Sun. "Didn't you tell them?"

"Not yet."

Mack raked his fingers through his hair. "We're working a case for the NSA and the FBI," he said bluntly. "We have reason to believe there's a nuclear bomb that will go off during the inauguration ceremony in roughly ten hours."

"A nuclear bomb?" Jarek repeated, shaking his head. "That's impossible."

"No, it's not impossible," Hana said softly. "It's very real."

"You know about the nuke?" Mack swiveled to face her. "How?"

Hana glanced at Jarek, then at Sun. "I've been working as an international spy. My last trip to North Korea revealed much dissatisfaction with the United States. There are so many disheartened by the lack of support. I heard rumblings of a nuclear bomb and made sure the chatter was sent through the appropriate channels."

"You're a spy?" Jarek gaped in shock.

"And you're the one who sent the original chatter to the FBI?" Sun added incredulously. "The female voice we heard? Small demonstration of what we are capable of? We are many, and we are strong? Big surprises come in small packages?"

"Yes. That was me. And I believe my last trip to the homeland caught the regime's attention." Hana tipped her chin in a stubborn look that mirrored Sun's. In that moment, Mack realized just how much Sun and her mother were alike. Hana turned toward Jarek, her expression stricken. "I'm sorry, Jarek. Please forgive me. I was afraid you wouldn't come if you knew the truth. I have put you in danger again, partially because I needed your help, but mostly because I wanted you to meet our daughter. All while saving the country. I know I had no right, but looking back, I believe this was God's plan all along. Especially as you were already in danger back in Chicago."

"But—a nuclear bomb?" Jarek still looked aghast. "Something like that would cause World War III!"

"Exactly," Hana said with a nod. "Which is why we must help Sun find this device, ASAP."

JANUARY 20 – 2:24 a.m. – *Washington, DC*

Sun had hugged her mother and had wanted to do the same with her father, but she had held back, unsure of how

Jarek Zeman felt about all this. She was thrilled yet also confused as to why she was finally meeting her father. She had dozens of questions, but there wasn't time to chat about their personal lives or all that had transpired over the past twenty-nine years.

But the most shocking news of all was that her mother had been spying on North Korea. No wonder they'd tracked her mother so relentlessly. And had come to find her too. Her thoughts whirled, but she forced herself to focus on the immediate issues at hand.

She eyed her mother. "You know for sure the regime followed you to DC?"

"We escaped from a North Korean at Reagan International Airport, thanks to Jarek's quick thinking," Hana said, tucking her hand in the crook of Jarek's elbow. Despite the surprising news, Sun noticed her father remained close to her mother, touching her frequently.

Almost as if they'd reunited after all this time apart.

Interesting how he was taking her mother being a spy in stride. But there wasn't time to worry about that now.

"There was only one of them?" Sun pressed. "That's unusual since they travel in pairs."

Hana's brow furrowed. "Yes, I thought so too. There may have been another stationed outside, but we didn't see anyone."

"I saw a man with dark hair outside when we escaped to find a taxi, but no way to say he was of North Korean descent," Jarek added.

"But you're sure you weren't followed here?" Mack asked.

"We don't know anything for sure," Jarek said. "I felt certain we lost the North Korean in Chicago, yet somehow they must have picked up our trail." He glanced at Hana.

"After seeing you in disguise, I guess I should have known there was more to why you'd arrived when you did. You have amazing skills, Hana. But I think it's clear now that your new identity has been compromised."

"Very likely," her mother agreed.

Sun didn't like the sound of that. "Okay, you can stay here in this room, it's under an assumed name that is not associated with any of us. You can get some rest, but Mack and I have work to do."

"You can stay here with your parents," Mack said, but Sun cut him off with a narrow glare.

"This is my case as much as it's yours," she reminded him.

He grimaced. "I just want you to be safe and to have time with your parents."

"Sun is right, there's time for that later. I plan to help find the bomb." Her mother's gaze was steady. "Trust me, I have been in many dangerous situations before."

Sun was still grappling with the idea that her mother had been spying on North Korea. "I know you have, but I would rather you and, uh, Jarek get far away from here. Before it's too late."

"No," Jarek's response surprised her. "Sun, I don't want to leave you like this. Not without getting to know you." Her father's voice cracked with emotion. "I didn't even know you existed until yesterday. I accept the danger. As Hana said, I was nearly killed in Chicago anyway. Life is short, Sun. Now that I've found you, I plan to stay. Please don't expect me to walk away from you now."

As touched as she was by his declaration, she wanted to scream in frustration. "Don't you understand? I need to know you and my mother are safe from all this."

"Better for us to stay together, Sun," her mother said softly. "You know the regime is close by."

They'd already fought off several attacks by the Russians, adding North Koreans to the mix only made things worse.

"The danger," Sun began, but her father interrupted, "is all around us, but as your mother said, better we stick together." His jaw firmed, and she fought the urge to hug him. For not having a father figure, she felt certain she could get used to this man being in her life.

If they had a life after today.

Her phone rang, and since the call was from Jordan, she quickly answered. "Do you have the security clearance IDs?"

"Yes, and I can meet you and Mack downtown," Jordan replied.

"Add two more, for Hana Yin-lee and Jarek Zeman. My parents are here and want to help."

"Your parents?" Jordan's voice rose incredulously. "Are you crazy?"

"First of all, my mother has been spying on North Korea, so she's already involved. She's the source of the chatter about the nuke. Besides, it's what they both want to do, and there isn't time to argue. It's going to take us time to get downtown to the National Mall area to begin checking out garbage containers."

There was a pause, then Jordan said, "Okay, I'll get two more security passes and join you in searching."

Sun wanted to protest, after all, Jordan had a wife, a daughter, and a baby on the way. Which made her understand why Mack had wanted her to leave.

The same reason she wanted her parents far, far away.

"Bring the passes, but after that, your time would be

better spent convincing Yates and the president to chuck the whole event." She disconnected from the call and glanced over to where Mack was packing up the sat computer. "Ready?"

"Yes."

She still wore her jacket and had the car keys, so she led the way outside. Her mother and father followed close behind.

Two Russians emerged from the darkness, each holding guns pointed at her. She stopped, and her heart thumped heavily against her chest.

The tables had been turned. Instead of tracking Mikhail and Kirill, the Russians had tracked her and Mack instead.

CHAPTER TWENTY-ONE

January 20 – 2:58 a.m. – Washington, DC

Mack unplugged the computer, packed it away, and was looping the computer bag over his shoulder when he heard Hana suck in a harsh breath and her whispered words in Korean warning of danger. He reacted instinctively, hitting the light switch off and dropping to the ground inside the motel room, using the computer bag as a shield in front of his head.

He pulled his weapon and noticed two Russian thugs both armed with handguns. Mikhail and Kirill, no doubt. From here, he couldn't see the telltale red-and-black star tattoo but felt certain they each had one.

There wasn't a lot of time to think things through, every instinct in his body indicated this was a do-or-die situation.

Taking careful aim from his location on the floor, he found himself praying that no one would move as he squeezed the trigger twice in rapid succession.

Deep voices howled in pain as he hit his marks, shooting both men in the lower abdomen. Not a kill shot, he hoped, but enough to prevent them from shooting back.

Or not. Twin gunshots rang out, and he watched in horror as Sun and Hana did some sort of gymnastic moves that had them dancing toward the gunman, each taking on one of the Russians. Why Sun didn't shoot them, he wasn't sure, but maybe because of her mother likely not having a gun.

With Sun and Hana in the fray, he couldn't shoot again, not unless he had a clear shot at the Russians. He reached up and yanked Jarek down beside him.

"Hana! Sun!" Jarek gasped.

"Stay down," Mack ordered, then sprinted to his feet and ran through the doorway of the motel room toward where the women were doing their best to disarm the Russians.

He saw Sun kick the guy she was tangling with in the lower abdominal area where he'd shot him and felt a surge of approval. He grabbed the guy's wrist, wrenched the gun away from him, and hit him in the back of the head. As the Russian went down, he caught a glimpse of the red-and-black star tattoo.

One down, one to go.

Mack whirled toward the Russian Hana was fighting with and was nonplussed to realize she was just as good as Sun in hand-to-hand combat. And Jarek hadn't listened to Mack's order to stay down but had rushed the Russian, using his head to hit the other man in the face. The Russian reared back, blood streaming from his broken nose, giving Mack the few seconds he needed to disarm him and put him down too.

But it wasn't over. The sound of police sirens indicated the gunshots had been called in, likely from the kid in the lobby.

"We have to go, now!" Sun said, pulling on her mother's arm.

Jarek was holding his head, having discovered headbutts weren't as easy as they looked on TV. Mack put a hand on the older man's shoulder. "The SUV is that way." He indicated where Sun had parked it.

Jarek stumbled after Sun and Hana, so Mack took a moment to scoop up the sat computer before following. Hana and Jarek had both gotten in the back, so he slid into the passenger seat beside Sun. Within seconds, they were barreling out of the motel parking lot and heading back toward downtown DC.

"How did the Russians find us?" Sun asked, wiping her hand over her brow.

"They may have somehow tracked the phone I used to call them," Mack admitted grimly. "I'm sorry, Sun."

"For what?" She shot him an exasperated look. "We had to follow up on the Russian lead, Mack. There isn't anything you could have done differently."

Logically, he knew she was right, but guilt plagued him anyway. He took the disposable phone he'd used to try to contact Mikhail and tossed it out the window.

"Jarek, are you all right?" Hana asked.

"I'll be fine, but where did you learn to fight like that?" Jarek asked. "Do they teach that in spy school? I almost had a heart attack when you and Sun did handsprings toward them."

"I learned to do what was necessary to survive long before I began spying on North Korea," Hana said softly. "I wish I had some ice for your head. I'm sure it's very painful."

"I'll be fine," Jarek said, a hint of obstinacy in his tone.

Mack turned to look at Sun's father. He looked pale and winced every time they passed a bright light. "You probably have a concussion. Maybe you would be better off driving Hana away from here until Sun and I can meet up with you."

"No," Hana and Jarek said at the same time.

Mack sighed and turned back to face the windshield. "Now I see where you get your stubborn streak, Sun."

A smile flitted across her features. "Apparently."

He shook his head wryly. "Do you want me to call Jordan? Find out where he's meeting us?"

Sun pulled her cell phone from her pocket and handed it to him. "Let him know about the incident with the Russians, just in case the lobby clerk gave the local authorities our license plate number."

"Okay." He dialed Jordan's number, thinking the locals were the least of their worries.

They still had the regime on their tail as well as a nuclear bomb to find.

This wasn't over, not by a long shot.

And it was humbling to realize only God could help them now.

JANUARY 20 – 3:21 *a.m.* – *Washington, DC*

Jarek closed his eyes against the throbbing pain in his head, trying to hold back the urge to throw up.

He would not look like a wimp in front of Hana.

Although he knew full well she was far more athletic than he. Sun too. When the two women had sprang into action, in what seemed to be identical choreographed moves, he'd been stunned speechless.

Then the gunfire and Mack pulling him down had

made him realize Hana and Sun had rushed forward to protect him.

How pathetic was that?

His cheeks burned with embarrassment, and he was certain Sun's young man thought him weak and ineffective.

And maybe he was, at least when it came to fighting and shooting.

He'd never even gone hunting, never understanding the allure of the sport.

"Jarek? Are you okay?" Hana's soft question made him feel even worse.

"Fine," he snapped. Then he softened his tone to add, "I wish there was more I could have done to help. You and Sun were amazing. Mack too."

He felt Hana's hand on his arm. "Jarek, you don't seem to understand that I'm the one that has caused you to be in danger. Not just my travels into North Korea to gather information, but because of who I am. That without me you would be free to live your life any way you choose without fear."

He turned his head to gaze down at her. "I choose you, Hana."

Their gazes clung for a long moment until he noticed Sun watching them in the rearview mirror. He smiled and tried to shake off his depressing thoughts of inadequacy.

He was here with his daughter and the woman he loved. Maybe they were in extreme danger, and maybe they wouldn't survive the day, but he would cherish every moment of time God granted to him.

This right here was all that mattered.

JANUARY 20 – 3:30 *a.m.* – *Washington, DC*

Getting one's hands dirty was not all it's cracked up to be. Disgusting really, but there was nothing else to do when surrounded by incompetence but take care of business yourself. Failure always deserved death.

There was not a moment to waste.

Things were spiraling way out of control, unraveling at the seams. If this mission was not successful, then the power holding North Korea would be at risk.

And that was an unacceptable outcome.

A quick swipe of the blade against the dead man's clothes was all there was time for, as time was of the essence.

Soon, very soon, all would be right. The survival of the regime and the planning of the successor was all that mattered. Some had even begun to suspect the truth about the man pretending to be the Supreme Leader. But that would be taken care of soon enough. The announcement would come right after the US Presidential Inauguration.

Speed and timing were most critical.

JANUARY 20 – 3:39 *a.m.* – *Washington, DC*

Sun peered through the windshield, trying to catch a glimpse of Jordan. He was supposed to meet them near the Capitol South Metro station. The area was quiet, but not for long as the trains were scheduled to start running as of 4:00 a.m.

People would be gathering in the area soon after, which added to the level of urgency. They desperately needed to find something very soon.

"There he is," Mack said, gesturing to the right. "He's in the SUV there."

"I see him." Sun had no idea where they could leave the

SUV, there was clearly no parking anywhere in the area. Although at this point, the way her parents kept refusing to drive to safety, they may as well allow the thing to be towed away. Easier than trying to deal with finding a parking garage that wasn't located on one of the closed streets.

She pulled up next to Jordan, noticing Sloan was seated beside him, and rolled down the passenger window and leaned past Mack to ask, "You have the passes?"

"Right here." Jordan held them up. There were the promised four security ID badges. "We have our own, too, and hope to pitch in, but not until after our meeting with Yates. I'm hoping to be finished within the hour."

"You have to convince him to call off the inauguration," Mack said somberly.

"That's the plan, but if you guys could find something, it would help," Jordan agreed.

"We'll do our best. One of you need to take the SUV, or it will be towed," Sun pointed out.

Jordan glanced at Sloan. "Fine, we'll find a place to leave the two vehicles, then join you here to search after we meet with Yates." Jordan looked as if he hadn't gotten much sleep either. "I'm hoping the news of the second attack by the Russians helps to sway him to cancel the whole thing."

"Good luck with that." Mack took the four security passes and handed them out to everyone in the SUV.

Sun slid out from behind the wheel, looping the lanyard around her neck. Her parents joined her as did Mack, still lugging the sat computer.

"We're not going to need the computer to search," she said with a frown.

Mack patted the bag. "I'm kinda attached to it. Besides, I have the garbage container information on here."

"All right." She crossed the street, heading toward the

expansive area in front of the Capitol known as the National Mall. The half-moon was bright, the air frigid enough to see their breath.

She tried to remain positive but couldn't help wondering if focusing on the garbage containers was the right thing to do. Yet what else was there? With all the security, it's the one thing that could be easily missed.

Surprisingly, there were not very many Capitol police out patrolling the area. Maybe because of the early hour. Still, she'd expected to be stopped and questioned as they approached the cordoned-off area.

A warning tingle snaked down her spine. If they could get in so easily, certainly others could as well.

The thought of someone within the Capitol building pulling strings even to the point of messing with security was sobering. It didn't make any sense, although again, maybe it was just too early for the police to be out in full force.

Sun hurried to the center of Fourth Street, standing directly in front of the Capitol. The lights were bright here, yet not nearly as much as she'd hoped.

"I suggest we start looking at the garbage containers closest to the Capitol building itself," Mack said. "We'll need to fan out to cover more ground."

"What exactly are we looking for?" Jarek asked. "I'm sure the bomb will be disguised in some way."

"We have reason to believe it may be in a backpack or some other carrying case," Mack said. "Small enough for a man to carry but big enough to be noticed."

"And if you do find something suspicious, don't touch it," Sun warned. "Once we verify something is here, we'll call the Feds and NSA, along with the bomb squad and any other local agencies that need to be involved."

"I understand, Sun," Hana said, resting a hand on her shoulder. "We do not want to be responsible for a nuclear tragedy."

This time, Sun couldn't help herself. She threw her arms around her mother, giving her a big hug, then moved on to do the same with her father, the tall man with graying temples who had clearly won her mother's heart.

"Stay safe," Sun whispered before releasing him. She glanced at her mother. "Both of you."

Her parents nodded and moved off to the right of the Capitol building.

She looked at Mack who was looking at her with a strange expression on his face. "What?"

He shook his head as if to indicate nothing was wrong, but then he hauled her into his arms for a kiss. A long, intense, powerful kiss that had the ability to wipe away all thoughts of the Russians, nuclear bombs, and even the regime.

When they came up for badly needed air, she leaned weakly against him. "Wow," she whispered.

"Ditto," Mack murmured back. "I need you to stay safe too, Sun."

She lifted her head and smiled up at him. "Ditto."

For a long moment, neither of them moved or said anything more. Reluctantly, she pulled out of his arms and drew in a ragged breath in an attempt to clear her muddled thoughts. "Garbage cans."

"Yeah. Let's hope we find something soon," Mack said.

She headed off to the left, with Mack going in the same direction but not as far. When she approached the first garbage bin, her pulse kicked up into triple digits.

It was the perfect size to hide a small nuclear bomb.

Holding her breath, she peered inside, but then let out a soundless sigh.

Nothing. The can was empty.

Refusing to become discouraged, she went over to the next garbage can. Also empty. She leaned over, patting the sides to make sure she wasn't missing something.

She wasn't.

Sun swallowed hard and moved on to the next one. She glanced around, noticing a few Capitol police officers were gathered in the center of Union Square.

Odd that they hadn't noticed her or Mack or her parents moving from one garbage container to the next. Then again, they were also moving farther and farther away from the Capitol itself. Maybe the darkness broken only by the lights of the Capitol and the moon was enough to put them in the shadows.

As she checked yet another garbage can without success, the niggle of doubt grew larger.

What if they were on the wrong track?

JANUARY 20 – 4:45 a.m. – Washington, DC

The knot in Mack's gut tightened as he searched garbage containers that were so far back from the Capitol he had a hard time believing the nuke was hidden in any one of them.

The four of them had been searching for the past hour without success.

Which meant this brilliant idea was nothing but a big, fat dud.

He figured they should finish searching the garbage cans before trying to come up with another plan. What that might entail, he had no clue.

The Russians had tried to take them out at the motel, which meant there had to be a Russian nuke here somewhere. And how would they place the blame on North Korea? No clue.

After finding two more empty garbage cans, he turned and stared back at the Capitol. The building seemed far away from where he stood near the Smithsonian Museum of Natural History, yet he knew it wasn't.

How much farther back should they go?

He pulled the satellite computer off his shoulder and powered it up.

What was he missing? The garbage can concept had seemed the most likely scenario, but he was forced to admit he was wrong.

But if not hidden in garbage cans, then what? How could anyone sneak a nuclear bomb into one of these heavily secured buildings?

The sound of some sort of scuffle reached his ears. He froze, then quickly shut the computer and slid it back into the case. He was so far back he'd lost sight of Sun and her parents.

Should he call out to her? Some deep intuition warned him not to.

Listening intently, he moved toward the direction he thought he'd heard the scuffling noise, staying hidden in the shadows as much as possible. He couldn't see any sign of a struggle, which was good and bad.

Good if he'd only heard Sun going through garbage cans. Bad if someone was under attack.

What if someone had managed to get the drop on Sun?

His instincts were screaming at him that something was wrong, but he did his best not to overreact.

Sun had proven herself more than capable of holding her own against any threat. Even two Russian thugs.

The scuffling sounds grew louder now, so Mack gave up trying to keep in the shadows. He darted toward a small group of trees and nearly choked in horror as he watched two men who appeared to be North Koreans fighting with Sun.

And from here? It looked as if they were winning. Why hadn't Sun simply shot them?

"Sun! Stop! Police!" Mack shouted, hoping the Capitol police who should be ensuring the safety of the area could hear him. He joined the melee, swinging the sat computer at the Korean's head, hitting him with a loud whack.

His shout must have provided Sun with a much-needed advantage because she slammed the palm of her hand up and into the nose of the North Korean he hadn't hit.

He finished off the guy he'd hit with the computer, chopping him in the back of his neck with enough force that pain shot up his arm. When the guy slumped to the ground, he quickly moved forward to help Sun.

Thankfully, she already had her guy under control as well. For a moment they stood, breathing heavily as the two North Koreans lay sprawled on the ground at their feet. He stepped forward, wanting nothing more than to haul her into his arms, but she pushed him away.

"My parents," she whispered.

A chill settled over him. Sun was right. If these two Koreans had come for her, there would be others going after her parents. "Where are they? At the Hirshhorn Museum?"

"I think so. Hurry!"

CHAPTER TWENTY-TWO

January 20 – 5:12 a.m. – Washington, DC

Hana felt the person behind her and spun away seconds before the attack. Still, she felt the slice of the blade along her arm but ignored the pain. She managed to kick and deflect the second blow, but then she felt another slice along her back. Not as deep as it may have been but enough to cause a flash of pain.

Two men flanked her now in the shadows of the Hirshhorn Museum, and she tried not to feel desperate in her attempt to fight them off. She was well trained, but still a woman, while these men had knives.

"No!" Jarek's scream caused one of the men to pause just long enough for her to plant her foot in his face. He stumbled back, reaching up to the blood gushing from his nose.

Inwardly she prayed for Jarek to stay away, knowing he'd likely be killed if he tried to help. She attacked again and again, moving instinctively, even as her heart squeezed in her chest for the brief love she was about to lose.

Better for her to die than Sun, who had her whole life

ahead of her. She'd made peace with her decision to infiltrate the land of her birth. Sun's future was here in America.

Blood congealed on the ground, the cold air turning it to slush. She slipped and went down, just in time to evade another thrust of the knife.

Anger spurred her into action. She gracefully leaped up, kicked the man in the groin, then chopped down on the wrist holding the knife. Hearing it clatter to the ground gave her a sense of satisfaction.

But the second man was on her now. She tried twisting from his grip, but he didn't budge. She stomped on his foot and threw her head back into his face, hitting his broken nose for the second time.

He swore at her in North Korean, and his hold loosened just enough for her to wrench free. But the first man was swooping up the fallen knife, and she feared she wouldn't be able to hold them both off much longer.

Suddenly two figures came onto the scene, each going after one of the two North Koreans. It took Hana a moment to realize Sun and Mack had come to their rescue.

She staggered backward, trying not to cry out in pain. Now that she was no longer under attack, the two knife wounds burned as if she were on fire.

Jarek, she needed to help Jarek.

Within moments, Sun and Mack had the two North Koreans flat on the ground, their weapons confiscated. Breathing heavily, Hana turned, sweeping her gaze over the area.

There was no sign of Jarek.

A stab of fear hit hard. "Jarek? Jarek!"

Nothing.

Sun crossed over. "You're bleeding, we need to get those wounds taken care of."

"Not until we find your father." Hana reached out to grab Sun's arm. "There's more I need to tell you, but not now. Hurry! We must find Jarek."

"Mack?" Sun called out. "We need to find my father."

"I have him," said a female voice. Hana froze when a slender woman stepped from the shadows with Jarek at her side. She was pinching the trigger point in his neck that basically rendered him useless to fight back. His face was twisted in agony from the pain the woman was inflicting. "So we finally meet face-to-face, sister."

Hana's blood ran cold. "Kim Jong-il. I can't believe you came all this way yourself just to execute me."

"You and your daughter." Kim Jong-il was the younger sister and second-in-command behind Kim Jong-un. Hana's real name was Kim Jong-ki, she was twenty years older than her younger sister.

And had never met her face-to-face until now.

"You being here must mean our brother is not doing well," Hana mused, trying to buy time. "I've suspected he's on death's door, his health has been terrible. Where did you find the imposter anyway? He is very skilled. Yet here you are. I'm sure you've come to tie up loose ends so that there is no one else who can take away the command of the country from your greedy little fingers."

"Yes, exactly," Kim Jong-il said as if they were talking about meal planning rather than a straight-up execution. "I'm glad you understand."

"But I don't understand." Hana took a subtle step forward, avoiding the fear and pain in Jarek's gaze. "I am no threat to you, sister, and neither is Sun. We want nothing to do with our homeland. There is no reason to kill us."

"There is every reason," Kim Jong-il hissed. "You have brought shame to our family, turned your back on our country, and worse, infiltrated the regime to leak information to our enemies! A swift death is too good for you. You deserve to die slowly and painfully."

Hana swallowed hard. Clearly, she had underestimated her younger sister's need for power. She wished she knew how her spying had been uncovered, not that it mattered. Still, Hana couldn't help wondering if she hadn't defected, she could have helped Kim Jong-il become a better person. To see the regime for what it was.

But it was far too late now.

"Let him go, sister," Hana said. "It's me and Sun you want. We will go with you peacefully."

"No. You will all need to come with me." Kim Jong-il tightened her grip on Jarek's neck, making him cry out in pain.

"Sister, listen carefully. If something happens to you, who will take over as the Supreme Leader?" Hana asked, risking another step forward. "Our brother is on death's door, the rumors are too many to ignore. I promise you on our mother's grave that I will never return to our homeland, that I will never attempt to take over or to gather information for your enemies. But if you don't leave now, then you risk failing the entire regime, all those counting on your leadership."

For a moment, Hana thought she'd finally gotten through to her sister. But then her sister pulled out a small yet lethal-looking gun.

"You will do as I say, or I'll shoot you all right here." Kim Jung-il smiled, but it wasn't pretty. "I am an expert marksman, sister."

Hana didn't dare tear her gaze away from the woman

holding captive the man she loved and took another step forward, surrendering herself.

She would have given her life, and had in a way, so that Jarek could live his.

Yet despite their best efforts, Hana knew with sick certainty they would both die here today.

Sun too.

JANUARY 20 – 5:28 *a.m.* – *Washington, DC*

Mack still had his weapon, but the idea of shooting the successor to the North Korean regime gave him pause. The political fallout was beyond comprehension.

Never in his wildest dreams had he imagined that Sun's mother was the older sister of Kim Jong-un. The stunning news was quickly followed by the realization that Sun was the ruler's niece.

Both mother and daughter had blood ties to the regime that couldn't be ignored.

And where were the Capitol police anyway? A gunshot would likely bring someone running, but Mack feared it would be too late.

"There's something you should know," Sun said abruptly. "There's a small nuclear bomb hidden somewhere in this area that will be set off during the inauguration ceremony, and the blame will be placed on North Korea."

"That's a lie. We haven't tested our nuclear rockets in over a year," Kim Jong-il said haughtily.

"I understand, however, the Russians are attempting to cause a problem for our respective countries," Sun continued. "If we don't find this nuclear bomb, North Korea will come under swift and ruthless retaliation from the United

States government. Just before you have time to take over as Supreme Leader."

Mack had to give Sun credit, the soon-to-be leader of North Korea appeared disturbed by this news.

"She tells the truth, sister," Hana said softly. "This is the information I uncovered during my recent trip to North Korea. You must know there is a faction of countrymen who will do anything to cause you and the regime harm, even if that means cooperating with a plan of this magnitude. And while I despise the regime, I cannot condone a global war."

"No," Kim Jong-il whispered. "That's not possible."

"Your men can vouch for the fact that we have been searching garbage containers in an effort to find this device," Hana continued. "If we are unsuccessful and it goes off, my death and Sun's will be meaningless. Do you really want to be in charge of a country that will be at war with the United States of America?"

For a long tense moment Kim Jong-il said nothing.

Mack decided to jump in. "We learned the Russians are responsible for smuggling in the nuclear bomb, but they have somehow set it up so that North Korea will take the blame. We're not exactly sure how, but we have been attacked several times by Russian men in an effort to stop us from finding the bomb. I can have you speak to my boss, Ken Tramall, in the National Security Agency if you want to corroborate our story."

"Why else would we be here in this place at this hour?" Sun added. "There is no reason for us to lie to you."

Kim Jong-il was silent for a long moment, then narrowed her gaze and abruptly nodded. "Okay, fine. I will take this man as my hostage as you continue searching for the device."

"No, let Jarek go, we will search regardless," Hana pleaded.

"Stop wasting time." Kim Jong-il waved her gun. "Go now."

Mack wasn't about to leave Jarek in this woman's hands. They'd already wasted enough time fighting off attackers. Time which would have been better spent searching.

Hana turned away, and Sun stepped up to embrace her mother. Mack was farther back, but he hefted the knife he'd taken off one of the North Koreans in his hand, wondering if he should take a chance. When Sun moved with Hana away from Kim Jong-il, he had a clear shot at her.

It was now or never.

In a swift movement, he threw the knife at Kim Jong-il, aiming for the vulnerable area between her clavicle and her right shoulder.

Her gun hand.

The knife blade spun tip over handle, then landed in the hollow of her shoulder. Kim Jong-il recoiled, letting go of Jarek and dropping the gun. Sun and her mother went over to grab her.

He had to give the woman credit, she didn't scream or cry out in agony. Apparently, those in the regime did not show weakness. Mack went over and helped Jarek to his feet, but the man was pale and shaky, and he hoped he wasn't having a full-blown heart attack.

The danger from the regime was over, at least for now.

But the nuclear bomb was still out there, somewhere. And Mack had no idea where to begin searching next.

JANUARY 20 – 5:59 a.m. – Washington, DC

Sun was still reeling from the news that she was actually related to Kim Jong-un and the long-presiding family ruling the entire North Korean regime. Easy to understand now why her mother had sent her away to Mensa school, stayed far away, and had begun to spy on her homeland. It also explained why her mother never told Jarek about her.

So many secrets and endless danger, all because the regime would stop at nothing to get what they wanted.

There wasn't time to worry about that now. She and her mother were holding on to Kim Jong-il, but they needed a plan.

There was still a nuclear bomb to find.

"Mack? Call Jordan, see if he can come take Kim Jong-il into custody." Sun couldn't come up with a better option of keeping Kim Jong-il out of their hair. Besides, the knife was still sticking out of the woman's shoulder, and she didn't dare remove it without medical advice. The vision of Chandler bleeding out on the sidewalk in front of the coffee shop was still far too clear in her mind.

Where had Mack learned that knife-throwing trick anyway? If they survived this, she planned on making him teach her how to do it. The skill would come in handy if their FBI consultant kept handing them impossible jobs like this one.

"Custody? I'm the Supreme Leader of North Korea!" Kim Jong-il shouted.

Sun tightened her grip on her aunt's arm. "Then act like it," she hissed. "You don't kill people because they leave your country and because they *might* do something you don't want them to do. Besides, the information that my mother took from your country eventually helps you too. Don't you understand? The longer you hold us up here, the more likely your country will be blamed for this bomb going off." A thought occurred to her. "And maybe the information about my mother's location was leaked at this specific time to assist in helping to blame your country. Can you imagine if they found out that an heir to the regime was killed during the nuclear blast?"

The more she thought about it, the more she believed all of this happening at the same time was no coincidence. Especially if the rumors of Kim Jong-un's severe illness were true. The conductor of this plan had covered all the bases.

"Stop wasting time and begin searching," Kim Jong-il commanded. At least her aunt had the whole issuing orders part of being in charge down pat. "And remove this knife from my shoulder immediately."

"I would keep searching, except I can't trust you. And you'll lose more blood if we remove the knife without medical help being nearby." As it was, Sun wanted to punch the woman in the stomach for hurting her father. Wanted to, but wouldn't.

Mack spoke quickly into his phone, then nodded and disconnected. "He and Sloan are on their way, they just returned from their meeting with Yates."

"And is Yates going to talk to the president?" she asked.

Mack grimaced. "He is, yes. But Jordan didn't sound hopeful that the ceremony would be called off."

Sun swallowed a surge of annoyance. Whatever happened to being hyperalert to possible terror attacks? Haven't they learned anything over the past year?

A wave of frustration hit hard. Complete idiots ran their country, no matter what side of the political fence they happened to sit on.

When Jordan arrived, Sun quickly filled him in on the highlights. The North Koreans that had attacked them were struggling to their feet, looking at Sun and Hana warily as they held their leader captive.

"You need to take her someplace for the next few hours," Sun told Jordan. "Get her medical attention while keeping her from calling any more reinforcements in yet another attempt to take us out of commission. I don't even know what happened to the two North Koreans who attacked me and Mack near the Smithsonian Museum of History."

Jordan frowned. "Four North Koreans total?"

"Five if you count her," Sun said, jutting her chin in Kim Jong-il's direction. "Oh, and take my parents with you, they've both been injured. My mother in particular needs her wounds looked at by Natalia. As you can see, she's already lost a lot of blood."

"Got it," Jordan agreed. "Let's go, Ms. Jong-il."

"Commander," Kim Jong-il shot back. "I will be addressed as Commander."

"Okay, then, Commander," Jordan replied smoothly. "We will be happy to put you on a plane back to North Korea once this is over."

Sun could tell her mother didn't want to go with Jordan for medical care, but this time she wasn't taking no for an answer. "You and Jarek both need to be looked at by Natalia, she's a very experienced critical care nurse. You're bleeding from two knife wounds, Mom, and Jarek's arm is still numb. If the injuries are bad enough, Natalia will make sure you get the hospital treatment you and Dad need." She hesitated, then added, "Please, Mom, I need you to do this for me. I need to know you and my dad are all right."

Hana nodded. "Sun, everything I have done was ultimately to protect you. I'm sorry you had to learn about our blood relation to the regime like this."

"We can discuss that more later," Sun said.

"You must find this device, Sun. Please," her mother

urged. "I can't bear for all of this to have happened for nothing."

Sun nodded, especially because she felt the same way. "That's the goal. Now go, get some help."

Her mother nodded and accompanied Jordan and Kim Jong-il, along with Sloan and her father, away from the Hirshhorn National Mall area.

Sun stood for a moment watching. Mack came up behind her and placed his hands on her shoulders. "Are you okay?"

The sweet concern in his voice was nearly her undoing. So much had happened in the past few hours, but the biggest shock was learning she was actually related by blood to the North Korean regime.

When she didn't answer, Mack came around and pulled her into his arms. "It's okay," he soothed. "Your parents are going to be okay. Natalia will take care of everything, better than any doctor."

Curling her fingertips into his winter jacket, she clung to him, resting her forehead on his broad chest. Mack may have broken her silly heart years ago, but he'd been nothing but incredible over these past thirty-six hours.

She'd never have made it this far without him.

"I . . . don't know what to say," she whispered. "I mean, to be related to a communist dictator regime? How insane is that?"

"You're still Sun Yin-lee, the most brilliant, talented, and lethal woman I know," Mack said, wrapping his arms around her and holding her tight. "Don't let this mess with your head."

She let out a choked laugh, thinking that being held in Mack's arms like this was far more likely to mess with her head. It felt so good, so right to be in his arms, but they couldn't just stand here clinging to each other.

There was a bomb to find.

With reluctance, she lifted her head and loosened her grip on his jacket. "Thanks," she murmured. "I needed that hug."

"Anytime. And I need this." He swooped in and kissed her. His lips were warm and sent a thrill of anticipation washing over her. She angled her head to deepen their embrace.

Mack's kiss warmed her from the inside out, and she leaned against him, returning his kiss with all the emotion she'd been keeping bottled up inside.

And trying not to think about the fact that they may not live to have a future.

"Hey, you guys can't be here," a deep voice said, rudely interrupting their kiss.

Sun leaned back and glared over her shoulder. Sure, now the Capitol police showed up. Talk about being a day late and a dollar short.

"We have clearance to be here," Sun said, pulling out her security badge.

"Why, so you can neck with your boyfriend?" the cop asked snidely without bothering to look closely at her badge. "I heard a ruckus over here and came to investigate. What's with all this red paint on the ground?"

It wasn't paint, it was blood. Her mother's blood. The cop was lucky she was feeling mellow after Mack's kiss or she may have been tempted to have him arrested for being stupid.

"We're checking things out for the FBI," Mack said. "Excuse us, we have more work to do."

"Work, yeah, sure," the cop said in a snarky tone.

Sun held her tongue with an effort, but as soon as they were out of earshot, she turned to face Mack. "What kind of cop doesn't inspect our security credentials on Inauguration Day?"

Mack smiled. "The lazy kind, but let's just ignore that for a moment. Do we keep checking garbage containers or do we move onto another theory?"

She blew out a breath. It was a good question. "How many more are out there to check?"

"Lots, if you go the entire length of the mall," Mack said wryly. "But I just don't see this bomb being triggered from a distance as far away as the Washington Monument."

Sun glanced around. "We're about halfway between the Capitol and the monument now. If none of these garbage containers are hiding the nuke, then I'm not sure where else to look. Every one of these buildings is closed because of the ceremony, so I don't see how anyone could have hidden a bomb inside."

"I agree." Mack sounded completely dejected, and she understood.

Dawn was still a good hour away, so there was still time for them to stop the attack from happening.

If they had any clue where to look next.

CHAPTER TWENTY-THREE

January 20 – 6:23 a.m. – Washington, DC

He'd heard nothing from the Russians, which could only mean bad news.

How could they have failed him? After he'd paid their astronomical fee?

Curling his fingers into fists, he tried not to panic. He'd been listening to the local news since he'd crawled out of bed, and so far there was no indication whatsoever that the upcoming inauguration ceremony had been canceled.

Either Yin-lee and Remington had been taken care of or they hadn't found the bomb.

Unfortunately, it was still too early to claim victory. He wanted to believe the Russians would deliver, but he was already regretting the deal he'd made with the devil. And if he tried to protest, they might try to silence him too.

His stomach was so tied up in knots he couldn't eat. Instead, he sipped his coffee to ward off the overwhelming fatigue. He hadn't gotten a decent night's sleep since everything started to unravel, and he needed to be on his toes.

Today was the day he'd been preparing for over the past few weeks.

His presence was required at the inauguration, but he had an escape plan lined up. Of course, his wife knew nothing about that, but there was no need to worry her pretty little head about the main event that would take place in roughly six hours. He'd simply get them both out of there and pretend to be shocked and horrified like the rest of the country. There would soon be new leadership, as was the plan he and two others had created.

After finishing his coffee, he went into the bedroom to dress. He'd wear his power suit, as this certainly was the beginning of a new era.

One in which only the very strong and the very smart would survive.

JANUARY 20 – 6:37 *a.m.* – *Washington, DC*

Mack and Sun had wasted almost an hour searching for the possibly fictitious bomb. Maybe it was time to call in the K-9s, although she wasn't sure the average bomb-sniffing dog would alert on nuclear material such as uranium and plutonium. As far as she knew, they were trained to detect TNT and gunpowder.

The semicircle area surrounding the Capitol was now teeming with people. Those who had come to watch this moment in history, those with press passes, and far too many governmental officials for his liking.

"We need to keep an eye out for the blond guy that spoke North Korean and disappeared into the building yesterday." Incredible to realize that twenty-four hours hadn't even passed since he'd followed the guy.

Sun grimaced. "I'll try, but trying to pick him out of this crowd will be like finding a penny in the Potomac."

He knew she was right, but what else did they have to go on? They'd walked the entire area of the National Mall, hoping some brilliant idea would come to him.

But there was nothing. Jordan had asked the Secret Service to double-check the rooftops of the Smithsonian museums, the Hirshhorn Museum, and the National Gallery of Art.

They hadn't found anything.

There were other buildings located outside the National Mall, and he had requested those be searched as well. But he doubted they'd find anything significant there either.

Deep in his gut, he felt certain the nuke would be close. Otherwise, there was no guarantee of success.

He shivered and stomped his feet to increase circulation. Being out in the cold for the past several hours had chilled him to the bone.

Which meant Sun was likely even more frozen. She didn't have the excess muscle on her frame that he did.

He could always kiss her again. The idea made him smile, despite the grimness of their situation. But the smile quickly faded as he realized if they didn't find this thing, they would never have the chance to kiss again.

To explore these feelings that had developed over the past day and a half.

Well, to be honest, his feelings toward Sun had always been complicated. But now they were clear as day.

He loved her. Why he'd ever dated Abigail, he had no idea.

Sure, both of them were beautiful, yet Sun was everything Abigail wasn't—maddeningly independent, competitive, and stubborn. Three traits he found oddly endearing.

Most of the time.

He gave himself a mental shake. He needed to remain focused or they'd never have a future together.

Where in the world was that bomb?

"Are we just going to stand here for the rest of the morning?" Sun asked with a shiver. "I'd like to warm up a bit."

"Yeah, let's do that." He gripped her hand and threaded through the crowd. His gaze narrowed on a small coffee and hot chocolate stand. "I didn't realize they'd have sidewalk vendors. Don't forget to take your antibiotic too."

"I will, but speaking of vendors, you think that one of them may have the bomb?" Sun asked. "I would think they'd be screened by the Secret Service prior to being allowed in."

"I don't know, but let's take a look. And get hot coffee while we're at it." Mack quickened his pace. Was this the key? Had one of the vendors managed to smuggle in the nuke?

And how many vendors would be allowed in anyway?

He found himself hoping and praying they had time to check them all.

JANUARY 20 – 7:12 a.m. – Washington, DC

Sun swallowed her antibiotic and clasped her cup of coffee close to her chest in an attempt to soak up the minute bit of warmth. Mack was going through the small vendor cart, returning a few minutes later.

"It's clean." He took a sip of his coffee. "We should split up to check the rest."

She gave a jerky nod, knowing he was right. Who knew

they allowed vendors? A flash of annoyance hit hard. Yates should have prepared them better.

Then again, Yates hadn't really bought into the whole nuke theory. If he had, she felt certain he'd have convinced the president to postpone the ceremony.

She'd never been to an inauguration ceremony before and couldn't believe how crowded the place was already, considering the main event was still several hours away.

Plenty of time to find the bomb. Except that every single idea they'd investigated had proved fruitless.

"I'll take the north side of the mall," Mack said. "You take the south side."

She'd held her coffee for so long it was already growing cold. She nodded and tossed the cup into the garbage. "Let's do this."

Mack pulled her in for a quick kiss. Before she could kiss him back, he released her and wove his way through the crowd to the other side of the mall.

She lightly touched her mouth, realizing how much she'd come to enjoy kissing Mack. Something to think about, if or rather *when* they put this case to rest.

Spurred by fierce determination, Sun lightly jogged to the next sidewalk vendor. Flashing her security badge, she eyed the man serving drinks warily. "I need to check your cart."

"Why? I have been granted permission to be here." He had dark skin, much like Jordan's, and spoke with a hint of an Indian accent.

"Security check, and the sooner you let me in, the faster you can get back to selling coffee and hot chocolate."

The man looked annoyed but stepped back to let her in. The setup was efficient, yet small and tight. No additional space to hide a nuke, even one as small as the potentially new and improved Davy Crockett. Still, she checked the small cupboards and looked into the large vat of coffee before stepping back.

"Thank you." She left and quickly moved onto the next one, even as she sensed they were on the wrong track.

Again.

It was incredibly frustrating.

She was on her fourth vendor when her phone rang. Recognizing Jordan's number, she quickly answered. "Please tell me the ceremony has been called off."

"I wish I could, but no. Everything is still a go at this point." Jordan sounded as exhausted as she was.

"How are my parents?"

"Okay, Natalia is taking good care of them." Jordan hesitated, then added, "We were able to arrange for a private plane to take Kim Jong-il back to North Korea, with several stops along the way."

She'd almost forgotten about her aunt. "That's good except there's no telling she won't make another attempt to come after my mother."

"We've taken care of that," Jordan assured her. "We secretly videotaped her and let her know that if anything ever happened to you or to Hana, we would release the video."

Sun found herself smiling at the news. "Well, that's one bright spot for the day."

"Natalia has just finished suturing your mother's injuries," Jordan continued. "She told me to tell you that the wounds were not as deep as yours and not to worry."

"What about my father?" Sun had only just found the man who'd sired her, and she desperately wanted more time with him.

With both of her parents.

Time they very well may not have.

"He's okay, still in pain from the nerve damage Kim Jong-il inflicted upon him, and he has a mild concussion too."

"Get him to the closest hospital, then, to have an expert examine him," Sun said sharply. "Tell him he needs to do this for me."

"I've been telling him that, but so far it's a no go. He insists he's going to wait until you and Mack find the bomb."

Sun raised her gaze up to the slightly lightening sky as dawn emerged slowly and surely over the horizon. "Can't my mother convince him to see a specialist? What if the nerve damage is permanent?"

"She won't go either," Jordan said on a sigh. "It's like dealing with two stubborn teenagers, only they're adults, so I've given up trying to get them to comply."

"Okay, fine. But, Jordan, if we don't find this thing in the next hour or two, I want you to force them to get out of DC, along with you and Sloan and your respective families. Traveling by subway would be best at least initially, because if this thing blows, the air will be contaminated for at least a hundred miles in all directions, maybe more. With a head start, you should be able to get far enough away to be safe."

"I'll do my best," Jordan promised. "At least as far as your parents go. But I'm not leaving you and Mack behind."

She'd almost reached the next vendor. "You have a family to think about, Jordan. Bryn deserves to grow up in a safe place with both of her parents and so does your unborn child. Sloan and Natalia and their baby too."

"Just find the idiotic thing, okay? Then we won't have to worry about it."

"We're not twiddling our thumbs here, we're in the

process of checking all the sidewalk vendors. Any ideas after that are more than welcome."

"Keep trying," Jordan said. "Listen, I have to go, Yates is on the other line." Before she could respond, he'd disconnected.

As Sun checked the vendor cart, she prayed Yates would pull the plug on this fiasco.

Canceling the event and evacuating the area may be the only thing that would save them, especially since they hadn't found the nuke. If there was a nuke.

She glanced at the time, feeling slightly sick to her stomach. There were already so many people here milling around, and it wasn't even fully light out yet.

How much time would they need to evacuate the area? An hour? Two hours?

And what if even more people showed up? Might it take even longer?

Sun jogged back to Union Square, searching for Mack. They didn't have until noon to find the bomb.

They only had as much time as it would take to evacuate the entire National Mall.

JANUARY 20 – 7:28 a.m. – Washington, DC

Mack silently admitted defeat. The bomb hadn't been smuggled in via one of the vendor carts.

It wasn't hidden in a garbage container or on any of the rooftops nearby.

Maybe it didn't exist at all.

Mack turned to scan the gathering crowd. There were even more people swarming around, and he felt certain he'd never be able to find the blond guy, if he even showed up.

And really, why would he if he knew there was a potential nuke going off?

The thought made him frown. Whoever had planned this would have to come up with some sort of escape route, right? Otherwise, they risked being nuked along with the current president, the president-elect, the current vice president, the current vice president elect, along with other members of Congress.

Considering the crowd that would likely only grow worse as the time of the actual inauguration approached, he wondered what that escape route might entail. Getting from point A to point B in the crush of people wouldn't be quick or easy.

His phone rang, interrupting his thoughts. "Hey, Sun, find anything?"

"No. Meet me in Union Square, we need to come up with another plan."

"Okay. While you're trying to come up with a place to hide a nuke, think about what the escape route might be for the blond guy, if he's the one involved in this."

"Good point. See you soon." Sun disconnected from the call.

He retraced his steps to Union Square, the trek taking longer than earlier thanks to the crowd of people. He must have said *excuse me* a hundred times before he made it to Union Square.

Finding Sun wasn't easy, she was so tiny he couldn't pick her out of the crowd. When she came up behind him, he pulled her close so they could talk without being overheard.

"I'm fresh out of ideas," he murmured.

"I know," Sun agreed, her gaze somber. "I told Jordan to get his family and Sloan's, along with my parents, out of here if we don't come up with anything within the next hour or so."

He stared down at her in surprise. "You think they'll leave?"

"No." She huffed out a breath. "He should, with a baby on the way, Sloan too, but he said they won't go without us."

Mack had to give Jordan and Sloan credit, if he had a baby on the way, he'd want his family protected no matter what. Even without a baby on the way, it was tempting to suggest they simply bug out of there.

But the moment the thought went through his mind he shoved it away.

He loved his country and didn't want to imagine the chaos that would ensue if there really was a bomb and someone actually set it off.

No way would he be able to live with himself if he left when there was even the remotest possibility of preventing a tragedy like that from happening.

Although considering the lack of proof they'd found so far, the entire bomb scare was likely nothing more than an elaborate hoax. One that would cause Russians to come after them and attempt to kill them?

Not likely.

"We might want to find the closest Metro stations," Sun said, interrupting his thoughts. "Just in case something does happen, we'll want to get underground."

"Along with everyone else," Mack muttered. He rubbed his hand over the back of his neck. "I remember there being several stations, one at the Smithsonian, one at the US Department of Energy, the L'Enfant Plaza station."

"Don't forget the Federal Central station and the Federal Triangle Metro Station," Sun added. She frowned. "It's interesting all of these stations are underground."

"Some of the stations farther out aren't underground," Mack felt compelled to point out. "Which makes it a dangerous way to escape a nuclear blast. I've been trying to anticipate what the blond guy has planned."

Sun shrugged. "There may be an underground area within the Capitol for all we know."

"There is, at least according to the blueprints," he acknowledged. "But no access to the subway from what I can tell."

Sun rubbed her hands together and blew on them. "We need to do something, Mack. Standing around and waiting for inspiration to strike is not going to get the job done."

He empathized with her frustration. Someone bumped into him from behind, and he rested his hands on Sun's shoulders to steady himself.

"Sorry," he said. "This crowd is giving me claustrophobia."

"We can try moving off to the side," Sun suggested. "Looks like some musicians are getting ready to set up. Once they start playing, we won't even be able to talk."

"Tell me about it." He gripped Sun's arm and threaded his way through the crowd. Sure enough, a group of musicians had gathered at the southeast end of Union Square.

He could see several musicians, one with a small square case that likely held a flute or a clarinet. Another carried a violin. His gaze lingered over one of the musicians who was lugging a large carrying case as tall as the man holding it. A cello.

Or something else?

Mack frowned, dodging around people, trying to get closer for a better view, but he felt like a salmon attempting to swim upstream. He pushed harder, using his elbows if necessary, ignoring the muttered curses in his wake.

His eyes were glued to the guy carrying the cello case. His heart thundered in his chest and every instinct he had was on red alert. Could this possibly be it? Hadn't the Secret Service vetted these guys?

The man set the cello down, then turned, revealing a dark mark along the side of his neck.

A tattoo? All the Russians they'd dealt with had sported a red-and-black star tattoo.

Desperately wishing for binoculars, he pushed forward, momentarily losing his grip on Sun. Still, he didn't dare look away from the cello guy.

He caught another glimpse, enough to see that the tattoo appeared to be a red-and-black five-point star.

Exactly like the one Morris, Igor, and at least one of the Russians he'd taken out had inked on their skin.

The nuke was in the cello case!

They had to move, now!

"Sun!" Feeling frantic, he looked around for her. She was several steps ahead of him, so he hurried to catch up. He pulled her close and spoke directly into her ear. "The cello case is in the hands of a Russian. I think he has the bomb. Call Jordan and tell him to notify Yates. I'm going over to grab it."

"Wait." Sun tightened her grip on his arm, preventing him from going. "Are you sure the guy is a Russian? And why would a Russian set it off rather than a North Korean?"

"He's got the red-and-black star tattoo, so I'm sure he's one of the Russians. And the cello case is huge, more than big enough for a new and improved version of the Davy Crockett. I don't know why they don't have a North Korean involved, but we have to go now. Hurry!"

"I'll call Jordan, but I'm coming with you." She pulled out her phone. "Jordan? There's a Russian with a cello case big enough to carry a modern Davy Crockett. We're going to investigate now."

Mack didn't want Sun to come with him, he wanted her far away from this thing. But there wasn't any time to argue.

If the nuke was in the cello case, the Russian wasn't going to give it up without a fight.

CHAPTER TWENTY-FOUR

January 20 – 8:33 a.m. – Washington, DC

"Jordan, you need to tell Yates to cancel the ceremony and begin evacuating the area!" Sun pushed through the crowd behind Mack, who was trying to get over to where the musicians were located. Why hadn't anyone mentioned they'd have musicians here?

Just like no one had told them about the food and drink vendors either.

"You really found it?" Jordan asked.

"We think so." She elbowed her way past a group of people who were clustered together and having a heated debate over politics. "Mack says the guy with the cello case has a Russian tattoo."

"I'll do my best but call me as soon as you have confirmation on the nuke."

"He's Russian!" Sun repeated, causing a few people to glance at her with a frown. "Shut it down!"

Without waiting for Jordan to answer, she hit the end button and slid the phone into her jacket. There was movement from the top of the steps leading up to the Capitol, and she caught a glimpse of a guy with blond hair standing next to a woman with long curly auburn hair.

She stumbled over someone's outstretched foot as her exhausted brain tried to fit the pieces together. There was something about the couple, then she remembered.

The woman was Joyce Clemmons, a congresswoman from North Carolina, who was the current Speaker of the House. And as such, she would become president if something happened to the current president and vice president. Her blood ran cold. Sun remembered reading that Joyce was married to a man named Cliff Watkins, but there hadn't been a photo of the guy.

Was it possible Cliff Watkins was the man who'd spoken in North Korean? If so, what business did he have within the Capitol?

Did he function in some role supporting his wife?

Had to be. Sun glanced around frantically, but she was behind several unusually tall men blocking her view. Rather than following Mack to the Russian with the cello case, she angled around for a better view of the couple.

She needed a better look at Cliff Watkins, if that's who the blond guy was. Her heart thudded in her chest, a combination of too much caffeine and not enough sleep.

A break in the crowd offered her a better view of the landing at the top of the stairs leading to the Capitol. The blond guy was definitely the same one Mack had followed from the coffee shop, and the way he placed his arm around Congresswoman Joyce Clemmons, pressing a kiss to her cheek, made Sun think they were married. She wondered why Watkins spoke North Korean instead of Russian since a Russian happened to have the cello case.

Maybe Watkins spoke Russian too.

The couple turned to walk back into the Capitol.

She glanced around to find Mack but didn't see him. Then she realized he was less than ten feet from the musicians.

Should she back up Mack? Or try to track down Watkins?

The nuke was the bigger threat at the moment, so she turned to head over to Mack.

First, they'd take care of the nuke, then they'd track down Cliff Watkins.

If Watkins was involved in this, she wasn't going to let him get away.

JANUARY 20 – 8:46 a.m. – Washington, DC

Mack was close enough now to see the upper half of a red-and-black five-point star peeking above the Russian's jacket.

As he considered how to approach the guy in order to get the cello case out of his hands, Mack realized he had no idea how easy it was to detonate a nuclear bomb.

Could the thing go off in a struggle? Maybe not if it was still in the case, right?

Okay, plan A was to keep the stupid thing inside the case. Plan B—he didn't have a plan B.

Mack risked a glance over his shoulder, searching for Sun. Hopefully, she'd convinced Jordan to convince Yates to shut this thing down, and fast.

He focused his attention on the Russian, formulating a plan to neutralize him while getting the cello case away from him.

But the crush of people surrounding them wouldn't make that easy. Especially since he feared the Capitol police would haul him off without waiting to hear his explanation.

Panic gripped him by the throat as he tried to figure out his next steps. He caught a glimpse of an instrument case lying on the ground a few feet from a musician checking his phone. Mack scooped it up and headed toward the Russian.

It was now or never.

With the borrowed instrument case in hand, he plowed into the Russian with enough force to knock him down. "Oh, so sorry, please excuse me," Mack said even as he dropped down on top of the guy.

"Get off me," the Russian hissed, but Mack reached up and pinched the same nerve in the Russian's neck that Kim Jong-il had used on Jarek.

"I don't think so," Mack whispered back in Russian. "I know what's in the cello case."

The Russian bucked against him with stunning strength considering the pressure on his nerve. Mack tightened his grip and kept up a monologue for those around them. "Really sorry, I'm such a klutz. Here, I'll help you up."

The cello case was leaning upright against the edge of the musician's platform. By the way the Russian glanced at it, Mack knew his guess was dead-on.

"Do you need help?" Sun asked, arriving somewhat breathlessly. She pressed the blunt nose of her gun into the Russian's side, using her body to block the view so that the sight of a gun didn't incite mass panic.

Mack grinned, relief making him a little dizzy. "Perfect timing."

The Russian went still when he realized Sun had him at gunpoint.

"What's going on here?" a harsh voice asked. Mack

inwardly groaned as he recognized the uniform of the Capitol police.

"This man is wanted for outstanding warrants," Mack said, improvising quickly. "We're part of the security team and are taking him into custody."

The Capitol cop's eyes were full of mistrust, but when Mack flashed his NSA credentials, he didn't protest as Mack hauled the Russian to his feet. Mack pointed at the upper part of the star tattoo. "See this? Indicates he's part of the Russian mob."

The cop's eyes widened, and he stepped back to give them room.

"Officer, could I borrow your handcuffs?" Sun asked with a smile. The cop shrugged and handed them over.

Once Mack had the Russian cuffed, he gestured to Sun. "Get the cello case and let's get out of here. But be careful."

"I'll try," Sun murmured, picking up the case, which was bigger than she was.

"Hey, where are you taking my cello?"

Mack turned to look at who'd spoken. It was a slender man, roughly his age, and his features indicated he was of North Korean descent. "I instructed that man to set it right here! We are to play as soon as the inauguration begins."

The final piece of the puzzle fell into place. The Russian was just the one delivering the bomb, while the plan was for the North Korean to open the case, which would likely set it off. A plan the blond guy who'd spoken North Korean in the coffee shop must have arranged. *Be on time or I'll retaliate.*

This was how they'd planned to place the blame on North Korea.

And it might have worked if he and Sun hadn't figured it out in time.

JANUARY 20 – 9:12 a.m. – *Washington, DC*

"Jordan, we need the bomb squad." Sun pinched the phone between her shoulder and ear as she lugged the cello case. She was strong and nimble, but this thing was bigger than her and twice as heavy. Not to mention the added challenge of trying to get it through a crowd without anyone slamming into it with enough force to accidentally open it.

"Are you sure it's in there?" Jordan asked.

She bit back a sarcastic reply. "Listen, we think it may be rigged to blow when the case is opened, so no, we haven't looked inside it. Which is why we need the bomb squad!"

The last words came out louder than she'd intended, drawing fearful looks from people around her.

"Did she say bomb?" someone asked.

"There's a bomb?" someone else echoed.

"A bomb!" a third yelled.

At that moment, a deep voice came through a microphone located in the area where the inauguration would normally take place. "Ladies and gentlemen, we respectfully ask that everyone walk slowly to the exits on each side of Union Square. There is no need to panic, please walk slowly and carefully to the exit closest to you."

Oh sure, now they were evacuating the area, while she was still trying to get the bomb out. Instantly, the crush of people grew worse as many ignored the request to move slowly but pushed and bullied their way toward the exit.

"Sun?" Mack's voice was barely audible above the din.

"Here!" She hoped he'd see the cello case in spite of the crowd.

But she felt herself being carried along with those streaming toward the exit and nearly lost her footing several times. If the cello case dropped down and opened, they'd all be toast.

Like literally burned to a crisp, toast.

"Mack!" She stumbled and by some miracle managed to remain upright. More and more people pushed against her as if they could force her to go faster despite the mass of people in front of her.

She needed help fast!

Please, Lord, help me through this! Keep us safe in Your care!

"Sun!" Mack's familiar face was a welcome surprise. She wasn't sure how Mack managed to thread through the crowd to get to her, but she was grateful for his presence. "I'll take the case."

She gratefully released her grip on the case but latched onto his jacket lest she lose him again. "Where's the Russian?"

"Handed him off to the Capitol police. Figured this thing was more important." Mack took the cello case and used it as a prop to get through the crowd.

"Where's the bomb squad?" Sun asked as they made some headway toward the south exit. "Do you see them?"

"Not yet." Mack's voice was grim. "I'm just hoping we can get out of here without this thing going off."

Sun felt the same way and wished once again Yates and the president would have called this off hours ago.

Then again, if they hadn't seen the musicians and identified the Russian, they may not have found the cello case at all.

A good reminder not to question God's plan.

Now if they could get this case handed off to the bomb squad, they could work on getting Cliff Watkins in for questioning.

She felt certain he was the mastermind behind all of this. Unfortunately, she didn't have any hard evidence to prove it.

JANUARY 20 – 9:39 a.m. – Washington, DC

Mack could see the exit just up ahead. He tried not to push people over as he edged through the crowd. Red and blue lights and a black square boxlike truck was pulling up, and he felt a surge of relief.

He couldn't wait to hand this thing off to those better equipped to handle it.

The crowd parted as people veered away from the red and blue lights and men dressed from head to toe in SWAT gear. Mack shoved the cello case at the SWAT officers closest to him.

"Do you have a way to test if there's a nuclear substance inside?" he asked breathlessly. "I have reason to believe it's rigged to blow upon being opened."

The two SWAT officers glanced warily at each other. "Let's get this into the truck and see what we have."

Mack wanted nothing more than to get out of Dodge, but he knew he couldn't. This was their case, and he and Sun needed to see this thing through.

He turned to look at her. "Are you okay?"

She nodded, although her pale skin and pinched expression told him otherwise. He completely understood, battling his claustrophobia had never been so difficult as he pushed through the crowd to reach Sun.

The SWAT team took the cello case into the back of the square box truck. He turned to glance back at the steps leading up to the Capitol. At least half the crowd had already dispersed, with streams of people still leaving the area.

A close call, really, considering the location of the musician platform. He could just imagine the North Korean opening the cello case and the missile shooting up into the sky right over the outgoing and incoming presidents of the United States.

"We need to find Cliff Watkins," Sun said.

"Who?"

"The blond guy who speaks North Korean," Sun quickly explained. "I saw him earlier with his wife, Congresswoman Joyce Clemmons. Watkins has to be the one who set this whole plan in motion. I think he hired the Russians and arranged for the North Korean cello player to be here today."

"Call Jordan," Mack urged. "Have Yates secure Clemmons and Watkins to question them."

"I'll try, but we don't have any proof," Sun reminded.

He blew out a breath because she was right. "No reason they can't be interviewed, right? Maybe we can get something from the Russian."

"Okay." Sun pulled out her phone and made the call.

Mack tried not to consider what might happen if the Russian refused to cooperate. Being tried and convicted of treason may be enough leverage, but there were no guarantees.

If Watkins and Clemmons were responsible, he wanted them arrested and punished to the full extent of the law.

Then it hit him. If Watkins and Clemmons knew about the nuclear bomb, wouldn't they already be making their way out of the city?

Of course, they would.

. . .

JANUARY 20 – 10:01 *a.m.* – *Washington, DC*

"We've confirmed there is a nuclear device inside the cello case," the SWAT officer announced in a grim tone. "I don't know how you figured out it was in there, but good job to both of you."

Sun glanced at Mack with a smile, feeling as if the entire weight of the planet had been lifted off her shoulders. They'd done it! They'd secured the bomb and kept the president and the vice president safe from harm.

It was over.

Except, of course, for Congresswoman Clemmons and her husband, Watkins.

"We need the computer case," Mack said in a low tone.

She stared at him, trying to think back to what seemed like eons ago rather than hours. "I think Jordan has it, we handed it off to him with my parents, remember?"

"We need to meet with him, ASAP." Mack put his arm around her. "If Watkins and Clemmons knew about the bomb, they'd get out of here well before the time it was set to blow. I need to hack into the Metro camera system to see if we can find them."

It was a brilliant idea. Sun made the call to Jordan who was already on his way over. "I told Yates about Watkins and Clemmons, but he claims no one has seen them."

"Because they're on their way out of town, but Mack thinks he can find them."

"Meet me at the McDonald's off Fourth Street, I'll be there in five minutes."

Sun grabbed Mack's hand. "Come on, we need to hurry. They may have gotten off the Metro by now."

They ran to the McDonald's in time to see Jordan pull up in the SUV. He had Sloan with him, who had the sat computer open and activated with a signal. She slid into the back seat with Mack as Sloan handed the computer over. "I hope your wives are somewhere safe," she said as Mack went to work.

"They're waiting for us back at the hotel," Jordan said. "They wouldn't leave without us, and we weren't leaving without you and Mack."

Sun shook her head. "Crazy, but thankfully it's okay now. In fact, there may still be time to hold the inauguration ceremony as planned."

Jordan shrugged. "Yates made it sound like they were going to do a smaller ceremony inside the Capitol and forgo the parade. It's probably a smart move, and thanks to the good work you and Mack did." Jordan hesitated, then added, "I heard from Tramall, he's impressed enough to offer Mack a raise."

"Huh," Mack grunted as he worked the keyboard. "For as much help as he was, he should pay me his salary and mine." There was a pause, then Mack said, "Got it! I'm in."

"That was fast," Sloan commented.

"Only because I've been in the video feed before, the Metro cameras are in the same system as the street cameras, just a different feed. Looks like they've taken care of my virus, too, which helps." Mack gestured for Sun to scoot over. "Tell me which lines to check first."

Envisioning the Metro map, she started at the most logical sites for Clemmons and Watkins to use. "Start at the distal location, first, in case they're already getting off."

"Okay." Mack turned the screen so they could both view the passengers. They went from one station to the next, and just when Sun was beginning to lose hope, she saw them.

"There! Call Yates, they're on the Red Metro near the White Flint station!" She glanced at Mack. "I bet you a buck they have a car waiting for them at the Shady Grove exit."

"You'd win that bet," Mack joked as Jordan made the call.

"Yates is sending a chopper to Shady Grove as we speak," Jordan announced. "Mack, sound the alarm if they get off sooner."

"They won't," Sun said. "I'm sure they wanted to stay underground as long as possible."

"I agree with Sun." Now that they had the congresswoman and her husband in their sights, they could relax and wait for the couple to be picked up for questioning.

"Oh, and Yates claims there are a couple of other key congressmen and women who are missing," Jordan said. "He thinks there's a small circle within the government who are all in on this thing."

There was a long, sobering silence in the SUV as they watched the train slow down, stop, then start up again for a few more stops before reaching Shady Grove. As predicted, the couple got off the train and stepped right into the hands of the Secret Service.

Jordan's phone rang. "You got them?" There was a pause, then he said, "Following the money always works. Thanks for the update, Yates. What about the others?" Another pause, then, "Okay, sounds like you're taking over from here."

Sun realized they not only had the congresswoman and her husband in custody, but the others who were also involved. And the reference to the money trail means they may even have the proof they needed to put them away forever.

She slumped against the seat. "It's really over."

"Yeah," Mack agreed softly. Then an impish grin

flashed across his features. "We saved the world from certain war today, Sun. We make an incredible team."

She had to smile back at him. "Yeah, thanks for your help with this one, Mack. We couldn't have done it without you."

"You held up your end of the bargain," Mack said modestly.

"No, she's right, Mack." Jordan turned in his seat to face them. "I know the NSA has just offered you a raise, and I'm not sure I can match what they're paying you, but if you'd like to jump ship and work in the private sector, Security Specialists, Incorporated could use your expertise. We'd love to have you join our team."

Sun shouldn't have been surprised by Jordan's offer, but she was. Mainly because she'd figured Mack would be glad to get back to New York and whatever hacking job the NSA had him doing.

"I'd love to be a part of your team, Jordan, but I have one condition," Mack said, reaching over to take her hand.

"And that is?" Jordan asked.

For an answer, Mack drew her close and kissed her. The two men coughed and turned back to face the windshield in a ridiculous attempt to give them privacy.

Kissing Mack was amazing, but she forced herself to pull away and look up at him. "You never said what your condition was," she pointed out breathlessly. "For taking the job."

"My condition is you, Sun." Mack's green eyes clung to hers. "I love you and want you to marry me."

"You—love me?" Sun knew she sounded like an idiot, but kissing Mack, then hearing his declaration of love had her brain neurons firing in all different directions. "Are you sure?"

"I'm sure," Mack said in a low husky voice. "But—maybe it's too soon for you?"

She shook her head. "No, Mack. I've loved you for a long time. I just never thought you felt the same way. After Abigail..."

"I was stupid to date Abigail, she bored me to tears." His gaze was sweetly earnest. "No one can compare to you, Sun."

She smiled and pulled him back down for another kiss.

"Come on, already, don't keep me in suspense," Jordan complained. "Are you working for us or not?"

It took a moment for them to break off from their embrace. Mack grinned at her.

"Yes, but I'm glad you don't have a rule about married couples working together. Because I want to work with Sun, and I plan on marrying her as soon as possible."

She thought about her parents and the fact that they were safe from harm, if still in need of medical attention they'd stubbornly refused, and nodded. "I'd like that, Mack. Very much."

"Good." He pulled her in for a hug. "I knew God brought us back together for a reason."

Sun smiled, thinking about her parents and how great it would be to not just have them escort her down the aisle at their wedding but to have them as a part of her life moving forward.

With God watching over them, she felt certain they would have a wonderful future, together.

Dear Reader,

I sincerely hope you enjoyed reading Mack and Sun's story in *Target for Revenge*. The entire Security Specialists, Inc. series has been so much fun to write. Touring the FBI in Washington, DC, several years ago gave me the idea for these books, and I'm thrilled to have received such a marvelous response from my readers. I'm truly blessed to have so many wonderful fans. A sincere thanks to each and every one of you.

Reviews are very important to authors, so if you enjoyed this book, please consider leaving a review on the platform from which you purchased it. I would be very grateful.

I adore hearing from my readers. I can be reached through my website at https://www.laurascottbooks.com, through Facebook at https://www.facebook.com/LauraScottBooks, and on Twitter at https://twitter.com/laurascottbooks.

Please consider signing up for my monthly newsletter through my website. I offer a free novella to everyone who subscribes. This is a book only available to my newsletter subscribers, it's not available for purchase on any platform.

Sincerely,
Laura Scott

Made in the USA
Monee, IL
13 September 2021